Jesse's mind was whirling, racing out of control.

If Sara's father caught them, this time he *would* shoot. If *his* father saw them, there'd be hell to pay.

Sara was too young, too innocent, too trusting. He should step back from her, he knew. And he would. In just a moment, another enchanted moment of tasting the sweetness she offered him so willingly, so freely.

Breathing hard, he pulled back to look into green eyes dazed with the beginnings of a surprising passion. Through a foggy cloud of desire, Jesse knew he'd never experienced a kiss like Sara's. Heart hammering, he bent to take her mouth again.

On a sigh of surrender, Sara kissed him back. She gave to him and, like a starving man, Jesse took. . . .

Dear Reader,

Welcome to Silhouette **Special Edition** ... welcome to romance.

Last year, I requested your opinions on the books that we publish. Thank you for the many thoughtful comments. For the next few months, I'd like to share quotes with you from those letters. This seems very appropriate while we are in the midst of the THAT SPECIAL WOMAN! promotion. Each one of our readers is a **special** woman, as heroic as the heroines in our books.

Our THAT SPECIAL WOMAN! title for October is *On Her Own* by Pat Warren. This is a heroine to cheer for as she returns to her hometown and the man she never forgot.

Also in store for you in October is *Marriage Wanted,* the third book in Debbie Macomber's heartwarming trilogy, FROM THIS DAY FORWARD. And don't miss *Here Comes the Groom* by Trisha Alexander, a spin-off from her *Mother of the Groom.*

Rounding out the month are books from Marie Ferrarella, Elizabeth Bevarly and Elyn Day, who makes her Silhouette Debut as Special Edition's PREMIERE author.

I hope you enjoy this book, and all of the stories to come!

Sincerely,

Tara Gavin
Senior Editor

QUOTE OF THE MONTH:

''I'm the mother of six, grandmother of ten and a registered nurse. I work in a hospice facility and deal with death and dying forty hours a week. Romance novels, light and airy, are my release from the stress.''

L. O'Donnell
Maine

PAT WARREN

ON HER OWN

Silhouette®

SPECIAL EDITION®

Published by Silhouette Books New York

America's Publisher of Contemporary Romance

This book is dedicated to my daughter, Julie, who, on her own, has perfected her talent with style and grace. From Mom, with love and affection.

SILHOUETTE BOOKS
300 East 42nd St., New York, N.Y. 10017

ON HER OWN

ISBN: 0-373-09841-3

First Silhouette Books printing October 1993

Books by Pat Warren

Silhouette Special Edition

With This Ring #375
Final Verdict #410
Look Homeward, Love #442
Summer Shadows #458
The Evolution of Adam #480
Build Me a Dream #514
The Long Road Home #548
The Lyon and the Lamb #582
My First Love, My Last #610
Winter Wishes #632
Till I Loved You #659
An Uncommon Love #678
Under Sunny Skies #731
That Hathaway Woman #758
Simply Unforgettable #797
On Her Own #841

Silhouette Romance

Season of the Heart #553

Silhouette Intimate Moments

Perfect Strangers #288

PAT WARREN

is the mother of four and lives in Arizona with her travel-agent husband and a lazy white cat. She's a former newspaper columnist whose lifetime dream was to become a novelist. A strong romantic streak, a sense of humor and a keen interest in developing relationships led her to try writing romance novels, with which she feels very much at home.

BOOK ONE

Chapter One

Jesse Morgan leaned against the thick white fence post and squinted into the late-afternoon sun. His sister stood on the makeshift pitcher's mound checking out the batting lineup. Nearly every day after school, she gathered several of her friends for an impromptu game on the grassy area in front of the ranch house. He knew Kay loved baseball and was good at it. He'd taught her himself.

Of course, he rarely joined them anymore. After all, he was much too old, much too mature and experienced to spend time with Kay and her little chums these days. He was also too busy with his own friends, his ranch chores and the breaking and training of horses, guided by his father. He couldn't be bothered with mere grade-school girls.

Jesse was a worldly-wise fourteen.

Still, he wanted to see how much of his teachings his little sister had retained, so he leaned forward to watch her wind up for the next pitch. Kay's hair, as curly and black as his own, blew about her thin face in a light breeze, but she scarcely noticed as she sized up the batter stepping up to the piece of tin that passed for home plate.

Jesse shifted his gaze and recognized the batter, surprised to see her since she rarely joined the other girls. When she did, he usually stopped to watch, intrigued with her long blond hair, worn today in one thick braid hanging down her back. Jesse's whole family had dark hair, which was probably why Sara Shephard's fair hair fascinated him.

Sara's father, Noah, kept a tight rein on her, hardly ever allowing his daughter to roam far from the Lazy-S Ranch, the one just west of the Morgan spread. Sara was small and delicate-looking, but her personality was anything but. She was feisty and defensive, perhaps because she'd been motherless since babyhood. Jesse admired people who stood up for themselves, male or female.

He watched Sara carelessly tuck the tail of her striped shirt into the band of her blue shorts with one hand, then curl her small fingers around the bat almost lazily. Yet he could see that her green eyes were narrowed in concentration.

Kay's pitch came fast and furious, if a little wobbly. Sara watched and waited, then whacked it a good one. The ball sailed high and wide, over Kay's head, skimming past the daydreaming second baseman. Then suddenly, it spiraled downward, looking as if it would drop neatly into the glove of the lone outfielder. But the chubby redhead fumbled, then scrambled to recover the ball.

Interested in spite of himself, Jesse pushed away from the fence and turned toward the crouching catcher. Sara's long, skinny legs were quickly carrying her home. She must have sensed that the outfielder had thrown the ball because, in a final burst of speed, she slid onto home plate a second before the toss thunked into the catcher's mitt.

The four other girls on Sara's team whooped with joy at the home run.

Because he was feeling expansive, Jesse ambled over.

"She's out, I tell you," Lisa Nagles shouted as she ran forward from the outfield.

At twelve, redheaded Lisa was the oldest one in the group and a whiner if there ever was one, in Jesse's opinion. Lisa's father had walked out on his family years ago, and just last Christmas, her mother had had a nervous breakdown. So naturally, Jesse's mother, Emily, who'd grown up with Lisa's mother, had unhesitatingly moved the child in with the Morgans. That had pleased Kay, who'd always wanted a sister. Jesse had been less than thrilled.

"You were too far out to see," Kay told Lisa as Jesse reached home plate. "Sara's safe." Even though Kay had thrown the pitch that had cost her team a home run, Emily Morgan had instilled a sense of fair play in her daughter that wouldn't be denied.

"You need glasses," Lisa countered. A head taller and quite a bit heavier, she glared at Kay, wrinkling a face that was already showing signs of one day becoming quite pretty.

"But *I* don't," Jesse intervened. "And I say she's safe." He watched Sara jump to her feet and look up at him in that hesitant way she had around him. "Congratulations, shrimp." He couldn't remember when he'd begun calling her by that silly name, only that it suited her.

Sara sent him a shy smile, then quickly looked away, as if hoping no one had noticed.

She was tough and independent around everyone, yet Jesse had noticed that when he was nearby, she seemed awkward and embarrassed. Pretty odd considering she spent most of her time on the Lazy-S with males, from her widowed father on down.

"Oh, yuk, you're bleeding," Lisa said, her voice filled with disgust as she pointed at Sara's knee.

Sara barely glanced at the scrape before looking up at Lisa, her chin raised defiantly. "Maybe so, but I scored."

"I still say you were out," Lisa answered, annoyed.

"Knock it off, Lisa," Kay said. Though she was two years younger than the girl she was trying to accept as a sister, she was always ready to speak up if she felt someone was wrong. "Time out while I get something for Sara's knee."

"I'll take her over," Jesse offered. It would probably be best to put some distance between Sara and Lisa. He wasn't sure why, but the two of them always wound up scrapping the few times they were together. "Come on, shrimp."

Kay waved the girls who'd gathered around back to their positions, then looked pointedly at Lisa as she started for the pitcher's mound. "Okay, let's play ball."

In the coolness of the barn, Jesse found bandages and disinfectant. At the sink, he wet a paper towel and turned to Sara, who had slowly followed him in.

"You don't have to do this," she said shyly. "It's just a little cut."

Feeling older-brother protective, Jesse shook his head. "You live on a ranch. You know better than to ignore scrapes that could become infected." He cleaned the cut, then sprayed on disinfectant. Though he knew it stung, she didn't flinch. Quickly, he attached a bandage. "That should do it. Now, for the rest of your medicine."

Sara stepped back warily. "What medicine?"

Jesse leaned down to open the small fridge and took out two frosty cans of soda. "This." He popped the tab on one and held it out to her. She gave him a relieved smile as she took it. He opened his own can, leaned his head back and drank thirstily.

Sara took a sip, watching his throat work as he drank. If she could have had a brother, she'd want him to be exactly like Jesse Morgan. He wasn't like the other older boys at her school. Of course, he'd graduated last June and was now going to Coronado High. She could no longer sit on the low cinderblock fence by the playground after lunch and watch him toss a football with his friends or sit behind him on the bus and just study him. She'd have to rely on catching him at home the few times she'd manage to sneak over to the Morgan Ranch without her father noticing.

"I saw your dad a while ago," Jesse said conversationally, since she'd been quiet so long.

Sara's heart leaped to her throat. "You did? Where? Was he looking for me?"

Jesse rubbed the deep cleft in his chin, a thoughtful gesture. "I don't think so. He was in his truck with Phil headed for town when I got off the school bus."

Unable to prevent it, Sara released a nervous breath, then tried to look unconcerned as her gaze skittered from his frowning face. "I forgot for a minute. They go to this meeting in town every Wednesday." Which meant that she was safe for a couple of hours yet. Gretchen knew where she was, but Gretchen wouldn't tell. To cover her embarrassment, she drank more cooling liquid.

"Where'd you learn to hit a ball like that?" Jesse asked, something he'd wondered every time he'd watched the girls play. "Your dad teach you?" He couldn't imagine that sourpuss playing ball with a little girl, but maybe with his daughter he was nicer.

Sara nearly choked at that. She couldn't remember her father spending a single leisurely moment with her. Carefully, she set the can down on the counter along the wall. "Phil taught me when I was young." Their ranch manager had never married or had children of his own, so he'd taken her under his wing, teaching her to swim, to ride a horse and to share with her his love of baseball.

Jesse hid his smile, not wanting her to think he found her reference to when she'd been young pretty funny, since she was only nine now. There was something about Sara Shephard that always made him feel protective. Maybe it was because of the things he'd heard about her father being a mean old drunk. "You're the best player out there," he said, and meant it.

Sara felt the glow of the compliment warm her, then tried to shrug it off. "Kay's a really good pitcher."

"Is that why you knocked her pitch into the woods?" He laughed at her attempt at modesty.

Reddening, not used to bantering with boys her own age, much less with one who was a freshman in high school, Sara didn't answer but instead reached for her soda can. Only her nerves made her hand twitch and the can tipped, spilling soda onto the concrete floor. "Oh, no!"

"No big deal." Jesse grabbed a roll of paper towels and began mopping up.

As Sara stooped to help him, her head bumped his and she pulled back, horrified at her clumsiness.

"Can't take you anywhere, can we, shrimp?" Jesse teased, wanting to put her at ease.

Misinterpreting his comment, Sara's back stiffened and her face went pale.

"Hey, I was only kidding." He stood, wondering why she was so touchy.

Sara rose to her feet and searched his eyes, finally deciding she'd read him wrong. It was just that she had to put up with so much criticism at home that it was difficult not to misinterpret a casual remark. She gave him a shaky smile. "I knew that."

Jesse grinned down at her, glad he was able to make her smile. She was someone who should smile more.

"Well, well," Lisa said from the doorway, her hands propped on her hips as she surveyed the mess on the floor and came to her own conclusions. "Aren't you the clumsy one, Sara? You may be able to hit a ball, but..."

"What do you want, Lisa?" Jesse asked, cutting her off. The girl was always creeping up on him, appearing out of nowhere when he least expected her. He was getting sick of it.

Lisa spoke to Jesse, but gave Sara a cool look. "I'm here to get Cinnamon, to lead her to the arena for my riding lesson. Pete's waiting for us. He says I'm the best student he's ever had and that one day I'm going to set the horse world on its ear."

"So go take her," Jesse answered, throwing the paper towels in the rubbish bin. That was another thing about Lisa—she was always bragging about the smallest accomplishment. She hadn't even been on a horse until she'd moved in with them nine months ago, and she totally ignored the fact that both he and Kay had been riding almost from the time they'd learned to walk.

He finished his drink as Lisa marched haughtily past them toward her horse's stall. "Don't let her get to you," he told Sara, noticing that her frown was back.

"She doesn't like me," Sara blurted out, then immediately regretted it. What had possessed her to say that to Jesse when Lisa Nagles now lived on the Morgan Ranch like an adopted daughter? Sara would have given everything she owned to change places with Lisa.

"She doesn't like *anyone,*" Jesse answered as they walked back out into the heat. Though it was September, the Arizona sun kept the temperatures hovering in the eighties. The nearest town, St. Johns, was over a hundred miles northeast of Phoenix, but sat at a much higher elevation, which allowed for a seasonal fluctuation of temperature. In the winter, in the nearby White Mountains, there was even skiing, a sport Jesse loved.

"She likes *you,*" Sara said, looking up at Jesse.

Squinting toward the paddock, Jesse stuck his hands into the back pockets of his jeans the way he'd seen his father do.

"I don't have time for girls. I've got to tend to my horses, and you'd better get back to the game. They need you."

She remembered her manners, the ones Gretchen tried to drum into her. "Thanks, Jesse, for fixing my knee and for the drink."

"See you later, shrimp." He started to walk away, then swung back. "You staying for dinner?"

"I...I don't know." She hadn't been asked, but her heart soared at the very thought.

She and Kay had suddenly become friends this summer, a fact that had literally changed Sara's life. She'd never had a girlfriend before, having had to content herself with the adults on the Lazy-S for company. Then one summer day, she'd gone for a swim in the river that bisected both ranches and found Kay already there. A friendship had been born. Although Sara couldn't visit the Morgan Ranch often, and certainly couldn't invite her new friend to her home, Kay seemed to understand.

But she'd never been invited to eat with the Morgans. If they did ask, could she dare accept?

"You ought to stay," Jesse called back. "Mom's making her famous chili. Best in the west." With a wave, he walked on.

Sara watched him until he disappeared into the back barn, then sighed. Why couldn't there be someone like Jesse living on her father's ranch, perhaps the son of one of the hands? A week ago when she'd been visiting Kay, they'd watched Jesse work with one of the show mares in the arena, and Sara had been so impressed at how good he was. Though he was young and almost too thin with those long legs, he was strong and had been training horses with his father directing from the sidelines for years. Having grown up with horses, Sara could tell that Jesse had the same wordless communication with the animals that she had.

For perhaps the hundredth time, she wondered also why her mother couldn't have had another daughter—someone like Kay—before she'd had to die? It simply wasn't fair.

She had only her father, and he was either in a bad mood or in a daze, sitting evenings in his worn leather chair in his den, drinking and talking to himself. Phil Howard really managed the ranch, and though he was nice enough, he was awfully busy. Gretchen, their housekeeper, was kind and let her have a lot of leeway when it came to some of Noah's overly strict rules. But Gretchen was old—at least fifty—and a terrible cook. Most every evening for dinner, Gretchen made what she called "surprise casserole." Sara's stomach churned at the thought.

But today, there was the possibility of being invited to dinner at the Morgans. Closing her eyes tightly, Sara sent a promise straight up to heaven that she wouldn't complain about raking out her allotted number of stalls tomorrow after school if only she could have dinner just once with Jesse and Kay.

Heaven must have heard her.

"Pass the grated cheese, please," Kay requested.

"Mom, this is soooo good," Jesse said around a huge mouthful.

"Emily, this cornbread gets better every time you make it," Hal Morgan told his wife, his dark eyes lingering on hers, giving the impression that they shared a marvelous secret that had nothing to do with cornbread.

Sara watched and listened, awestruck by the warmth, the laughter, the congeniality of the people seated at the round table with its red-and-white checkered tablecloth and matching napkins. The dishes were sparkling white, and the silverware all matched. In the center was a set of tapered candles that smelled faintly of vanilla.

She'd never in her life had a more elegant meal.

"So, Sara," Emily Morgan said, smiling softly at the shy little girl who seemed both nervous and excited, "how do you like fifth grade?"

Before Sara could answer, Kay jumped in. "She's disgusting, Mom. Sara gets all A's even though she's skipped a grade." She sent her friend a look that meant she was giving a backhanded compliment. Though Kay was a year older, now they were in the same grade.

Unused to the attention, Sara looked down at her bowl of chili. Even though it tasted wonderful, she was too jittery to eat much.

"That's great, Sara," Hal commented. "I'll bet your father sees to it that you study every night." He was no longer friends with Noah Shephard, but Hal knew the man was strict.

"Yes, sir," Sara said into her plate.

Under the table, Emily touched her husband's knee, a silent warning, for she could see the child was uncomfortable at the mention of her father. Perhaps better than anyone present, Emily knew Noah, knew how difficult he could be. "Your hair is lovely, Sara. Just like your mother's."

Sara looked up, her green eyes filled with curiosity. "You knew my mother?"

Emily nodded as she passed the basket of cornbread to Hal. "She was a sweet woman and a marvelous cook. Not that we ate together, but I remember that every fall her canned fruit and jellies won prizes at the fair."

"I wish she'd have taught Gretchen how to make something besides surprise casserole," Sara said, earning her a smile from Jesse who was dishing out his third bowl of chili.

"Have some more lemonade," Lisa said to Sara, pouring from the pitcher, "and try not to spill it all over."

"Lisa," Emily reprimanded quietly, and said no more. But the silent rebuke was enough to bring color to the girl's face. Folding her napkin, Emily found herself wondering again if she'd done the right thing by bringing Lisa Nagles into the family. She could be so sweet at times, yet she had a stubborn, almost mean streak that surfaced often enough to worry Emily.

"That was a great workout today with Domino," Hal told his son, thinking a change of subject was in order.

Jesse swallowed noisily. "Thanks, Dad. She's really catching on. She's way quicker than Frolic."

"I think that's because you're getting better as a trainer."

Sara listened, amazed at how often compliments flew across the table in the Morgan dining room. She couldn't remember the last one she'd heard in her own home. Mr. Morgan talked to his son as if he considered the boy an equal. Sara watched Mrs. Morgan reach out to brush back a lock of Kay's hair with a loving touch. It was like watching a make-believe family on television. She hadn't believed real people acted like this, and her young heart longed to be a part of it all.

Except for Lisa. Why Lisa was always trying to embarrass or criticize her was a mystery to Sara. She made up her mind to steer clear of the girl.

When the dinner plates were cleared and Mrs. Morgan brought out a banana cream pie she'd made for dessert, Sara was sure she'd died and gone to heaven. Afterward, when she and Kay were in the kitchen doing dishes together, she couldn't keep her impressions to herself. "Your mother's so wonderful. You're really lucky."

"Yeah, she's pretty great," Kay answered, rinsing a sudsy dish, then handing it to Sara. "She gets along with everyone." Well aware that Sara had never known her mother and able to imagine how devastated she'd feel if she lost hers, Kay decided to switch topics. "Mom said I could have a pajama party Saturday night. You want to come?"

Sara kept polishing the already dry dish, wondering what on earth a pajama party was, yet reluctant to reveal her ig-

norance, even to Kay. "I...don't know," she answered
hesitantly.

"Oh, come on, it'll be fun. I get to ask four more girls
from our class." Kay yanked on the stopper and released the
soapy water. "We can stay up late and make popcorn and
watch TV. I checked, and *The Wizard of Oz* is on."

Sara's eyes widened. It was her favorite movie.

"Do you have a sleeping bag? If not, you can use Jesse's.
We're going to all sleep in Dad's den, but we can't touch his
desk."

She was being asked to spend the night, Sara realized. Kay
was one of the most popular girls in school and she, Sara
Shephard, was one of the chosen few Kay had selected to
invite to her pajama party. For a moment, Sara felt an
overwhelming rush of joy. Then reality set in, and she swallowed hard over a lump of disappointment. "Thanks, but I
can't."

"Why not?" Kay had known forever that Sara's father
was strict, but surely he couldn't object to a silly little
sleepover. "How about if I have my mom call your father
and..."

"No!" Sara almost dropped the dish she'd finished dry-
ing. "No, please don't."

Seeing her friend's suddenly pale face, Kay was at a loss
for words.

With trembling hands, Sara carefully placed the dish on
the counter and hung up the towel. She glanced pointedly
out the window. "It's almost dark. I have to go." Even
Gretchen could be pushed only so far. And there was always the hideous possibility that her father had decided to
return home early from his Wednesday meeting, though he
rarely did.

Kay's empathies, inherited from her mother, were always close to the surface. "Sara, I didn't mean to upset
you."

Straightening her back, Sara turned from the window and raised her chin a notch. She wouldn't let Kay see she was hurting, just like she never let her father see how his many criticisms hurt her. "You didn't, honestly. The dinner was great, but I have to go home."

Emily Morgan stepped out of the shadows of the dining room and walked through the archway into the kitchen. She hadn't intended to eavesdrop, yet couldn't help overhearing the last few minutes of the girls' conversation. Her heart went out to the small blond child who was trying so hard to be brave, for she knew only too well why Sara couldn't accept Kay's invitation.

"It *is* getting late," Emily said, "and they'll be worrying about you." It had been years since she'd witnessed Noah's displays of temper, but she well remembered his short fuse, and she hoped he wouldn't turn his wrath on his daughter.

Sara nodded, wanting desperately now to escape from these well-meaning people who were too kind. Their obvious happiness and acceptance of one another only pointed out to her the contrasts of her own life. She turned to grip the back doorknob, not trusting her voice to answer Mrs. Morgan.

"I'll have Jesse give you a ride home," Emily said, moving out onto the porch with her. "Sundance needs the exercise." She knew perfectly well that her son never failed to exercise his horse, but she hoped Sara couldn't see through the excuse.

"I can walk. It's not far." She'd come across the east pasture and through the old gate between the two ranches, a good mile. She couldn't let them know that she'd have walked twice that distance to spend this evening with the Morgans.

"No, I won't hear of it." Emily glanced toward the corral nearest the horse barn and spotted her son. "Jesse, I need you to do something for me."

Jesse would guess that something was wrong, Sara thought as her knees began to shake. She'd caught him studying her with those serious gray eyes several times tonight. She couldn't chance it. "I'll be all right, really. I'll run and..."

Gently but firmly, Emily took her arm. "I can't let you do that, Sara. It isn't safe."

With a sinking heart, Sara watched Jesse running over.

"You won't tell on me, will you?" Jesse asked Sara in mock seriousness.

Sitting in front of him astride Sundance, feeling unusually safe despite her skittery nerves, Sara shook her head.

Jesse felt her thick braid skim along his chest. There was an early moon overhead turning the golden strands to silver. He decided he liked blond hair best. "Dad's always telling me not to ride bareback, but I don't see what's wrong with doing it, if you're careful."

"I ride this way a lot." Phil had warned her, too, and her father had threatened to sell her horse, Shadow, if she didn't cut it out. It was her one major infraction of his rules. That and, more recently, sneaking off to the Morgans'.

The evening breeze was balmy, brushing across their faces. Jesse held the reins loosely, keeping Sundance to a leisurely pace. "Do you get to ride much?" he asked her.

Sara had never been this close to a boy, yet with Jesse, she didn't mind. He didn't smell sweaty like some of the boys on the school playground, and he didn't yell the way a lot of them did. "Most every day. I like to go really fast, so I can feel the wind blowing through my hair."

"You mean where you lean over and feel like you and the horse are one and the same?"

Sara angled her head back to look up at him. "How did you know that's how I felt?"

He smiled. "'Cause I do, too."

They rode in silence, both a little amazed to find a bond, considering their age difference.

"Is your knee okay?" Jesse asked. "I don't want your dad to get mad 'cause you got hurt at our place."

"He won't be." With any luck, she'd be in bed long before her father returned home. She wasn't sure what the Wednesday meetings involved, but she knew he always came home full of drink. She'd learned to stay out of his way on Wednesdays.

At the gate that years ago had been set into the fence dividing the two ranches, Jesse slid off and shoved it open, then jumped back up behind Sara and nudged Sundance into unfamiliar territory. The Lazy-S was quite a bit smaller than the Morgan Ranch, but a neat spread. Like his father's ranch, the main function here was the breeding and training of quarter horses for show and racing.

"Will you be coming to Kay's birthday party sleepover next Saturday?" he asked.

So that was the reason for the party, Sara realized. Kay hadn't mentioned the birthday, maybe because she didn't think Sara could manage to get a gift. Did everyone know about the way she lived? "I can't make it," she answered, hoping he'd drop it.

Jesse's father had told him some time ago that Noah Shephard hated all the Morgans and wouldn't allow Sara to have anything to do with them, either, which was why Jesse had been surprised to see her coming around lately. Maybe the poor kid was so lonely that she'd finally decided to defy her father. "I could come get you," he offered. "I'm not afraid of your father."

Sara felt shame redden her cheeks and hoped he couldn't see in the dim twilight. It was true; they all knew about her father's unreasonable ways. She had to try a bluff. "It's not that. I'm just real busy on Saturdays."

Jesse wasn't buying it. "You're lying, and you don't have to. Not to me. I know your dad doesn't like my family. He told me once never to step foot on his land again. It isn't fair of him to not let you be friends with us because he's upset about something that happened a long time ago." Which was all his father had given Jesse by way of explanation for Noah's animosity.

Sara sat up straighter, so her body wasn't touching his quite so much. "I don't need you to feel sorry for me."

"I don't. I like you, or I wouldn't bother with you at all."

She didn't know what to say to that but was saved from answering by the loud banging of a screen door coming from the direction of her house. As she tensed, Jesse pulled Sundance to a halt. They sat listening. She could make out her father's voice, loud with drink, but couldn't make out the words. Which was probably just as well. "I better get off here," she said, feeling a sudden knot forming in her stomach.

"I'm not afraid of your father," Jesse repeated. "I'll take you all the way."

Her hand clutched his as he held the reins. "Jesse, please. You'll only make it worse for me."

She was older than her years, Jesse realized, and the thought saddened him. That was the thing that set Sara Shephard apart from the other little girls who'd been at the ranch today. That and the oddly haunted look that was sometimes in her big green eyes.

Gritting his teeth, he reluctantly slipped off Sundance and held up a hand to help her down. A short distance beyond the small cluster of trees, he could hear old man Shephard's drunken rantings and the occasional shout of his daughter's name. "Does he ever hit you?" Jesse asked, the overwhelming need to protect this small person a new and unexpected feeling.

"No. Never." She was telling the truth, and she hoped he believed her. She was desperately afraid Jesse would insist on going with her and causing a scene. The last such scene, when one of the hands had overheard Noah berating her and had rushed to her defense, had pushed her father into a drinking binge that had lasted several days.

In the moonlight, Jesse searched her eyes, finally satisfied that she was being honest. "If he ever does, even once, you call me or come to me. Promise me you'll do that, Sara." He hadn't the foggiest idea what he'd do, but he knew he'd find a way to shield her. She didn't deserve to live like that. No one did.

Her throat felt clogged, partly from fear and partly from emotion. No one had ever offered to take on her father for her. Even the hand who'd tried to reason with Noah had backed down quickly. In one instant, Jesse became ten feet tall for Sara. "I promise."

Clumsily, he patted her shoulder. "I'll wait here to make sure you get inside safely."

Unable to say more, Sara skittered through the trees and circled around the barn, heading toward the front while her father wove around the backyard, raving and gesturing.

Jesse watched her until she disappeared through the front door into the house. He hoped the housekeeper was there to hustle her to her room before Noah went back in. Maybe they'd make up a story that Sara had been asleep all along.

Turning away, Jesse realized his hands were tightly clenched into fists. Slowly, he forced himself to relax his fingers. In one fluid movement, he climbed up onto Sundance and turned her around, his mind racing, his lips a thin line.

He didn't know what was eating at Noah Shephard, what had caused him to turn into a drunken, neglectful father. But he sure as hell meant to find out one day.

Chapter Two

She didn't want him to leave. Of that much, Sara was absolutely certain.

She swatted at a buzzing fly and leaned back against the white fencing, recently put up around the gazebo that stood in the center of the grassy area alongside the main house. It was the exact spot where she and Kay and the other girls had played baseball way back when. At least, it seemed like all that had taken place a long time ago.

Now, those tomboy days were behind her and she was getting ready to start high school in a week. And Jesse was going away to college.

Standing off to the side, Sara gazed across at the crowd of family, friends and ranch hands who'd gathered on this Sunday afternoon in late August to wish Jesse well in his university studies. Long picnic tables were almost groaning beneath the weight of enough food to feed an army. Even enough for Jesse's huge football friends and former high school baseball teammates.

There were tin tubs of cold soda and beer, pitchers of lemonade and iced tea, and a big urn of coffee alongside an enormous sheet cake decorated with white frosting and shiny blue letters spelling out Good Luck, Jesse. There was another table at the edge of the greenbelt piled high with gaily wrapped packages. Everywhere she looked, people were laughing, smiling, happily talking.

Sara felt like weeping.

No one else seemed even mildly upset about Jesse going away. While it was true that Arizona State was only a three-hour drive, it might as well have been on the far side of the moon. But then, the people here hadn't spent the last four years risking the wrath of a tyrannical father just for a glimpse of Jesse. They wouldn't know how empty her life would be knowing he'd be coming home only on holidays and the occasional weekend, nor could she count on seeing him even then.

They—the cheerful, laughing guests—weren't aware that her thirteen-year-old heart was breaking.

But Sara would sooner have gone headfirst down the old well at the back of the property than let anyone know how she felt. So she stood on the sidelines unobtrusively watching Jesse. He was wearing a blue shirt with white denims and was easily the best-looking guy here. Most of her friends thought Aaron Strong, Jesse's best friend and the former football quarterback, handsomer, but they were wrong.

Polite as always, Jesse was going around to the various clusters of people, accepting handshakes and pats on the back in his usual calm, friendly way. Sara longed to tug him away for a walk where she could have him all to herself, somewhere quiet, like by the river. And she'd listen to that wonderfully deep voice and hear that laugh that sent shivers through her and made her feel funny and squirmy inside. Then she'd fling herself into his arms and beg him not to go away.

Sara sighed. Jesse would likely drag her back and turn her over to Dr. Owens, now filling his plate by the food table, sure she must be coming down with heatstroke or something. She was certain that Jesse knew nothing of her real feelings for him. Truth be known, she wasn't sure exactly what they were, either. She only knew that when she was with Jesse, the sun shone brighter and she felt good about herself, more alive. Happy even.

Earlier in the summer, Kay had accused her of having a crush on her brother, pointing out that she'd caught Sara staring after him often. At the time, she'd gotten mad and hotly denied the insinuation. Yet privately, she supposed there was some truth in what Kay had said.

Yet she was honest enough to admit that she was nothing to Jesse except his kid sister's best friend, someone who hung around when she was able, a girl who played ball well and made him laugh occasionally. While it was true that he seemed to enjoy talking with her and that he was never, never unkind to her, Jesse was nice to everyone. Sara was sure that he hadn't a clue that to her, he was a hero. Especially since the incident three months ago.

He'd ridden her home more than once after that first time she'd stayed for dinner. She'd honestly tried to obey her father, to stay away from the Morgans, though she couldn't imagine why she should. But she'd found compliance impossible. The entire family drew her like a magnet. Kay was bright and quick and fun to be with. Mrs. Morgan was the dearest woman Sara had ever met. And Mr. Morgan was so kind, never raising his voice, not prone to wide mood swings the way her father was. She'd even learned to tolerate Lisa, though she couldn't honestly say she liked her.

But it was Jesse she really longed to be with.

She'd worked out a routine, managing to *accidentally* be at the river when he'd come along for a swim. Or to be riding bareback on Shadow the very same late afternoon Jesse would be taking Sundance for a run. And nearly every Wednesday, she'd hurry home from school, quickly complete her chores and tell Gretchen she was going for a long walk.

Gretchen knew where Sara was going, knew also how badly she needed to be in a loving family atmosphere. Sara would play ball with Kay, or just go up to her room and talk, then stay for dinner. And Mrs. Morgan would always insist that Jesse escort her home.

He'd ease Sundance slowly along the mile or so between the two ranch houses, and they'd talk. Sara was certain heaven couldn't be better than those precious moments she spent alone with Jesse. But, always aware of Noah's temper, she'd made sure they'd start out well before her father was expected, and luck had been with her. Until that terrible evening this past June.

It had been a particularly clear night, the stars winking above them in a cloudless sky. They'd dismounted at their usual parting spot and Jesse had been explaining about the constellations, pointing out the formations of the Big Dipper and the Little Dipper. They'd both been absorbed, looking up, and hadn't heard someone approaching.

Suddenly, he was there, her father, with a shotgun in his hand, his eyes bloodshot and filled with rage.

Frightened beyond belief, acting on impulse, Sara had instantly positioned herself in front of Jesse, her only thought that she couldn't allow Noah to hurt her friend. But that had only angered her father more, and he'd begun cursing the Morgan name, then ordering Jesse off his land. She, too, had urged Jesse to leave, fearful Noah would do something terrible.

But Jesse had remained calm, slowly moving her behind his much larger frame as he explained to her father that he'd been riding along the fence that separated the two ranches when he'd seen Sara out walking. Suddenly, she'd twisted her ankle, and he'd insisted on escorting her home. Sara had known he'd told the lie to protect her. No one had ever done that for her before.

In his woozy state and filled with his inflexible anger, her father hadn't believed Jesse. He'd begun weaving and haranguing again. Sara's legs had trembled so badly that she'd scarcely been able to stay upright. Her father was a tall man, nearing fifty but strong from working outdoors all his life. Yet years of drinking had clouded his mind and sharpened his temper.

At eighteen, Jesse was over six feet tall, lean and hard with muscular arms and broad shoulders, and he had youth on his side. Jesse would probably win in a fight between the two of them. But there'd been that shotgun that made the odds terribly uneven. She'd never known her father to threaten anyone in person, but suddenly she feared he'd gone over the edge.

Then Jesse had done the most astounding thing.

Turning his back on Noah, he'd whispered into her ear to just follow his lead, then helped her up onto Sundance's back. Next, he'd swung up behind her. Almost senseless with fear, she'd whispered back that her father would shoot him for not obeying. "No, he won't," Jesse had murmured, then he'd turned to Noah. "I'm taking your daughter home," he'd told him. Seemingly unruffled, he'd nudged Sundance forward.

Perhaps her father had been too stunned to do anything in the face of Jesse's quiet defiance. Or maybe he'd been too drunk. In either case, he hadn't raised the shotgun or followed them, nor had he said another word.

Jesse had ridden her right up to the front porch where a distraught Gretchen had been waiting. As if he'd been used to confronting a wild drunk wielding a shotgun every evening, he'd unhurriedly dismounted and helped Sara down.

Uneasily she'd ventured a glance toward the cluster of trees and seen that Noah was nowhere in sight. Unable to meet Jesse's eyes, she'd mumbled an apology, shamed to her core at her father's behavior. She'd also thanked him repeatedly for standing up to her father, as Gretchen urged her to hurry inside.

Ignoring the housekeeper, Jesse had reached out and touched Sara's hair, then tipped up her chin. On his face she'd seen a look of brotherly affection. "I've told you before, if you ever need me, all you have to do is call. Don't be afraid."

If she lived to be a hundred, Sara now thought, she'd never ever forget how Jesse had made her feel that evening. Protected. Special. Cared for.

He, on the other hand, had probably forgotten the entire incident. Girls, she'd discovered through the friendships Kay had exposed her to, tended to make more of the little things than boys. Still, secretly in her heart, she knew that Jesse was the special one, not her. He was afraid of no one, and when he was around, the world was a better place.

The trouble was, he wasn't going to be around for four impossibly long years.

Pushing off from the fence, Sara walked to the buffet table, picked up the nearly empty bowl of noodle salad and headed for the house to refill it. Kay had asked her over to see Jesse off, but also to help serve, and here she'd been outside daydreaming.

Entering the kitchen, she passed Lisa on her way back outside with two handfuls of napkins. As usual, she didn't say a word to Sara, dismissing her with a cool glance as if the younger girl were a bothersome pest to be merely tolerated. At the counter, Kay was loading the new dishwasher that had been installed recently. And Mabel, the Morgan's part-time housekeeper, was removing a steaming bean pot from the oven.

"There you are, honey," Mabel said in her faintly southern accent, a smile on her flushed face. "You'll find more noodle salad in the fridge. They're waiting for these beans."

"Okay, Mabel." Sara set the bowl she'd brought in on the counter and went to get the new one.

"Did you see what Lisa was carrying?" Kay asked, struggling with a look of annoyance. "Napkins! Do you believe that girl?" Everyone was only too aware that Lisa was allergic to work, especially in the kitchen.

Sara shut the refrigerator door. "I hope she doesn't strain herself with that heavy load."

"Heaven forbid she should wrinkle her sweet little party dress or hang around the kitchen and get so warm, her makeup will run." Kay dropped silverware into the dishwasher rack with a satisfying thunk. She'd tried, she'd *really* tried, over the past four or five years to accept Lisa as her mother had requested. But the girl was impossible, always maneuvering her way out of chores, quick to take credit when none was due, looking innocent whenever anything went wrong. "How does she manage to snow so many people with those big, innocent-looking blue eyes?"

"Maybe when we get to be sixteen, we'll be oozing charm, too." Actually, Sara didn't want to be like Lisa, but she surely envied the girl's looks. Gone was Lisa's baby fat, revealing a body to die for. Her skin was unfreckled and porcelain pure, her hair was a rich auburn, thick and long. And the most unforgivable thing was...Lisa had breasts. Not huge, but definitely there. Glancing down at her own flat chest, Sara wondered if she ever would.

"I hope she steps in a gopher hole and falls on her butt in front of the entire football team," Kay said as she slammed shut the dishwasher door.

"And, for good measure, her boobs disappear." The two girls giggled conspiratorially.

"What are you two laughing about?" Jesse asked from the doorway.

Startled, they turned as one. "Nothing," they both said.

"Uh-huh." He walked to the counter, picked up a spoon and dipped into the noodle salad bowl Sara was holding. Tasting it, he rolled his eyes appreciatively. "Boy, that's good." He looked down at Sara. "Have you eaten?"

He was so tall she nearly had to lean her head back to look up at him, making her feel like the shrimp he'd always called her. "Not yet. I'm helping out."

"I say it's time you took a break. They can get along without you for a spell." He took her arm, turning her toward the back door as he looked at his sister. "Okay if I borrow Sara?"

"You're the man of the hour, so I guess so," Kay answered, her forehead wrinkling with curiosity.

His grip on her arm light but firm, Jesse led Sara outside.

"Where are we going?"

He nodded toward a picnic bench under a green-barked palo verde tree. "Just there. I took a couple of cold drinks over for us."

Nervously trotting along, trying to keep up with his long strides, Sara glanced toward the gazebo where most everyone else was sitting and eating. "But you're the guest of honor. I can't take you away from your own party."

"*I'm* taking me away from my party." At the bench, he stopped and looked into her wary green eyes. "I can see those guys anytime. Half of them live here, and most of the others are going on to ASU with me." He let go of her arm and sat down on one of the benches. "I won't be able to see *you* for a while, and I wanted to talk."

Hesitantly, Sara slipped onto the bench opposite him. Needing something to ease her suddenly dry throat, she reached for the closest can of soda. Jesse looked so serious that he was scaring her.

Jesse watched Sara's trembling hand pick up the cold drink. He'd thought she'd gotten over this nervousness around him, but for some reason, he still made her uneasy. Which was the last thing he wanted.

He hadn't the faintest idea why, but he felt more of a brotherly concern for Sara Shephard than he did for his own sister. Certainly more than for Lisa Nagles. But then, Kay had a loving family always ready to support her. And Lisa— well, Lisa would always land on her feet. She was goal-oriented and occasionally ruthless. Lisa pretended helplessness, but that was just one of her many ploys. Jesse had seen through her in the first week she'd lived with them.

But Sara was another story.

She was such a sad, funny little kid with that solemn, thin face that contrasted so startlingly with those huge green eyes and all that terrific blond hair. She was wearing a floppy red shirt, white shorts and tennis shoes, looking younger than thirteen. Until you looked into her eyes. She was moody and giggly, quick-witted and stubborn, feisty and vulnerable— all at the same time. For years now, he'd kept an eye on her, making sure she didn't get hurt, even ready to do battle with that pathetic father of hers. Come tomorrow, he'd no longer be around to watch over her.

And that worried him—a lot.

"Are you going to be okay?" he asked gently.

The thing to do was to act as if she didn't know what he meant, Sara decided as she carefully set down the can of soda. "You mean in high school?" She rushed on to answer her own question. "Oh, sure. My grades were always good, so I think I can make the adjustment okay. The math might be a problem, especially when I get into geometry and trig. But I figure I can always send you my homework problems by smoke signals and you can signal back the answers." The little joke fell flat and she knew it, but she couldn't think of a clever follow-up.

Silently he stared at her until she finally raised her eyes to his. "That's not what I mean, and you know it." He watched her a long moment, then went on. "How are things at home?"

Sara shrugged. She might have known that Jesse would see through her. Why, when she wanted to talk with him about so many things, was this ugly subject of her father and his drinking always getting in the way? "About the same," she finally answered.

"How'd you get away today?" Jesse knew that Sundays on a ranch were slow, which meant that Noah would be hanging around the house much of the day.

She decided it was useless to pretend with Jesse. Not after last June. "I told him I was going to take Shadow for a nice long run and maybe stop for a swim in the river." She glanced over to the corral nearest the Morgan house. "Instead, I came here and tied her up over there." Sara stared down at her hands twisting in her lap, hating the need to lie.

"You lied to him so you could come to my party?" he asked, only it wasn't really a question, but an obvious summation.

Sara looked into his gray eyes. Didn't he know by now that she'd walk on cut glass for him? "You lied for me last June."

He remembered, all too well. "Has your father stayed off your back since then?" Jesse hadn't seen much of her this summer, working extra hours, saving his money.

"Pretty much."

"Does he ever mention me?"

"No." Which was only a half truth. Noah never mentioned Jesse to her directly, but she'd heard his drunken babbling the evenings he shut himself in his den, and his complaints generally centered on the Morgans, all of whom he'd get around to cursing before falling asleep.

"Do you have any idea why he hates my family?" He'd tried repeatedly to discover the reason, questioning both his parents. Hal dismissed Noah as an eccentric who held a lot of unreasonable grudges. Emily would sort of look off in the distance whenever Jesse brought up the subject, then say that it was a long story, and one she didn't want to go into. His mother knew something, Jesse was certain, but she sure wasn't talking. At least not to him.

In answer to his question, Sara shook her head. "I've asked everyone, and they just give me stupid reasons. Phil says things like, 'your father's not an easy man to understand.' And Gretchen, who's lived at the house forever, even back when she was taking care of my sick mother and me when I was a baby, clams up when I ask. 'It's not for me to say,' she tells me." Sara gazed off into the treetops with a puzzled frown. "Do you suppose that years ago your grandfather shot my grandfather, and that's what this is all about?"

"Could be. Dad did say that your father claims there was a land dispute at one time between our grandfathers, and mine won. I suppose your father could still be upset about that. Talk about carrying a grudge! The man really can't let go, if that's it."

"Sort of like the Hatfields and McCoys, right?" She had to make light of it, or otherwise the unfairness would make her terribly angry.

"Yeah, sort of." She sounded better, which cheered Jesse. He knew she had a core of toughness, or she'd never have been able to survive living with Noah as long as she had and still be as innocent as he knew she was. He picked up his can and tossed his head back to drink deeply.

Watching him, Sara reached for her can. And tipped it over, the contents spilling onto the grass with a gurgling rush. She moaned aloud. "I can't believe I did that. What is there about you that makes me so clumsy? I *never* act like this around anyone else."

Rising, Jesse grinned down at her. "Face it, shrimp, I'm a big college man, and you're a mere high school freshman. You're probably nuts about me and don't know how to tell me."

Sara angled her body away from him as she stood, unwilling to let him see her face and discover how close to the truth he'd come with that casual comment. "You're getting a swelled head, Morgan, and you haven't even left for college yet."

"Yeah, swell, that's me." Jesse reached down to the bench to pick up a small box that he'd left there when he'd brought over the sodas earlier. He removed the hand-tooled leather belt and held it up so she could see it. "I opened this a few minutes ago. You made it, didn't you?"

She felt her face flush. She'd deliberately left the small box at the back of the pile of gifts, thinking she'd be long gone before he'd get to it. "Phil's been teaching me to work in leather for a couple of years now. I know it's not as good as some..."

He stepped closer. "It's the neatest belt I've ever owned. Thank you."

"You're welcome." Self-consciously, she glanced back toward the house. The people were milling around, probably looking for the guest of honor. "It's getting late. I probably should go. And you should get back to your party."

"Not until you give me a goodbye hug."

Had she heard right? Swallowing on a thick throat, Sara looked up at him. No, he wasn't teasing. His expression was the one he generally wore around her. Yet she hesitated.

"Hey, come on, kid. I'm practically your brother." Sliding his arms around her thin frame, Jesse pulled her to him. He held her close, hoping no harm would come to her in his absence. She deserved a chance to grow up, to have people around her who loved her, to be happy.

Sara felt her heart pound as she inhaled the unfamiliar masculine scent of him, her face pressed hard against his broad chest. If she died right now, it would be all right. Jesse cared for her, at least a little.

Then suddenly, panic overwhelmed her as tears came to her eyes. She mustn't let him see, mustn't let the others spot her emotional reaction. Pulling back, she swung away. "I have to go. Tell Kay I'm sorry, will you, please?" She began to walk away.

"What's your hurry?" Jesse called after her. "You haven't even eaten."

"I'm not hungry. Good luck at ASU." And she broke into a run. Peripherally, she saw Mrs. Morgan come out onto the back porch, but she didn't dare stop. If Emily came after her, Sara would be mortified.

At the fence, she untied Shadow and hurriedly climbed on, turning the horse toward home. With a swift nudge, the mare took off, her rider leaning forward and urging her on.

Slowly walking back, Jesse watched Sara ride away, her blond hair flying behind her. In moments, she was sailing with the wind, the way she'd told him a long time ago she liked to do.

She was an odd child, he decided. What a shame that no one at her home seemed to appreciate her gentleness, her intelligence. He wondered what would happen to her, living the way she did. Maybe he'd talk to his mother tonight after everyone left and ask her to keep an eye on Sara Shephard.

"Hey, man, where you been?" Aaron Strong called out as he caught up with Jesse.

Putting his concern for his sister's little friend on the back burner, Jesse turned to his friend and joined the party.

"I think I'd catch on faster if we started on a car instead of a truck," Sara said, squinting up at Jesse as he yanked open the door to his pickup.

"Probably so," Jesse agreed patiently, "but all I've got is my truck. You want to learn to drive or not?"

She had little choice, she supposed. There certainly were no others lined up offering to teach her, with cars or trucks. She'd turned sixteen in March and here it was August, yet she still wasn't able to get her license. Undoubtedly she would be the only person to ever start her senior year unable to drive if she didn't accept Jesse's offer.

She'd timidly asked her father to teach her and he'd grudgingly said he would. When he had the time. Next she'd asked Phil, who'd taken her out on the range in his truck a couple of times and explained the mechanics of driving and let her take the wheel for a while. But that had been a month ago and Phil hadn't found free time since. School was starting in two weeks and she'd be the only senior riding the bus if she didn't do something about it.

"Yes, I want to learn." Sara hopped up into the cab and slid over so Jesse could get behind the wheel.

She was a little nervous, not so much about driving but about being alone with Jesse in the close confines of the truck's cab. She'd seen very little of him this summer, and he was going back to ASU next week. She'd deliberately stayed away because it was simply too difficult for her, watching him from a distance, unable to share private moments with him as she had when they'd been younger.

Jesse worked all summer every day, earning regular wages from his father. He did everything from training the horses, to breeding them, to attending auctions and arranging sales along with Hal. Sara knew Hal was grooming his only son to take over the operation of the ranch one day, and she had no doubt that Jesse would be up to the task. But that left little leisure time for quiet walks and shared horseback rides.

She missed that aspect of their relationship and had felt it best to stay away rather than hang around pining for something she couldn't have. It was a little like window-shopping without having the money to buy. Jesse Morgan would forever see her as a child, not as someone he could date like all the coeds she was certain hovered around him at college. He was five years older and light-years more experienced than she.

Sara had never even been out of Apache County.

Her head snapped back as Jesse shot the truck forward. "Out on the range would probably be best," he told her as he headed for the open acreage. Jesse wasn't sure why he'd agreed to take an hour or two off to give driving instructions.

He had precious little free time and what he did have he preferred to spend sleeping. Or going into town with his friend Aaron. This summer, the two of them had been casually dating two sisters who lived in Springerville just south of St. Johns. Joyce was eighteen and Kathy, twenty. Nice enough girls, but demanding more time than either he or Aaron had to spare. Personally, he wouldn't be saddened at having to bid them a fond farewell when he and Aaron went back to ASU.

Downshifting, Jesse glanced over at Sara, staring out the side window, lost in thought. She'd changed a lot since he'd first left for college. Her freckles had disappeared and her face had matured. Those huge green eyes of hers still took on that haunted look occasionally, and her blond hair was still fabulous. He wondered if it was as soft as it looked.

She'd moved from skinny to slender and filled out some, though it was hard to tell exactly what was under the over-size white blouse she wore over her jeans. She used to chatter away at him, asking questions, introducing new topics as if her mind raced ahead of her voice. Yet now, she sat quietly studying the landscape that was as familiar to her as the palm of her hand.

"Penny for your thoughts," Jesse said, wondering if perhaps there was something wrong.

Sara had been thinking that he smelled good. It was about five in the afternoon, and he'd gone in to clean up before taking her out. His thick, dark hair was still wet from his shower and his scent was a mixture of soap and undeniable masculinity that she was seldom near enough to appreciate in anyone her own age. He had shaved and nicked his chin alongside the dimple. She had a crazy urge to kiss it and make it better.

Obviously, she could tell him none of that. "I was just wondering if it was going to rain," she lied.

Pointedly, Jesse angled to peer out the windshield and glanced up at a cloudless sky. "Highly doubtful." He sent her a concerned look. "Everything all right at home?"

Sara's nerves felt strained. "Could we spend just one hour together without talking about my father?" She lived with him, even loved him in her own way, but she didn't want to waste the little time she had with Jesse discussing Noah.

"Okay by me." He'd much rather see her annoyed than hurting. After all these years, he'd learned to read her pretty well. At the point where the land leveled, Jesse brought the truck to a stop and shoved it into park. "I'm going to walk around while you scoot behind the wheel."

Sara grabbed his arm before he could jump out. "Wait. Don't you want to go over some things with me before I get in the driver's seat?"

"This isn't something you can learn any other way except by doing it." He waved to include the open land stretching on all sides of them. "There's no other vehicle in sight. You can't possibly hurt yourself or the truck. Trust me. I'll talk you through it."

Sara released an anxious sigh and slid over after he got out. She studied the gauges while he climbed in beside her. Placing her hands on the wheel, she forced herself to relax.

"This is an automatic," he began, "so there's very little you have to learn other than how to work the pedals and to steer." He watched her nod nervously. "You remember anything that Phil told you?" He hoped the Lazy-S ranch manager had already taught her the basics.

"Yes, everything."

He'd forgotten how bright she was. "All right, show me."

Taking a deep breath, Sara put her foot on the brake and shifted from park to drive. Gently she touched the gas pedal and they began inching forward.

"Just go around the bushes and try to dodge the tumbleweed."

They were moving along nicely. Sara was thinking it wasn't all that difficult. "Should I avoid the ruts in the ground, too?" she asked, trying for some levity she was far from feeling.

"Not a bad idea. This truck isn't paid for yet." He felt her pick up speed. Getting cocky, was she? "This isn't a horse. It's not as easy to control as Shadow."

Sara slowed, then swerved around a bush directly in their path that she'd swear had just appeared out of nowhere. "I thought there were lots of horses under that hood."

"Yeah, but they're wild horses. You've got to learn to tame them."

"Think I'd be good at taming wild horses, Jesse?"

He glanced over at her. Was Sara flirting with him? After a moment, he decided he'd merely read something into her innocent remark. "Don't you remember, shrimp? I always told you you could do anything you set out to do." He felt more comfortable using his childhood nickname for her. After all, this was Kay's best friend, someone who was like another sister to him.

Sara turned the wheel gradually, heading toward the river. "Yes, you always did have faith in me." They rode along in silence for several minutes. Through the open truck window, she could smell the heat of the day still on the land. In the distance, she could see a black vulture circling overhead. Perhaps it had found the carcass of a steer or a dead horse.

She turned sharply to avoid another wild shrub, and they both jerked to the left.

"You might want to try slowing down on your turns, tap lightly on the brakes. It'll be a smoother ride that way."

"Yes, sir."

Jesse angled his body to face her, studying her profile. He had to admit she was more attractive than either Joyce or Kathy. And she wasn't finished developing yet. "Have you decided what you want to do with your life? Will Noah want you to go on to college?"

She let out an exasperated breath. "He wants me to go to the University of New Mexico where he went, but I'm not sure I want to do that."

"What, then?"

"All I've ever known is the Lazy-S," she admitted. "But already I can see so many things I'd do differently than my dad if I had a chance to run the ranch."

"That's good. I'd alter things at our place, too. Without change and growth, a ranch can easily go under. You have to keep up with the times."

At the river's edge, she touched the brakes and eased the truck to a bumpy stop alongside a tall piñon pine. "I don't believe my father's made a change since before I was born." She shifted into park. "You know, I'd always thought driving was difficult. You made it easy."

"I didn't do anything. But this isn't all, either. Wait until tomorrow when we go out on the roads, into traffic."

Her heart picked up its pace, not because she was excited about driving in traffic, but because he was going to be with her. "Can we get out for a few minutes?"

"Sure. Turn off the engine." Jesse stepped out, wondering at her pensive mood.

Sara walked along the grass bordering the rushing water. Yellow and purple wildflowers in random clusters nestled among the red rocks and thin grass. The air smelled of pine. A sudden movement through a clump of trees had her looking up and smiling at a spotted deer scurrying from sight. "I love it out here," she commented as Jesse fell in step beside her.

Hands in his pockets, Jesse gazed up at a sky dimming with approaching dusk. "Me, too. I can't imagine living anywhere else. Ranching sort of gets in your blood."

"I agree."

His thoughts returned to Noah who hadn't let go of his absurd prejudices in all these years. "Do you think your father will turn the ranch over to you after you graduate from college?" The man had no other heirs, but he was contrary enough to burn it to the ground if the mood struck him.

Sara shrugged. "Your guess is as good as mine. He doesn't like me very much." Probably not at all, if she were to face the bare facts.

Touching her arm, Jesse stopped them both and waited until she turned to him. "I don't think it's you. Something happened years ago to sour your father, but I don't believe it had anything to do with you. He's unable to get past it, and he's made you and everyone around him miserable. I kind of feel sorry for him.''

Sara looked down as she kicked at a pebble with the toe of her shoe, realizing that the disgust and anger she felt for her father crowded out everything else. ''You don't live with him. I know he's unhappy. No one drinks as much as he does except to escape. But he won't let anyone get close to him.''

''Maybe it would be best if you went away to college.''

''Most likely. But not to New Mexico.''

''Lisa loves it at the University of Arizona, and Tucson isn't all that far.''

The last thing she'd do would be to go anywhere where Lisa Nagles was. Lisa had been even ruder to her this summer than in previous years. ''I want to go to ASU with Kay, but I don't know if I can convince my father.'' Because the conversation was depressing her, Sara shook her head and smiled up at him. ''Oh, well, I have a year to work on him. Do you believe in miracles?''

''In a way. Kay thinks it's a miracle this fellow named Mark asked her out tonight. What do you think of him?''

''He's a jock, but he's all right.''

''You don't date jocks?'' he asked, his tone teasing. When she didn't answer, he came back with another question. ''Who *do* you date, Sara?''

No one, she wanted to tell him, though she'd been asked out several times in her junior year. No one seemed to measure up to the image of a certain man that wouldn't leave her mind. ''I don't go out much,'' she said evasively.

He should have known her father wouldn't allow her such freedom until possibly the day she turned forty. ''I thought it was just the Morgans he was against?''

Sara had never in her life done a bold thing, but she decided to take a chance this time. ''I'd defy him to go out with a Morgan, if one asked me." She watched the awareness move into his gray eyes as he caught her meaning. "I've been defying him for years just to be near the Morgans."

A light breeze toyed with the ends of her hair. Jesse's hands itched with a sudden yearning to bury his fingers in the thick blond waves. "You have, haven't you? I suppose because of how nice my mom and dad are."

"Partly."

"And Kay. You two are such good friends." He found his breathing going shallow at her nearness, at the womanly scent of her wrapping around him. Her mouth looked soft and inviting. Oh, Lord, what was he thinking of? She was just a kid.

"Yes, I love Kay like a sister." Sara saw a muscle under his eye twitch with nerves and suddenly felt calmer. She took a step closer. "And you. There was always you."

His hand touched her shoulder, whether to draw her nearer or push her away, he wasn't sure. "Sara, I'm not sure I should do what I want to do."

"What do you want to do?"

"Kiss you."

"I want that, too, Jesse." She swayed toward him just a fraction, needing, wanting to feel his hard arms envelop her.

It would take a stronger man than he to resist what she was offering, Jesse thought as his head dipped and his arms went around her. The first touch of his mouth to hers was hesitant, almost wary. Then he felt her rise on tiptoe, pressing closer, her lips incredibly soft and opening to him. With a deep moan, he dragged her to him.

He could tell she was inexperienced, but her curiosity made up for the lack. Her hands slid up and over his shoulders, sliding across his nape, her slim fingers tangling in his hair. Jesse felt her breasts crush against his chest and became aware that she was fuller than the loose clothing she always wore would indicate. He cupped the back of her neck, holding her head steady for his kiss, while his other hand slipped down her slender back and settled low, pressing her nearer.

His mind was whirling, racing out of control. If her father caught them, this time he *would* shoot. If *his* father saw them, there'd be hell to pay. Sara was too young, too innocent, too trusting. He should step back from her, he knew. And he would. In just a moment, another moment of tasting the sweetness she offered him so willingly, so freely.

Sara felt as if she'd been tossed into the vortex of one of the dust devils that often swirled in the open Arizona fields. Jesse could probably tell she'd never been kissed before, but she didn't care. He was here, locked together with her, where she'd dreamed of him being through countless lonely nights. And she didn't want anything to spoil this enchanted moment.

Finally, he pulled back, breathing hard, to look into green eyes dazed with the beginnings of a surprising passion. Heart hammering, he bent to take her mouth again. Stronger even than before, needs awakened in him. Through the foggy cloud of desire, Jesse knew he'd never experienced a kiss like Sara's. When her lips parted, he slipped his tongue inside and heard her surprised intake of breath. He'd been about to lift his head when the tip of her tongue touched his hesitantly. On a sigh of surrender, she kissed him back with all the pent-up feelings she'd saved only for him. She gave to him and, like a starving man, Jesse took.

The galloping thunder of horse's hooves nearby broke through their absorption with each other, and they jumped apart like guilty children caught at the cookie jar. Jesse turned to see Lisa reining in Cinnamon, then holding the mare steady while she stared at the two of them. Even across the distance, he could see the cold fury in her gaze. Yanking her horse about, Lisa took off in a swirl of dust.

"Damn," he muttered. "Of all people to come along." Jesse ran a shaky hand through his hair. It wasn't for himself he cared; he could handle Lisa. But she was already just short of ugly to Sara. He'd have to talk with her before she said something, perhaps to Sara's father. He wouldn't put it past her.

"Why is she so angry? Are you and her...?" Sara couldn't complete the question.

"No. Never." How could she think he could kiss her like that if he and Lisa meant anything to each other?

"We weren't doing anything wrong," Sara said, more to convince herself than him. Why did Lisa have to come along and spoil the most beautiful moment of her life?

Jesse trailed his fingers along her smooth cheek, then cupped her chin. "No, we weren't doing anything wrong, and we're not going to let anyone make us feel as if we were." But if he stayed here in this isolated spot and kept looking into her eyes, he'd kiss her again. And maybe more. He dropped his hand. "Come on. I'll take you back. It's getting late."

Walking with him, seeing his frown, she began to worry. "Are you angry with me?"

"No. I'm angry with me. I shouldn't have let things get so far."

At the truck, Sara turned to face him. "Why, Jesse? Why is it wrong for you to want me?" She was a virgin, inexperienced and innocent. But she knew she hadn't mistaken his desire. Nor her own.

He softened immediately, as only she could make him do. He had to make her understand so she wouldn't feel rejected. "Because you're too young, under the age of consent. There are laws to protect young girls."

"But how do you turn your feelings off?"

She had him there. Slowly, Jesse smiled. "Damned if I know."

Opening the truck door, he faced a new worry. Now that he'd tasted her, could he forget her?

Chapter Three

Jesse wiped his damp forehead with the sleeve of his plaid shirt, then squinted into the blazing sun of a June afternoon. The temperatures usually didn't climb to ninety until July, but today was unseasonably hot. He propped a booted foot on the new wooden fencing that stretched as far as the eye could see enclosing the Morgans' west pasture, and nodded in satisfaction. "They look good, don't they?" he asked his father.

Next to him, Hal Morgan gazed out on four hundred head of holstein roaming the range. He had to agree. "I sure never dreamed I'd turn into a cow man instead of a horse man."

"You're both, Dad." Jesse shifted his tired shoulder muscles, trying to loosen the kinks. Though it was only four o'clock, he'd been up twelve hours, overseeing the finishing touches on the new cattle barns and instructing the newly hired cowhands, some of whom he could see patrolling the pasture perimeter on horseback. "It just plain makes sense to diversify, and holsteins give off an abundance of low-fat milk."

Hal knew his son was right. Already the Arabian horse market was shaky, and word was that the thoroughbreds would follow. Show horses would always need training, but there wasn't the money in that aspect of ranching that there was in breeding and selling. Jesse had studied animal husbandry, agriculture and business administration for four years. It would be foolish to ignore his educated advice. "I agree. I think the ranchers in our area who don't vary their stock and the services they offer are going to be the ones to crash first."

Jesse brushed a lock of hair off his forehead as he started back to the truck they'd parked on an incline. He badly needed a shave and shower, along with something cold to drink. He was tired and grungy, but he felt good. He'd always felt confident that he had his father's love and affection, but since graduating from ASU last month, he sensed Hal's respect and admiration as well. His vote of confidence in Jesse in allowing him to lead the Morgan Ranch along a new, innovative path spoke volumes.

"It's not too late for any of them. They can plant crops, a winter harvest and a different summer one to keep the soil rich. Or they can add cattle, either for milk or beef. I've heard that a couple of ranchers have added sheep. Lots of choices."

Walking with Jesse, Hal felt a rush of pride. At twenty-two, his son was a fine-looking man, hard-working and strong. But more important, he was honest and caring. Though Hal was only fifty, he decided it was nice to be able to share the ranching responsibilities with Jesse. "I doubt if many of them will, though the newspapers are full of some sad predictions. Trouble is, we've got some real old-fashioned ranchers here, men who work the same land once owned by their fathers and grandfathers and some go even further back. Stubborn men who don't accept change."

At the truck, Jesse opened the driver's door. "Then they'll fold, Dad. It's as simple as that."

The father studied the son a moment before climbing into the truck. So easy for the young to initiate change, to embrace new ways quickly. Not that Hal didn't agree with Jesse's plan. But he also understood that some of the oldtimers wouldn't, *couldn't,* make instant transformations comfortably. "I'd really hate to see that happen. Ranchers depend on one another. What hurts one hurts us all."

Jesse turned on the engine and headed back to the house. "You're on the board of directors of the Show Commission. You know horsemen from Albuquerque to Louisville, even Canada. Maybe you can talk some sense into the holdouts."

"Maybe." Hal waved out the side window to one of the hands heading out, then resumed his concerned thoughts. "I'd be willing to wager Noah Shephard wouldn't listen. Certainly not to me, perhaps not to anyone."

As always, at the mention of their closest neighbor, Jesse felt the heat of anger. He hadn't actually run into Noah in a year and, though he'd been home a couple of weeks, he hadn't seen Sara come around. After that afternoon last August by the river when he'd kissed her, he'd continued teaching her to drive until he'd left for school. But he'd made certain they were out in traffic and that people were around the house when they set out and returned.

It wasn't that he didn't like Sara, that he didn't want Sara. He wanted her *too* much. But she was still very young, and as his buddy Aaron was always reminding him, she was jailbait. But that hadn't stopped Jesse from allowing her to star in more restless dreams than he'd care to count. Then he'd awaken filled with guilt. How could he be longing to make love to a girl younger than his kid sister? Men like him simply didn't do that sort of thing.

"How is old Noah?" Jesse asked.

Hal fingered the cleft in his chin, a duplicate of his son's, as he pondered his reply. He'd known Noah Shephard all his life, yet he didn't really know the man. What he knew of him, he didn't like. The land dispute their fathers supposedly had been involved in was a fabrication of Noah's twisted thinking without a shred of proof. Yet the stubborn fool continued to insist that the Morgans had cheated the Shephards.

The other matter that Noah carried a grudge over was something a man of pride and integrity would have set aside long before this. Nonetheless, what irritated Hal the most was how Noah carried his resentment over into the second generation. His daughter was the one paying the price for her father's inflexibility.

"I haven't heard anything to the contrary, so I assume Noah hasn't changed."

They were nearing the compound, and Jesse's curiosity won over his reticence to discuss Sara. "Does Sara still come around?"

Hal had been wondering when Jesse would ask. He'd known for years that his son was sweet on Sara. And anyone with two good eyes could see that the girl worshipped Jesse. But Noah's shadow was between them. "Now and then. Her father bought her a car for graduation. Just a little four-cylinder Ford. Afraid she'll get wild, I guess, so he limits her every which way he can. Your mother said Sara has a job in town at the Valley Bank. Something to do with computers, as I recall. She's a smart little thing."

"She *is* smart. I hope he's going to let her go on to college in the fall."

Hal grunted. "Can't imagine Noah letting his daughter out of his sight for nine months of the year." As Jesse parked the truck by the barn nearest the house, Hal glanced over toward the wide front porch. "There's Sara now."

Jesse stepped out, narrowing his eyes against the glare of the late-afternoon sun. He saw his mother on the porch seated in the glider she loved while Kay relaxed in the white rattan chair. Half standing and half seated on the railing was a young woman wearing a loose yellow dress that hung nearly to her ankles and white sandals. She was turned away from him, but he could see that mass of golden hair falling down her back. "No. That can't be Sara, can it?" He'd managed to avoid seeing her his last visit home at Christmas, deciding it was in both their best interests not to start something they couldn't finish.

Hal grinned. "Little Sara's grown up."

Jesse slammed shut the truck door and followed his father to the house. Suddenly, as if sensing eyes on her, Sara turned and saw them. Slowly, she removed her sunglasses and eased to her feet. He never took his eyes from her, even as he stopped by the porch steps.

Emily greeted her two men, then raised an eyebrow in surprise when Jesse didn't respond. Kay's welcoming smile turned to one of amazement as she watched the unbroken look between her brother and her friend go on and on. Jesse just stared, his face hard and unsmiling. Sara met his unwavering gaze, her expression unreadable.

Emily and Hal excused themselves and went inside. Then, Kay muttered something about getting something cold to drink, and followed them. And still, neither Jesse nor Sara spoke.

She wanted to let out a whoop of joy at the sight of him, wanted to rush into his arms, wanted to feel that hard mouth take hers. How could he have grown even handsomer? Sara asked herself. His thick, dark hair just brushed his collar and his skin was deeply tanned, making his gray eyes appear almost silver. He needed a shave, which gave him a slightly dangerous look, something she'd never noticed before. Rumpled, dusty and sweat-stained, he was the most beautiful man she'd ever seen.

But he wasn't smiling, and he seemed angry.

She had no right to be so damn beautiful, Jesse thought with a surge of unreasonable fury. He'd been remembering a pretty girl, sweetly innocent and naive. He'd come home to find her so much more. Her skin was creamy and unblemished, her hair like a silken crown. Her eyes were a deep emerald green, eyes a man could easily drown in. Even the cotton dress couldn't disguise the curves that had seemingly overnight filled out her slender frame.

Beautiful. And still off limits. Deliberately, he made himself remember that she'd just turned seventeen a couple of months ago, that her father hated the Morgans, that he shouldn't be longing after Sara Shephard.

Sara could stand it no longer. "Hello, Jesse," she said, wishing he'd smile or say something. Why was he being so cold? The Jesse she remembered had always been so gentle and caring.

At last, Jesse tore his eyes from her and ran a hand along his day's growth of beard. He would have to run into her the first time looking like a bum and smelling like a cow while she was fresh as a spring morning. He cleared his throat, trying to find his voice, wondering what in hell to say to her.

"Hello, Sara," he finally managed to say.

"I heard you graduated. Congratulations." *Strangers. They were like strangers. What was wrong?*

"Yeah, you, too." Jesse felt torn. Perhaps if he'd have had some warning, if he'd known she was going to be here today and be so…so much a woman and so little like the girl he remembered, perhaps then he could have prepared himself. He'd have known what to say to her. As it was, his emotions were in a jumble. More than ever, he wanted to take her by the hand, drag her off somewhere where the two of them could talk and he could hold her and . . .

Damn! How could he explain that to *his* father, let alone hers?

She had to try to break through to him somehow. Maybe he was just hot, tired and caught off guard. "I still ride Shadow down by the river almost every evening. Would you want to meet me there later tonight?"

No, he couldn't do that. If he wanted her this badly in sunlight on his mother's porch, how could he fight his desire for her in secluded moonlight? He turned to her, still unsmiling. "What for?"

Sara couldn't have been more shocked if he'd struck her, but she raised her chin a notch. "I just thought we could talk."

"'Fraid not. I'm awfully busy. Managing the ranch now, in case you haven't heard." He nodded his head toward the smaller house on the other side of the greenbelt. "I've moved into the manager's cabin. I start my days at four in the morning, usually finish up around ten at night. We've got cows now, too, you know." He was rambling on like a madman, something he never did. He couldn't risk looking at her. He just wanted to get this over with. "I need a shower. See you around." Not a great exit line, but coldly efficient. Without another word, he took off for his cabin.

Stunned, Sara stepped from the porch and stood staring after him a long moment, her eyes filling, destroying her careful composure. She didn't know what she'd done or how she'd managed to anger him, but evidently she had.

Behind her, she heard a screen door slam. She couldn't face any of the Morgans right now. Quickly, she dashed to her car, her vision blurred by her tears.

"Sara, wait," Kay called after her.

But Sara was already behind the wheel, jamming her key into the ignition. Hurriedly, she pulled out of the driveway and turned onto the road.

Alongside the house, Lisa pushed away from the tree she'd been leaning against. She'd seen and heard everything, and been elated at the turn of events. At last, Jesse had gotten rid of little miss goody-two-shoes from next door. Maybe now that he was back to stay and Simple Sara was out of the picture, Jesse would notice her.

She'd be around all summer to make sure he did. Tossing back her long auburn hair, Lisa smiled to herself as she sauntered toward the show barn.

Work was the best cure, Jesse decided as he tossed a cube of baled hay down from the barn loft. Work would empty the mind and tire the body. Why then was he still having so damn much trouble sleeping?

"Hey, buddy," Aaron Strong called up. "You want to watch your aim?"

Jesse adjusted his thick haying gloves as he glanced down and saw that Aaron had had to jump out of the way of his last pitch. "Sorry." He'd been pleased when his father had agreed to hire his friend and put him in charge of the cattle. They needed a man of Aaron's experience, and Aaron needed a job since his father had recently sold the ranch he'd nearly bankrupted. Another stubborn rancher unwilling to adjust to the times. Aaron had had a rough year. Woman troubles. Suddenly, Jesse could relate.

Since he'd seen Sara Shephard.

Jesse swore under his breath as he hooked the clamps into another cube. Why was it that no matter which path his thoughts took, they kept coming back to one or both Shephards?

"You going to pitch that down to me or play with it a while?" Aaron called up.

Not bothering to answer, Jesse tossed it over, his aim better this time. He watched Aaron shift the cube to the side, then stop and pull off his gloves.

"Let's take a break," he said, walking over to the refrigerator in the corner. "It's so damn hot I'm soaking wet."

Jesse climbed down the ladder and went over to pop the tab on a cold can. He nearly drained the contents in one long swallow, then swiped at his mouth.

Aaron eyed his friend speculatively. "You want to tell me about it?"

At six-four, Aaron was two inches taller and a good twenty pounds heavier than Jesse. He was blond and good-looking, a man who'd never lacked for female companionship. The two had become friends the first day of high school. Aaron probably knew Jesse better than anyone. Yet the thing that was eating at him now wasn't something he was willing to discuss, even with Aaron who'd gone through something similar lately. Yet he wouldn't insult his friend by pretending he didn't know what he meant. "No." He dabbed at his damp face with a red kerchief.

"Can I wager a guess?"

"No." Jesse drank the rest of his drink and tossed the can aside.

"Damn, Jesse, this isn't like you. I can understand a bad day or two. But it's been over a week now, and your disposition's on a par with that mean old bull we got penned next door."

"I'll be fine. Just got a lot on my mind, is all."

"Yeah, right." Aaron crushed his can in his big fist. "Why the hell don't you go on over there and make up with that girl, 'cause you aren't going to be okay again till you do." Only a long, close friendship allowed Aaron to speak his mind.

Even so, Jesse whirled around, glaring. "Why the hell don't you mind your own business?" Turning on his heel,

Jesse stormed out of the barn, walking past his father with only a curt nod.

Hal ambled over to where Aaron stood frowning. "A mite touchy, is he?"

"You got that right."

Hal clapped his hand on Aaron's shoulder. "Don't take it personal, son. If it's any consolation, he's the same with all of us these days. We both know what's eating at him, but we can't help him with it. A man's got to work that sort of thing out for himself."

Aaron made a sympathetic sound. "Yeah, I know." Pulling his gloves on, he went back to work.

The wind whistled past her ears, and her long hair whipped about her head as she flew across the plain on her horse. Leaning forward on Shadow, gripping the mare's thick mane, Sara saw the outbuildings of the Lazy-S swim into focus through her narrowed eyes. It was nearly dusk and she supposed she'd best head for the barn and let Shadow cool off, although she'd liked to have stayed out a while longer.

The problem was that no matter how many hours she put in on her job or what she did at home afterward, she couldn't seem to tire herself enough to sleep.

Slowing the mare, she sat upright and aimed her for the open corral gate, feeling weary. She could wear out her body, yet couldn't turn off her mind.

Inside the fenced area, Sara slid off the horse and fastened the gate, then took the reins and began walking the heated mare along the fencing, talking softly to her. As she turned the corner near the barn, a shadow separated itself from the building, and she stepped back, startled.

"Where you been, girl?" Noah Shephard asked his daughter.

"Out riding." She would have thought that was obvious, even if he'd begun drinking since early afternoon, which he seemed to be doing more and more.

"Who were you with?" he persisted.

"No one. Just Shadow and me." Sara was used to his interrogations and answered almost automatically. He'd been quizzing her like this for years.

"I thought I saw someone with you when you were up on that hill, then he rode off the other way." Noah stepped closer into the spotlight that shone on the corral from the barn entrance. "You been seeing that Morgan boy again? Answer me, girl."

She hated it when he didn't use her name, almost as if he didn't remember it. She saw that his white hair was askew, his clothes wrinkled and his eyes bloodshot. *Oh, Dad, how did you let this happen to you? And why?* He'd been an attractive man once, tall and straight, lean and strong. She'd seen the pictures in the family album. Now he was stooped, his skin an unhealthy color, and his hands trembled badly. At forty-eight, Noah looked sixty. She was amazed that he still put in a day's work, still called the shots around the ranch. It was the nights that tormented him.

"No, I was alone," she answered patiently. The thing to do was to wait him out and soon he'd tire of the repetitious questions and go back to his den and his beloved bottle.

"I don't believe you," Noah stated in his deep, rumbling voice. He'd always been able to make Sara tremble with his voice alone.

Her nerves had about had it. She'd spent two miserable weeks since her last encounter with Jesse, worrying and wondering why he'd gone to so much trouble to hurt her. She'd spent her days in a fog and her nights wrestling with the sheets, only to fall into snatches of sleep where she saw Jesse's face everywhere. On top of all that, she didn't need her father's ridiculous accusations. "I'm sorry if you don't, but it's the truth."

After another turn around the corral, she led Shadow into the barn and turned her over to William, the groom who was still hanging around. Outside, Sara drew in a deep breath and made her way to the back door. Perhaps she'd feel better after a shower.

But in the kitchen, Noah stepped in front of her again. "I told you I didn't want you going anywhere near those Morgans again."

This time, at least, she could be honest with him. "I haven't been. I was out riding alone. I swear it."

"They're no good, you know. Thieves, all of 'em. They only want more of my land." Noah poured coffee into the ceramic mug he carried around the house with him. Sara knew it was heavily laced with whiskey.

There was no use talking with him when he started in on the Morgans. She was in no mood to discuss them herself this evening. "I'm going up to shower."

Noah followed her to the stairs, but before she started up, he took hold of her arm and peered into her face in the dim light. "You're not...not her. You're blond. She's not blond, and the eyes are all wrong. Hers are gray."

"Who do you mean?" Sara asked. He'd rambled on about someone before, but drunk or sober, he never revealed much. She knew from old snapshots that her mother also had been blond, which made her doubly curious about this woman who seemed to linger in her father's memory.

Dropping his hand, he waved her away. "Never mind. Just leave me alone."

More than happy to oblige, Sara started up the stairs.

"That Morgan boy don't want you, either," Noah called after her. "He's just using you to get me. He'll only hurt you. Mark my words, girl. He's going to hurt you real bad."

Sara ran the rest of the way as she heard Gretchen come out from her downstairs bedroom and try to persuade Noah to lie down. She closed her bedroom door, shutting out the disjointed mutterings that she knew would go on for hours. Fighting tears, she flung herself on her bed.

She would not cry. She would bide her time, then leave this house as soon as the fall school semester began. She loved the ranch and had hoped one day after college to be able to help run it. But she needed to leave this unhappy home, even if it meant giving in and attending the university her father had chosen. She was slowly dying here.

She needed to be with friends, yet after what had happened with Jesse, she didn't feel right about going to visit Kay, nor could she ask her friend over. She was stuck in an impossible situation, and she'd even lost Jesse's affection.

For nine long months since the time he'd kissed her, she'd hoped and prayed that Jesse returned the feelings she had for him. He hadn't written from school, but she knew he was busy with his senior year, and she hadn't expected him to. Always before, they'd been able to pick right up where they'd left off. But this time, he'd rebuffed her so coldly, so deliberately.

He couldn't have known how she'd planned for all those months, how she'd hoped things would be when he returned. She'd wanted to find a way to be alone with him, to see if he would kiss her again. To see if she'd read more into that first kiss than she should have.

To see if the deepening feelings she had for Jesse Morgan were real. To discover if what she felt could be love.

She'd been so certain he'd return the same old Jesse, smiling down at her, touching her hair, his gray eyes filled with concern. In a short few minutes, he'd shattered all her dreams. Now there was nothing to stay for.

Soon, Sara thought, she'd be gone. Gone from a father who didn't care for her and a man who didn't want her. In the meantime, she'd go to work, do her chores and try to stay out of Noah's way.

He'd been a sonofabitch and he knew it. Jesse guided Sundance along slowly in the moonlight, having come to the conclusion that solitude was all the company he deserved. For weeks, he'd been abrupt and unkind to his family, distracted and surly to his men, acting like a bear with a wounded paw. He'd been so self-absorbed that he hadn't listened to Aaron or Kay or even his mother's pleas. But earlier tonight, when his father had taken him aside and told him to shape up or take some time off, he'd had to face a hard fact.

He was crazy about Sara Shephard, and the feeling wasn't apt to go away.

Sundance knew the terrain along the fence well and easily avoided a low barrel cactus. Jesse scarcely noticed, so deep in thought was he. He'd set out after dinner and ridden hard, like the devil himself were after him. Then he'd slowed, cooling his stallion and his own fevered brain. He'd decided not to return to the barn until he'd thought things through and had come up with a plan.

He cared about Sara more than he'd planned. More than he probably should. He hadn't been able to admit that until tonight, always trying to force himself to remember that she was a teenager, his kid sister's friend, too young for him. But he couldn't hide from the truth. He not only cared, he wanted her as only a man who is serious about a woman can want.

He needed to tell her that, to apologize for his behavior, to win her trust and friendship again. Then they'd have something to build on, something that might lead to a future together.

Jesse had known his share of girls and women, but had never even once thought of permanence with any one of them. Until tonight, he'd never conceded the fact that always, as far back as he could remember, Sara had been there hovering in the background of his mind.

But he had some making up to do.

He'd thought that maybe he'd drop in on Sara at her job and ask to talk with her privately there, on neutral territory. But he'd dismissed that idea as too calculated. Then he'd thought he'd wait until the next time she dropped in to see Kay and take her aside. But he realized after the way he'd treated her, she probably wouldn't come over again.

He'd wondered if he should call over to the Shephard house, hoping she'd answer the phone, or maybe the housekeeper would. Anyone but Noah. Not that he would mind having it out with her father, but he didn't want to risk getting Sara in trouble. Yet that plan didn't appeal to him much, either.

A new thought struck him. What if he'd ruined everything, and she wouldn't talk to him again? No, that couldn't be. He would convince her, that's all. Jesse stared up at a full moon and inhaled the rich scent of nearby ponderosa pines. Things would work out. He'd see to it that they did.

A sound suddenly broke through his thoughts, the sound of horse's hooves nearby. Stopping Sundance, he gazed in the direction of the noise and saw in the moonlight that a brown mare was streaking across the pasture on the other side of the fence he'd been trailing. The Shephard side.

For a moment, he thought it was a runaway horse. But as he peered intently, he saw a bareback rider leaning forward onto the horse's thick neck, racing as one with the animal. Only one person he knew rode like that.

Sundance was straining, chomping at the bit to give chase, and Jesse gave him the chance. The wooden fencing was low at this point and after a few minutes, he felt the stallion's speed was sufficient to clear it easily. On the other side, he urged Sundance to go even faster.

Sara was a good horsewoman, but Jesse's stallion had been groomed as a racehorse and had no trouble closing the gap. He saw her become aware of someone following, saw her turn and look back and knew the moment she recognized him. "Stop, Sara," he called out.

But instead, she put forth a burst of speed.

So much for the thought that she was going to make this easy for him, Jesse thought, as he swore ripely in the hot night air. Nudging Sundance's sides, he pushed on. When he pulled alongside the mare, he shouted again for Sara to stop. Again, she ignored him. Jesse decided to take matters into his own hands.

Watching carefully, he waited until the moment was just right, then leaned down and gripped Sara around her waist. With a shocked yelp, she dropped the reins instantly, and he lifted her off Shadow. He plunked his angry armload down in the saddle in front of him.

Sara struggled, but Jesse circled her squirming body and held her close while he bent down to grab Shadow's reins with his other hand before the mare moved out of reach. "Stop it, Sara," he warned her as he slowed both horses.

Furious, Sara shook her head, feeling her long, loose hair swipe across his face. She hoped she'd momentarily blinded him. Maybe then, he'd let her go. Seething, breathing hard, she forced herself to relax, letting him think she was complying. She was in no mood to listen to whatever Jesse had to say.

She'd gone another round with Noah tonight, more repetitious accusations, and she felt drained, whipped. She'd waited until her father had drifted into a drunken sleep, then she'd left the house. She'd simply had to get out where she could breathe, away from that stifling atmosphere.

And now Jesse was confining her.

With no small effort, Jesse brought the two horses to a stop near a thick cluster of pine trees. He could tell Sara was still aggravated, though she was putting on a show of meekness. It wasn't in her nature to give in so readily. "I'm going to lower you to the ground," he said evenly.

"I can get down myself." And she did, arcing her leg over and jumping down. She knew every inch of this ranch, every tree and bush. And she knew she didn't want to stay here and have a chat with a man boorish enough to yank her from her own horse. If he was planning to apologize, he was about two weeks too late. The moment her feet hit the ground, she began running into the woods.

"Dammit, Sara," Jesse yelled as he climbed down. Quickly, he tethered the mare to a tree limb and Sundance upwind so the stallion wouldn't get restless. Then he took off after Sara.

He had reason to be grateful that the pine trees here weren't dense and that the moonlight sprinkled down from a nearly cloudless sky. Like the stallion, he was bigger and faster and caught up with her easily. Circling her with his arms, he pinned hers tight to her body and backed her up to the trunk of a tree where she stood glaring up at him.

"Why are you doing this?" Sara spat out, angrier than she could ever remember being.

"Why are you running from me?" Jesse countered.

"Why would I want to talk with you when you've made it very clear you don't even want to be near me?"

"You're wrong. I want to be near you so much I ache with it." He saw the sudden confusion in the rich green of her eyes. But the wariness remained, along with the distrust.

"You have a funny way of showing it."

"I hurt you that day, and I'm sorry. Very sorry." To show he meant it, Jesse loosened his hold on her and straightened, taking a step back.

In the dappled moonlight, she studied his face. "Why were you so cold, so deliberately rude?"

"I didn't mean to be. I want to make it up to you." He dared reach out and place his hands on her, running his fingers along her bare arms, gentle, soothing.

"I want to know why you did it." He owed her that much for putting her through two solid weeks of hell. Perhaps she didn't deserve his love, but she hadn't deserved that cool indifference.

"Don't you know why?" His throat was dry, and his voice sounded anguished. "For so long now, I've denied what I feel for you, telling myself you were off limits, too young for me, all kinds of excuses. I pushed you away because I didn't think it was right to reach out for you the way I wanted to."

He saw the surprise on her face, still mingled with disbelief. "I can't fight this anymore, Sara." His hands slid around her back, drawing her fractionally closer, relieved when she didn't resist. "I've never felt like this about anyone but you." When she didn't answer, just continued to stare up at him, he felt a jolt of fear. "Have I waited too long? Have I messed things up too badly between us, Sara?"

Had she heard right? Dare she believe him? "Oh, Jesse," she whispered, and rose on tiptoe, her mouth reaching for his. She would depend on her body, her senses to tell her if this was real, if this was right. Words couldn't always be relied upon, but as her eyes drifted shut, she decided to trust her instincts.

He was too emotionally fired up by the wild ride and the vigorous run through the woods to go gently. His arms wound around her so tightly not even a shadow could have gotten between them as he felt her heart pound against his own.

At the touch of her lips on his, passion flared instantly, fiercely. Then he was kissing her and she was kissing back—small nips, long lingering brushing of lips, tongues twining intimately. Sighs, murmurs, throaty moans as their hands

stroked everywhere, cheeks and hair and shoulders. The
need for physical contact and for words to reassure, was
huge within them.

"I thought you were angry with me, that you didn't want
me near you," she whispered against his seeking lips.

"No, never that."

"I thought I'd lost you forever."

"You could never lose me, never."

"I've been so miserable."

"I've been a bear because I couldn't have you," Jesse
admitted as he stroked her hair.

"You have me. You've always had me."

And then Sara eased back, her fingers fumbling with the
buttons of his shirt, needing to touch that strong, broad
chest. Though he hesitated, she did not, moving to shrug out
of her own shirt. When they were both bare to the waist,
their eyes feasted on each other.

Jesse's hand trembled as he raised it to cup one perfect
breast. He watched Sara close her eyes, letting the feeling
take her. He heard the soft sound she made low in her throat
as she swayed toward him. "Are you sure, Sara? I . . ."

Slowly, she looked up at him as she placed her hands in
the thick, curly hair of his chest. "Yes. This feels right, so
very right."

Struggling with needs that hammered at him, Jesse lowered her to the fragrant bed of pine needles and followed her
down. Clumsy in his haste, he finally managed to pull off his
boots and hers, then rid them both of the rest of their
clothes before returning to kiss her again. And again.

She felt his lips skim down the line of her throat and lower
to claim the breasts his hands had lovingly prepared. She
couldn't lie still as he teased and tasted, his clever fingers
touching everywhere, setting her on fire.

Sara was whirling away on a sea of sensation. She'd nurtured needs deep inside her for years, storing them away

greedily, and he was answering each one in turn. From a distance, she heard an owl hoot, heard the soft swish of the pine branches overhead swaying in a light breeze. Helpless to do anything but allow him, her limp arms fell away and she gave herself up to each savage new pleasure.

Breathing hard, Jesse paused to let his eyes roam down the length of her incredible loveliness. "You can't know how many hours I've lain awake dreaming of looking at you like this." His eyes returned to hers. "But you're far more beautiful than my dreams."

Sara couldn't reply, could only look at him with her heart in her eyes, and trail her fingers along the hard line of his jaw. Gently, she traced the deep indentation in his chin. She still couldn't believe he was here, hers to touch freely, hers to love at last.

He lowered to her, his lips distracting her with deep, open-mouthed kisses while his fingers found her. She arched and froze. He waited until she relaxed, then moved on. So aroused was she that in two tender strokes, he had her soaring as her hands clenched at his back.

The rippling pleasure had Sara sighing, had her moaning his name as her breath shuddered from her. She'd heard her friends talk and she'd dreamed, but she hadn't believed. Until now.

Jesse knew he was close to the end of his endurance. His legs trembling, he raised himself above her. "This may hurt a little," he warned.

"I know. It's all right." She was floating in such euphoria, she couldn't believe anything could hurt her now.

It did hurt, for a brief moment. Then Jesse's hands lifted her hips and he joined with her more fully. The movements were slow and steady, then suddenly long and sure, and finally unbridled in their intensity. Her hands clutched at his biceps as she hung on. Then there was only a mindless pleasure that rocketed through her and went on and on. Sara let herself go, let the sensation take over.

And when long minutes later she opened her eyes, Jesse was smiling down at her. She didn't say the words aloud, but only to herself. *I love you, Jesse.*

Chapter Four

Sara awoke on a rainy Saturday morning in mid-August and knew something was terribly wrong. She'd suspected for several weeks now and finally had to face the disturbing facts.

It had been such an idyllic summer, the best she'd ever known. Small wonder that she'd put aside every small worry, every possible problem, unwilling to allow anything or anyone to taint the beauty of this magical time. Since that wonderful night she'd given her innocence so eagerly to Jesse, life had taken on a rosy hue.

She'd spent her days working at the bank, though her concentration had been somewhat marred by thoughts of Jesse that intruded regularly during the endless hours she was separated from him. Evenings after dinner and the completion of her chores, she'd watched her father, waiting for the moment when he'd fall into his alcohol-induced slumber. Then she'd sneak out of the house, lead Shadow out of the barn and take off to meet Jesse.

Throughout the long, unseasonably dry summer, they'd met frequently, usually every other evening. By prearrangement, they'd rendezvoused at the river and enjoyed a swim at midnight. Or they'd ridden side by side on horseback in the moonlight, quietly talking as they'd always been able to do. And they'd returned often to the site of their first encounter and fallen wordlessly onto the now-familiar bed of pine needles.

There they'd made love. Frequently, passionately, lovingly. Sometimes, as the first time, with pounding need and haste that left them both panting and breathless. Other times, sweetly and slowly, savoring the pleasure they brought each other. But always, Sara thought, with stunning beauty.

Their conversations had run the gamut from childhood memories to teenage uncertainties and on to nebulous dreams of the future. They got along surprisingly well throughout this intense period of love newly discovered and emotions peaking. They argued over only one topic: Noah Shephard.

From the first night on, Jesse had wanted the two of them to go to his parents and to her father, to bring out in the open their feelings for each other. He hated the sneaking around, the lying, the furtiveness. While Sara hated the deception, too, she feared Noah more.

She'd begged Jesse to wait, to see if she could soften Noah. Barring that, she knew she'd be leaving the last week of August for Albuquerque, for she'd agreed to her father's choice of college in an attempt to keep him happy. Living on campus—which Noah had finally agreed to— she'd be free to have Jesse visit her, and there'd be no need to hide their relationship. All too often, she'd seen Noah's temper in full flare and she had no doubt, with his nurtured hatred of the Morgans, that he would find a way to harm Jesse if she couldn't win her father over.

Jesse had given her a multitude of arguments, but in the end, he'd reluctantly agreed to wait. But only until Christmas. If she couldn't persuade her father to allow them to see each other publicly by the holidays, he'd insist she consider moving out of Noah's home and into the Morgan compound where she'd be shielded by Emily and Hal.

That thought also worried Sara. Years ago, she'd have given anything to move in with the Morgans. But now, as their son's lover, how would his parents look upon her? And, although he'd repeatedly told her how much he cared, Jesse had never once mentioned love. Or marriage.

Sara's stomach rolled queasily. Moving slowly, she punched the bed pillow behind her head and swallowed down the nausea. Which brought her to the acknowledgment of her new problem on this rainy morning.

After their first night together, Jesse had begun to carry protection in his wallet. Small foil packets that were used up rapidly, for they couldn't seem to get enough of each other. No matter how interruptive, they'd used them faithfully.

Except that first time.

Sara ran a shaky hand over her damp face. Surely not. This simply couldn't have happened to her, not in the midst of the happiest weeks of her life. Surely the gods wouldn't punish her for one small slip.

But as the meager contents of her stomach threatened a reappearance, she faced the truth with a heavy heart. She'd just missed her second period. Even an optimist would hold out little hope at this point that she was suffering only from a case of nerves. The thought had her breaking out in a sweat, and she made it to the bathroom just in time.

Afterward, when she'd showered and dressed, Sara decided it was time to make sure. Nearly everyone in town knew her and her father, so going to a nearby doctor was out of the question. But driving to Springerville and buying a pregnancy test kit at a drugstore wasn't.

With trembling hands, Sara picked up her car keys.

The rain splashed down on the Ford's windshield and bounced off, sliding down the pale gray hood as the car sat in the Shephard driveway. Sara scarcely noticed. She sat staring unseeingly, more worried than she'd ever been.

Just hours ago, she'd gotten the pregnancy test and taken it upstairs to her bathroom where it had confirmed her worst fears. She was pregnant.

Because of the rain, her father was in the house, supposedly working on the books in his den, the door open. She pleaded a headache when Gretchen had called her for lunch, which had been no lie. She'd stayed in her room, lying in bed and staring at the ceiling as if an answer to her dilemma would magically appear there.

She'd dismissed one wild notion after another, finally deciding that this was more than she could handle alone. She had to talk with Jesse. He'd know what to do.

And she had to do it now because on Monday, Jesse and his father were heading for Texas, driving the big gooseneck trailer rig. They'd made arrangements on the phone with a rancher Hal had known for years to purchase a young, healthy bull. Jesse had told her Thursday night when they'd met at the river that Saturday would be their last evening together for a while. The trip would take a week.

But with this rain, she and Jesse probably wouldn't be meeting tonight. She'd have to do something now. Impatiently, she'd waited around until her father had been called out to the barn by Phil. Then she'd run to her car and driven to the Morgan Ranch.

Only to run out of luck.

When she'd knocked on the door of Jesse's house and realized he wasn't there, she'd gone to see Emily. Desperately hoping her anxiety didn't show, she'd chatted with Jesse's mother for several minutes before getting up the nerve to ask about Jesse. That was when she'd learned that, because they couldn't do much work on the ranch during this rainy weekend, Hal and Jesse had set out early this morning for Texas. It'd be slow-going, but at least they'd be on their way, Emily had explained. Jesse had asked his mother to let Sara know he'd be away a week or so, a message Emily delivered with a curious smile. Sara had known that Jesse's family had surmised that there was something between him and Sara, but she didn't know how much he'd told them.

Today wasn't the day to enlighten them further. She hadn't known she'd had it in her, but Sara had actually managed to stay and have a cup of tea with Emily, who'd been in a chatty mood, going on about how Kay was out shopping for school clothes since she'd be leaving next week for ASU. Yes, Sara had lied, she also was looking forward to starting classes at the University of New Mexico. Finally, she'd said her goodbyes and driven home.

Sitting in her car in her own driveway now, she wondered how she'd made it. Though it was a short distance between the two ranches by road, she had absolutely no recollection of driving it.

The rain pinged and slithered. Sara wished she could cry. It wouldn't solve anything, but it might make her feel better. What in the world was she going to do now? Gripping the wheel, she ran through her options.

She could try to reach Jesse, but she hadn't a clue what route they were taking, nor would she be able to ask Emily without a pretty good explanation. No, she still had some pride left. She could tell her father so he'd have the satisfaction of knowing that she'd done the very thing he'd been accusing her of for years. No, that would be akin to suicide.

She could leave for school next Wednesday as planned with no one the wiser. Then, settled in, she could wait till Jesse returned and call him, ask him to come visit her. Together, they'd work something out. Yes, that was the only answer that made sense.

Sara felt better as she hurried from her car to the porch. But once inside, the cup of tea she'd swallowed a short time ago churned in her stomach and she rushed into the downstairs bathroom.

Weak from nausea and her jumpy nerves, Sara saw in the mirror that her face was ashen, her skin damp. She splashed on cold water and dried herself, wishing she could think of an excuse to curl up in bed. Maybe she could convince Gretchen and her father she had a summer virus or a case of the flu, though she so rarely was sick they probably wouldn't believe her. Hanging up the towel and studying her pale mirror image, she decided they might today.

She opened the bathroom door and found her father waiting for her, a deep scowl on his weathered face.

Blanching, unused to the guilt she'd been carrying around, she took hold of the door frame for support. "I'm not feeling too well," she managed to say.

"Is that a fact?" Noah asked. His eyes were unusually clear today, his stance erect. He actually looked sober.

"The flu maybe," Sara offered. "Or a virus."

Noah's eyes narrowed. "Tell me another one." His hand shot out and his strong, thin fingers grabbed her arm in a steely grip. "You think I was born yesterday, girl?"

"Dad, you're hurting me." Her father had never so much as spanked her when she'd been a child, which only added to her fright.

Half pulling, half dragging, he maneuvered her down the hall to his den and shoved her onto the brown plaid couch. "You think my mind's foggy and I'm too old or too busy to know what's going on around here?'' Noah asked, his face reddening with rage.

Sara huddled in the corner, her eyes wide, not answering.

Her silence seemed to infuriate him more. "I heard you, two or three mornings last week, in the bathroom, sicker than a dog, and now again. I see you can't eat, you're pale and shaky. You think I'm too stupid to figure out what you've gone and done?''

Disgusted, he began to pace the width of the book-lined room, needing to walk off his anger. "I warned you over and over. But would you listen? No. You think that boy cares about you any? Hell, no, he doesn't. He's no good, like his father before him, and his grandfather before that.''

Her stomach muscles quivering, Sara pulled her legs up, swallowing hard. There wasn't anything inside to come up, yet she felt the nausea twist at her insides. How had this happened? Why wasn't Jesse home?

Noah picked his mug up from his desk and took a long swallow of whiskey-laced coffee. Then he turned on his daughter.

"You've shamed me. I never thought I'd live to see the day.''

She had to try to reason with him. "Dad, please listen. I know you hate the Morgans, but I love Jesse.''

Noah slammed his fist onto the desk hard enough to make his mug bounce, the contents nearly spilling over. "The hell you say. The Morgan men don't know how to love. They kill love. They use women for their own gain. You think that boy'll make an honest woman of you? Ha! It's this ranch he wants, girl. Not you and not that bastard you're carrying.''

Sara cringed at his words, pressing her fist to her mouth to keep from crying out. *He was wrong. He had to be wrong.* "No. Jesse isn't like that.''

"Keep still," he snarled. "Not another word. You go on upstairs to your room till I decide what I'm going to do with you."

From somewhere, Sara found a spurt of courage. "No. I want to contact Jesse. I have a right..."

"You got *no* rights, girl. In case you don't know the law, you're under the age of consent. With one phone call, I could have your precious Jesse in jail for statutory rape."

Sara drew in a startled breath. "You wouldn't!"

"Wouldn't I? Try disobeying me one more time, and you'll find out. Now get in your room and don't you dare leave it till I come get you. You hear, girl?"

Trembling, Sara left the den and ran upstairs.

It was dark outside, nearly nine at night, before Sara saw her father again. Gretchen had brought up her dinner on a tray around six, offering tea and sympathy as well, but she'd been able to eat very little. Too frightened to do much besides cower in her room, she was a bundle of nerves by the time Noah unceremoniously opened the door and walked in.

Sara scooted off the bed and turned to him, her heart sinking further when she noticed his hard expression. In his hand he carried a suitcase which he set on the floor with a thud.

"Get your clothes packed," he commanded. "You're leaving tomorrow morning on the eight o'clock bus."

She'd never seen him so cold and unrelenting. Always, even when he'd been full of drink, there'd been more of a pathetic edge to Noah than this unyielding manner. This coolly determined man frightened her. "Where am I going?" Sara asked, unable to keep her voice from trembling.

"To your Aunt Margaret's in San Diego," he replied.

Surprised and confused, Sara blinked up at him. "I...I didn't know I had an Aunt Margaret."

"She's your mother's sister. They were never close, but I called her, and she said she'd take you in." He sent her a look of deep disappointment. "God knows, I don't know who else would."

She didn't want to go to California miles from everyone and everything she knew, to some stranger's house, a woman who'd been talked into taking her in. She hated humbling herself, but she saw no other way. "Please, don't do this. Let me go to the Morgans. Emily will let me stay until Jesse gets back from his trip." Sara shuddered at the thought of seeing disappointment in Emily's eyes, but she'd run out of good choices.

That suggestion seemed to infuriate him. "No! You won't disgrace me further by bringing the Morgans in on this."

"But I have to. It's Jesse's baby, too, and..."

"We're going to do this *my* way, girl. You got no say-so." He reached into his pocket and tossed several things onto her bed. "There's your bus ticket, twenty dollars and Margaret's phone number. When you get there, you call her and she'll come pick you up. I offered to send money for your care, but the damn fool woman refused it. Fine. Truth is, you don't deserve a cent the way you've dishonored me."

She stood, needing desperately to get through to him. "Dad, I'm sorry if I hurt you. Please let me go to Jesse, and I'll never bother you again." She was taking a terrible chance that Jesse would want her, but the alternative was so much worse.

Reaching for the doorknob, he shook his head. "I've got your car keys and I'm going to be sleeping right next to the phone, so don't be thinking about calling anyone. Phil will drive you to the bus stop in the morning. Don't you dare try to leave this room before then." He swung wide the door, then turned back to look one more time at his daughter, on his face a look of infinite sadness. "Goodbye, Sara." Noah walked out, closing her in her room.

Were those tears in his eyes? Sara asked herself. No, they couldn't have been. Her father didn't care about her, or any other living soul that she knew of. He cared only about his ranch and his bottle. At that moment, she hated him fiercely.

Walking unsteadily to the window, she stood gazing out at the steadily falling rain. If only she could sneak out somehow, but she knew Noah would be keeping watch this night. Just as he could control his drinking during the daylight hours while he worked, he'd not let himself get drunk tonight. If only Jesse hadn't left early on his trip, she'd have found a way to get to him. If only she weren't seventeen, but a year older.

No matter what, she couldn't let Noah have Jesse arrested. His family had been so good to her; they'd be embarrassed, humiliated, angry. She couldn't risk hurting the people she loved. She'd have to pull herself together, travel to the home of the aunt she hadn't known she had, and wait until things quieted down so she could contact Jesse.

She'd be pretty much on her own for a while, a thought that frightened her. But she was strong and she had a tiny life within her to take care of now. She'd find a way to work things out somehow.

Turning, Sara picked up the suitcase and opened it onto the bed.

Perhaps it was fitting that she leave in what was almost a torrential downpour. The falling rain reminded Sara of the tears she seemed unable to shed. She climbed up into the truck alongside Phil and turned back for a final look at the house where she'd spent all seventeen years of her life.

Noah was standing at the window of his den, watching her leave. She was certain he was dry-eyed and relieved to be rid of her. Gretchen had made her a breakfast she'd only managed to down a few bites of, then hugged her fiercely and told her not to worry. Good advice, Sara supposed, if a bit hard to follow, under the circumstances.

The truck moved down the driveway, heading for the road. Sara's heart was like a heavy lead weight in her chest. She glanced over at Phil and saw he had his unlit pipe clenched tightly between his teeth. She had to try.

She put all her suppressed need into her voice. "Please, Phil, would you stop at the Morgan house. I…I need to talk a moment with Kay." She'd thought about it through the long sleepless night. She'd have to risk taking her friend into her confidence. Kay wouldn't betray her.

Phil stroked his neat beard nervously. "If your daddy finds out, he'll blow a gasket."

"I won't take but a minute. I swear to you." She was beyond shame, willing to beg.

He didn't look at her, but at the turnoff to the Morgan Ranch, Phil swung in and pulled up close to the porch. "Two minutes. That's all."

Gratefully, Sara jumped out and ran up onto the porch. She knew the door was usually left unlocked. She turned the knob quietly. It was seven o'clock on a rainy Sunday morning. She hoped Kay was awake.

Stepping inside, she saw Lisa walking into the foyer sipping a cup of coffee. Her heart lurched. Of all the luck.

"What brings you over so early?" Lisa asked, her wide blue eyes narrowing suspiciously.

"I need to talk with Kay a minute," Sara answered, moving toward the stairs.

"Too bad. She's spending the weekend in Phoenix with a friend. Orientation begins tomorrow at ASU." Lisa's gaze took in Sara's outfit—dress slacks, white blouse and a linen jacket—not her usual jeans and shirt. Growing more curious, she glanced out and noticed Phil waiting in his idling truck. "Going somewhere?"

Sara swung her eyes in the direction of the kitchen. "Is Emily up yet?" She didn't know what she'd say to Jesse's mother, but she was feeling her last chance slip away.

"She's in the shower. Do you want me to tell her you're here?"

Suddenly, it all was too much for Sara. Her father's words echoed in her mind. *With one phone call, I can have your precious Jesse in jail for statutory rape.* She believed him.

Releasing a hopeless sigh, Sara shook her head. "No, it's not important. I've got to go." She turned to leave.

Lisa followed her. "You seem upset. Are you sure I can't help you?"

"Positive." All she needed right now was Lisa's interference. Hurriedly, she ducked her head against the rain and jumped back up into the truck.

As Phil pulled away, she saw Lisa watching her curiously. She hoped the nosy creature would let sleeping dogs lie.

Leaning her head back, Sara pushed a fist into her queasy stomach, praying she wouldn't embarrass herself on the long bus ride. Resignedly, she let her thoughts drift to San Diego and an aunt she'd never met.

She couldn't do it. She couldn't call a stranger, a woman who, despite being related to her, would likely resent an unknown niece intruding on her life. And rightly so.

Sara stood on the curb outside the San Diego bus station and wondered what on earth she should do. She had about ten dollars left of the twenty her father had given her, having spent the rest on food at the many stops the local bus had made through the seemingly endless trip. And she had another fifty she'd had in her wallet from her last paycheck. The small stake wouldn't last her long. She looked up and down the busy thoroughfare, her weary mind in a jumble.

It was Monday morning, the sky a bright blue with occasional puffy white clouds floating by. The weather was warm, but not as hot as it had been in Arizona. Thank goodness they'd left the depressing rain behind. Slipping off her jacket, she walked over to an empty wooden bench, dropped her suitcase and sat down to consider her options.

Staring at Margaret's phone number, Sara shook her head. No, she wouldn't burden that poor soul with her problems. She'd find a place to stay, then get a job. Once she had those two things, she'd make a plan.

Someone had left a newspaper on the bench. She picked it up and turned to the classified ad section. There were several rooms for rent and a long column of furnished apartments available. The problem was, they all required a security deposit and the first month's rent. Discouraged, Sara was about to set the paper aside when something caught her eye.

There was an article about a woman named Lacie Stone who ran a home for runaways and homeless women. She'd apparently talked a friend on the city council into getting an appropriation to fix up and use an old three-story home that some benevolent soul had donated to the cause. Lacie called the home Christopher House, a halfway residence for people needing a second chance, a temporary helping hand.

If ever anyone qualified, Sara thought she was the one.

Studying Lacie's picture, Sara was impressed with the heavy-set woman's kind eyes and unpretentious look. At the end of the article was the telephone number for Christopher House. Taking the newspaper with her, Sara went to the bank of phones.

Shrewd blue eyes looked Sara over, peering out from a round face that had yet to develop a single wrinkle, although Lacie looked to be somewhere in her fifties. She wore a shapeless print dress that had seen better days and scuffed tennis shoes that had probably once been white. Tufts of red hair liberally streaked with gray stuck out all over her head.

Oddly, Sara didn't mind the inspection for she sensed an underlying generosity spilling forth from Lacie. Her gaze steady, she waited.

At last, Lacie smiled expansively, revealing a set of sparkling white teeth, and reached out to hug Sara. "Welcome to Christopher House, honey."

Releasing a relieved breath, Sara gave her the first genuine smile she'd managed in two days. "Thank you."

"Now," Lacie said, slipping her ample arm around Sara as she drew her inside, "like I told you on the phone, you got to earn your keep here. We need help in the kitchen, in the laundry and in our garden out back. Are you any good with growing things?" The older woman rushed on, not waiting for an answer. "Don't matter. You'll learn. If you can't cook, one of us'll teach you that, too. I don't suppose you know what to do with a needle? We sure could use a seamstress. We get all sorts of donated clothes, but they generally need altering."

At that moment, a girl who looked impossibly young, no more than fourteen, came through the swinging doors leading from the kitchen, walking sway-backed to accommodate her very late pregnancy. "Lacie, you got the grocery list made out?" she asked, brushing back a strand of thick brown hair. "Cindy's ready to go to the market."

"It's on the counter next to the fridge, honey. This here's Sara, Gemma. Come say hello."

Gemma came over, a smile on her friendly face. "Hi, Sara. You like spaghetti? That's what we're having tonight."

Sara felt herself relaxing by inches. "Yes, thank you, I do."

After Gemma had left, Lacie led Sara into what she called the parlor. A big, old-fashioned room, it had a red brick fireplace at one end, worn carpeting in a truly ugly shade of green spread in the center of the creaking floorboards and an asssortment of odd-lot chairs and tables set off by two long plastic couches. Sitting herself down on the nearest sofa, the woman gestured to Sara to join her.

"All my girls are here because they have problems, some more serious than others," Lacie began, running thick fingers through her scraggly hair. "Your business is yours and none of us will stick our noses in it, 'less you invite us in. We got just a couple rules we go by. I can't harbor no criminals, so if you're running from the law, we need to talk. I don't put up with drugs, drinking or men visiting. Anything else, we can work out later if not sooner."

Sara found herself leaning back on the couch, the two nights she'd spent without sleep wrestling with her worries beginning to take its toll. "I'm not running from the law, and I have no problem with your rules."

Lacie gave her another dazzling smile. "Good, then let me show you to your room. You'll have to share, of course."

She needed to tell Lacie just a bit more. "I don't have much money, but I'll get a job. And I'll do anything around the house you want me to. I'm not afraid of hard work."

"Glad to hear it. We can always use two good hands. You look strong and healthy." Lacie stood.

"I am, but I'm...pregnant. Just two months." There was no use hiding it, for Lacie would find out soon enough.

"Half my girls here are, honey. And the baby's father?"

Sara stood, meeting her eyes, her chin held high. "He lives in another state."

"I see. And your folks, will they be giving us a problem?"

Sara shook her head. "My mother's dead, and my father threw me out." Hard words to say, but she had to face the hard facts.

Lacie pulled the girl's slender form close to her. "It don't matter, honey. You got family here now, and we take care of our own."

Tears blurring her vision, Sara let herself be led upstairs.

"Oh, God, Lacie, it hurts. It hurts so much." Drenched in sweat, Sara clutched the bedclothes, her swollen body damp and straining.

Lacie wrung out the cool cloth and lay it on the girl's forehead. "I know, honey. I know." She'd been a nurse-midwife for twenty years and she didn't like the way things were going with this delivery. Sara had been in labor ten hours already, yet she was only dilated three centimeters. And just now when she'd listened, the baby's heartbeat had seemed even fainter than the last time.

Sara swallowed around a dry mouth. "You look worried. Is . . . is something wrong?"

"I'm not sure," Lacie answered. Obviously, honesty was important to her.

"Here comes another one," Sara said, and tried to remember to breathe the way Lacie had taught her. She puffed away, but still the pain felt strong enough to rip her apart. When it finally passed, she grabbed Lacie's arm. "What do you mean? Is my baby all right?"

"So far, honey." Lacie wound the blood pressure cuff around Sara's thin arm and placed the stethoscope in her ears. Minutes later, she put the instrument away, trying to keep her face from revealing her fears. Sara's pressure was falling and that wasn't a good sign. "I think we're going to need a little help here. I'm going to get one of the girls to call Dr. Hemmings."

"But why?" Sara's voice had a frantic edge despite her fatigue. "Tell me what's wrong."

Lacie wiped the feverish brow again. "Maybe nothing, but I don't want to take a chance. I've delivered hundreds of babies, but there are times I need assistance. You'd rather we be safe than sorry, wouldn't you, honey?"

"Yes, but..."

Standing, Lacie took Sara's small hand in her own. "One other thing. I want your permission to call Jesse."

Sara struggled through another shattering wave of pain before she was able to answer. "But why? We've talked about this before, Lacie. We agreed we wouldn't call him unless...unless there might be a serious problem." Slowly, her eyes widened as the implication sunk in. "You mean..."

Lacie squeezed the girl's hand. "I mean it's time we brought him in on it. You turned eighteen two weeks ago. You're of age now, so I doubt your father would press charges. Let me call Jesse, Sara, please?"

She closed her eyes a long minute, then finally nodded. "His number's in my purse over there. If he's not home, talk with his mother, Emily Morgan. She...she'll know what to do." At least, Sara prayed she would, that Emily wouldn't turn against her, too.

"I'll be back in a couple of minutes," Lacie told her. "I'll send Ellen to sit with you till I return." Leaving, she hurried to the phone downstairs.

Sara seemed to drift in and out of a haze of pain. There was a dreamlike feel to things, Sara thought, with her body doing things she had no control over, and her mind drifting as she fought to give birth. She opened her eyes and at times saw Ellen with her, then Lacie beside her. Finally, there was a man, an older man with thinning hair and a thick mustache. His voice was soothing as he filled a syringe. Her last plea, croaked out in a voice she didn't recognize as her own as he slipped the needle into her arm, was to beg him not to let her baby die.

Then there was only blackness.

The pale light of a March morning was drifting in through the window the next time Sara opened her eyes. She was lying in the same bed she'd slept in at Christopher House since she'd first arrived. The sheets were clean and cool and her body was no longer hot and straining. Raising her head slightly, she saw that the bulge she'd carried around for months was gone.

Panic slammed into her. "My baby!" she cried.

Lacie moved into her line of vision from the old rocker where she'd been sitting. Smiling, she walked over to Sara. "He's right here, and he's beautiful." She placed the small bundle in the soft blue blanket into Sara's waiting arms.

"He's... he's all right in every way?" Sara asked, touching the impossibly soft cheek with a trembling finger.

"Yes, indeed. A healthy boy born on St. Patrick's Day. I checked him out myself, and he's perfect."

Sara was unaware of the tears that trailed down her face as she admired the perfection of her son. After several minutes, she turned to Lacie. "Did I dream it, or was there a doctor here?"

Lacie nodded. "Dr. Hemmings delivered your baby. You remember I insisted we call him. The cord had somehow wrapped around the baby's neck and as he moved into the birth canal, his air supply would have been cut off if we hadn't acted quickly."

Flooded with gratitude, Sara reached out to grip the woman's hand. "Thank you."

"All the thanks I need is watching you with that sweet little boy."

Sara cuddled the baby for several minutes, then remembered something else. "You called Jesse. What did he say?"

She knew her heart shouldn't be swelling with hope, but it was.

Lacie dropped her eyes to the blanket as she fussed with its folds. "He . . . he wasn't at home."

There was more, Sara felt certain. "Who answered the phone?"

"Emily Morgan."

It was probably a mistake, but she needed to know. "What did she say?"

"She said that Jesse had made a new life for himself with another woman and that you weren't ever to call him again," Lacie answered hesitantly.

Sara closed her eyes, struggling to absorb the sharp shaft of pain. Through the long months since leaving, she'd wanted so badly to phone Jesse. She had imagined that he was hurt, confused, angry. She knew her father would never tell him where she was or why she'd left. Besides, Noah didn't know how to find her. She hadn't contacted Jesse because of her father's threat, and now it was too late.

What else had she expected? Life goes on, and Jesse had found someone else. Painful as it was, she wished him well. She'd left to protect him. She'd do it again.

Opening her eyes, she gazed down at Jesse's son sleeping peacefully in her arms. Such a beautiful boy, right down to the tiny cleft in his small chin. "I think I'll name him Christopher," she said to Lacie. Christopher House, which Lacie had named after her late husband, had saved Sara and her baby. It was only fitting.

Her own eyes not too dry, Lacie nodded. "It's a fine name."

Sara nuzzled the top of the baby's fuzzy head. "We'll be fine, Christopher. Don't you worry. We're on our own, but we'll be just fine."

BOOK TWO

Chapter Five

Sara Shephard turned off her computer for the day with an anxious eye on the clock. If she didn't hurry, she'd be late for Chris's pitching debut in the first Little League game of the season. At age eleven, her son was tall and loose-limbed, perfect for a pitcher, with keen eyes and excellent coordination. Of course, she thought with a smile as she switched off her laser printer, she could be a tad prejudiced.

Carefully, she stacked the work she'd run off into piles on the long table that ran along the back of her small office. She'd opened her graphic arts studio four years ago after working for the previous three from her home. Though it had been tough-going for a while there, she was finally comfortably in the black.

The two assistants she'd been able to hire, Lila and Ginger, had left for the day just a short time ago. They were both bright, talented and pleasant to work with, which made the days pass quickly. And her evenings were spent with the young man who was the focal point of her life, Christopher J. Shephard, who was this minute probably wondering where she was. Sara hurriedly put away her pens and straightened her drafting table, then grabbed her keys.

Just as she reached for the doorknob, the phone rang. For a moment, she debated about letting her answering machine take a message. But maybe it was Chris asking her to pick up something he'd forgotten. She walked back to grab the receiver. "Shephard Design Studio," she said.

"Would this be Sara Shephard?" a man with a slight western twang asked.

Sara hesitated, trying to place the vaguely familiar voice. "Yes," she answered cautiously.

"The Sara Shephard who grew up in St. Johns, Arizona?" he asked.

Now she recognized him, a voice from her past. "Phil, is that you? Phil Howard?"

"Sure is," Phil replied. "I've had the devil's own time tracking you down, Sara."

Sara sat down in her swivel chair, a little shaken by the quick jolt of memories brought into focus just hearing Phil's voice. "Why have you been looking for me?"

Phil cleared his throat in that slow way he had. "I got some news for you. We found your daddy yesterday morning slumped over his desk. 'Pears he died in his sleep, quiet like. His heart just gave up."

Sara leaned back, closing her eyes against the rush of more memories. She wished she could mourn her father's passing, as any loving daughter would do. But she'd grieved for both of them when he'd sent her from his home twelve years ago at age seventeen with nothing more than a bus ticket, twenty dollars and a phone number. "How did you find me, Phil?"

"I looked in your daddy's address book and run across the name of Margaret Anderson in San Diego. Next to it,

Noah had written that she was your mother's sister. I remembered when I took you to the bus stop that day that you were heading for San Diego, so I put two and two together. I just hung up from talking with your aunt. Nice lady."

Phil hadn't been much of a talker, as Sara recalled, so that had been quite a speech for him. She could picture him stroking his well-trimmed gray beard or smoothing back his thinning hair while he waited for some reaction from her. Unfortunately, she couldn't give him what he was probably expecting. If she couldn't feel a renewed sense of loss, at least she could admit to some curiosity. "How'd my father been since I left?"

"Not good, Sara. What he did, sending you away like that, it ate away at him."

"Yes, well, it didn't do much for my peace of mind, either." But she'd let go of her anger and resentment a long while back.

"He drank more and more," Phil went on. "This last year, I don't know how he stayed alive, hardly eatin', too shaky to work much."

"Did he ever mention me?"

Phil made an embarrassed sound. "Not to me. He was a hard man to know, Sara."

Amen to that, she thought. A hard man whose narrow viewpoint kept him from knowing his only grandson. "Thank you for letting me know."

"Hold on. You need to come back. I found the name of your father's attorney and called him out here. He's the one told me to find you. You're Noah's only heir. You got to return to settle his estate."

Sara slumped in her chair. The thought of returning to that unhappy place nearly caused her to moan aloud. "Can't we do this by mail? It's difficult for me to just pick up and rush back there, Phil. I've built a life here." And I have a son no one in Arizona knows about.

Phil went on to shore up his argument. "Everything's in a mess here. The men don't know what to do—stay or go. The ranch either needs to go on or be put up for sale, this here lawyer told me. Noah wasn't real good at record-keeping. His den's full of papers and files, all sorts of things. I can't make head nor tails of most of it. Sara, you got to come."

Sara pressed a hand to her forehead where the beginning of a headache was making itself known. Dear God, she didn't want to return, to face all those memories, to be thrust back where she'd been so unhappy. And there was another thing.

Jesse Morgan would be right next door, undoubtedly married to that woman Emily had said he'd found just months after Sara had left. Perhaps he'd had children with her and was in charge of the Morgan spread by now. How would she feel if she ran into him, if she saw him happy with another woman and their children?

Here, she had the advantage of time and distance on her side, eleven years and hundreds of miles separating them. But there, so close again, how could she keep control of her emotions? How could she prevent her treacherous heart from wanting him again when even now, so many years later, occasionally she awoke wrapped in the remnants of vivid dreams? Dreams where Jesse was holding her, kissing her, loving her.

"Did you hear me, Sara?" Phil asked into the silence. "I got to tell this lawyer something. What're you going to do?"

What, indeed. "I've got to give this some thought, Phil. I'll phone you tomorrow and tell you what I've decided."

"That's fine. You remember the number?"

"Yes, I remember." She remembered all too much.

"I got Hal and Emily Morgan coming over in a bit to help with the funeral arrangements. You want we should hold off till you get here?"

"No. You do what you think is best. If I decide to re-turn, it'll take me a couple of days." She said goodbye and slowly hung up the phone. Why hadn't she left the office before this disturbing call? But she'd only have put the news off for another day. If there was one thing Sara had learned and learned well, it was that postponing bad news rarely improved the situation.

She'd have to think it through, to see if there was any other way around this. Tonight, she'd go to Margaret's and talk things over. Margaret was always so sensible, so level-headed.

But for now, she had a ball game and a curly-haired pitcher to cheer on. Rising, Sara left her office.

Emily Morgan sat down in the kitchen chair and grate-fully accepted the frosty glass of iced tea that Jesse handed her. Closing her eyes wearily, she took several swallows, hoping the cold drink would revive her somewhat. She'd been feeling so tired lately. Or was it less fatigue and more the unease she'd felt at spending several hours in Noah Shephard's den just now?

"The house is an absolute mess," Emily told her son. "Noah never should have let Gretchen go after Sara left."

After topping off his own tea, Jesse sat down at the table across from his mother. "A man living alone for over ten years. I'm not surprised." And not just any man, but the most narrow-minded, stubborn, offensive man he'd ever known.

"Poor Phil's at a loss, and the men are confused. It'll take someone weeks to go through all the papers on Noah's desk and scattered around his den. His attorney says he'd kept after him, but Noah hadn't gotten around to making out a will." Emily released an exasperated sigh.

"The mean old coot thought he'd live forever, did he? Might have, too. They say only the good die young."

Frowning, Jesse drank tea and tasted his own lingering bitterness.

Emily raised her eyes to her son's face. She knew only too well how much he'd suffered because of Noah's stubbornness. But she'd also thought she'd instilled compassion in both her children. "Jesse, there's an old Indian saying that goes something like, don't ever criticize a man until you've walked in his moccasins. I believe there's a lot of truth in that."

Jesse's scowl deepened. "There are exceptions to every rule. Tell me one good thing Noah Shephard ever did. Just one."

"It isn't for us to judge him, or anyone else."

"Yeah, well, it's easy for you to think kind thoughts of him. He didn't put you through the hell he did me." Rising, he felt anger surge through him as he walked to stare out the kitchen window.

It was dusk, Jesse's favorite time of day. It had always been at dusk that he and Sara had ridden to their meeting place among the pine trees or by the Little Colorado River. It had been at dusk that he'd held her and they'd talked, then as if by silent signal, made love till they'd both been limp and breathless. He'd watched the dusky sunset turn her yellow hair to gold and darken her pale skin. They'd spent that whole glorious summer sharing their thoughts, their passions.

And suddenly, it had all ended.

He and his father had returned from Texas hauling a trailer containing a strapping young bull they'd bought, making plans for further expansion. The Morgan Ranch was thriving and the future looked golden. Locked in the intimacy of the truck during the long drive, Jesse had finally told his father that he loved Sara Shephard and that he wanted to marry her.

Hal had warned him that Noah wouldn't be pleased, that he would undoubtedly feel Sara was too young and that she should go on to college. Jesse knew all that and was even willing to wait while she finished school. If only Noah would allow them to see each other, to publicly date instead of forcing them to meet secretly, which they both hated.

He'd been so filled with his visions of the future and his need to share them with her that he'd phoned the Shephard house as soon as he'd walked in the door. Gretchen, sounding strained, had told him that Sara had left for the University of New Mexico. Undaunted, Jesse had driven to Albuquerque the first chance he'd had—only to discover that Sara wasn't there, wasn't even registered. Confused and growing worried, he'd rushed back to confront Noah.

The old man had been oddly sober, but then it'd been only midafternoon. Sara had stolen money from him and left in the stealth of night, Noah had said. He'd pointed to the garage to prove that her car was gone, even offered to take him upstairs to show him that her closet and dresser drawers were empty. His sudden, almost affable cooperation had immediately aroused Jesse's suspicions.

He hadn't believed Noah. Sara wouldn't steal, wouldn't leave like some thief in the night without good reason, without leaving him some word. When he'd asked her father if she'd left a note for him, Noah had shaken his head. Something didn't add up, Jesse was certain, so he'd lost his temper and yelled at the stubborn old fool. He'd demanded to know what Noah had done to Sara, certain that something terrible had to have happened.

"If she went away, it's because you caused her to leave," he'd screamed at Noah.

"Get off my land, boy," Noah had bellowed back. "Get off and stay off."

Feeling rage, feeling helpless, he'd gone back home and done some sleuthing. He'd learned that Sara's car had been

sold while he'd been in Texas, the transaction handled by
Phil Howard, the manager of the Lazy-S. So he'd hunted
Phil down, catching him out on the range. It had taken him
a while, but he'd finally worn Phil down and learned that
Sara had caught a bus to San Diego, but Phil didn't know
why she'd left or who she might know there. He only knew
that she and Noah had quarreled, and Sara had left. The
following Monday, Noah had instructed Phil to sell her car.

Jesse had been frantic. He'd questioned his mother and
father, both of whom had known Noah in their youth, but
neither knew of any relatives or friends Sara's father had in
San Diego or anywhere else. He was back to square one.

But he hadn't given up. He'd felt so certain that Sara
cared for him as much as he did for her. Although he didn't
know where she was, *she* knew how to reach *him*. So he'd
waited for word from her by phone or mail. Weeks went by,
and there'd been none. Jesse had lost weight, lost his patience, his sense of humor. Still, nothing.

Desperate, he'd gone back to challenge Noah again, less
afraid of the old man's wrath than of losing Sara. But the
stubborn bastard had stuck to his story that he had no idea
where Sara had gone. Jesse had wanted to talk with
Gretchen, hoping she'd seen or heard something, but the
housekeeper had been let go and had left for parts unknown.

Fighting discouragement, he'd gone to see Phil again,
knowing the manager was usually the first to get the mail
that came to the ranch. But no note had come from Sara.
He'd tried one more long shot. He'd left a letter with Phil,
a letter he'd written to Sara, and asked Phil to mail it to her
if he should somehow discover her address. In the event Phil
knew more than he was revealing, Jesse thought the ranch
manager might get a pang of conscience and mail her the
letter, which he could do without giving away where she'd
gone.

Finally, with weeks of hope turning into months of despair, Jesse had given up and forced himself to face the unvarnished truth. Sara had left him without a word, had had ample time to contact him and hadn't bothered. Apparently, he'd been the biggest fool of all time. He'd loved her, but he hadn't known her at all. He'd loved the girl he'd watched grow up and the woman he'd thought she was. The callous creature who'd stolen from her own father and snuck away in the middle of the night was a stranger.

With that realization, he'd stopped anguishing over her. But the experience had left an indelible mark on Jesse. He would never again trust easily, love spontaneously or let himself be hurt by another woman, he'd vowed.

And he'd kept that vow these long lonely twelve years. Several had tried, but no woman had gotten close to him. And he intended to keep it that way. Work and the ranch, his family and friends, were enough for him.

That, too, was Noah's legacy. Perhaps he should have thanked the man for waking him up.

Watching her son, noticing the small muscle in his hard jaw clench in remembered anger, Emily's heart went out to Jesse. Noah Shephard had put her through hell years ago, and Hal, too, with the so-called land dispute and other disagreements. But no one had been hurt as much as Jesse. She knew her son blamed Sara as well. Emily didn't know what had transpired between father and daughter that fateful weekend to cause Sara to leave, but she didn't believe Noah's version. She couldn't be as harsh a judge as her firstborn. But then, she'd lived longer and had had to forgive more.

Studying his ramrod-straight back, she wondered how Jesse would take the news she was about to tell him. "She's coming back, Jesse," Emily said softly. Though Phil had told her that Sara would call tomorrow to let him know, Emily felt certain Sara would return. She was Noah's only heir, the only one who could settle his estate, which had certainly been left in shambles.

Slowly, Jesse turned, wearing a questioning frown. He'd been concentrating so hard on the past that he'd lost the thread of their conversation. "Who's coming back?"

"Sara Shephard." She watched the shock register in gray eyes so like her own, saw him struggle to accept her words. "Phil located her. Apparently, she lives in San Diego."

Jesse felt as if he'd just taken a neat punch in the gut. So Phil hadn't lied to him way back when. All this time, she'd been a day's drive away.

Emily knew he wanted to know more but was too proud to ask. "Phil found an address book of Noah's. Evidently, Sara's mother, Rose, had a sister who still lives in San Diego. Phil called her, and she gave him Sara's number. She owns a graphic arts studio."

Jesse wasn't sure he could trust his voice, but he had to say something, then get out where he could be alone. "I hope the hell she stays away from us." He started for the back door.

She rose, wanting him to understand. "Jesse, please listen. You've seen what carrying a grudge for years did to Noah. Couldn't you at least hear Sara out? Maybe she has a perfectly reasonable explanation."

Jesse closed his fingers tightly around the doorknob. "Reasonable explanation? I can think of no acceptable excuse for what she did."

"But I . . ."

"Please, Mother. I can't handle one of your lectures on compassion just now." Without turning, Jesse left.

Emily sank back into her chair, feeling more tired than she had been in a long while. It was beginning all over again, the tension between the Morgans and the Shephards, moving into the third generation.

When and how would it all end? she wondered.

* * *

"Pizza is the best reward for a game well played," Margaret Anderson told her grand-nephew, as she handed him a plate with two huge pieces.

The boy grinned at her. "Thanks, Aunt Margaret." Chris grabbed a slice and took a big bite.

"Did I tell you Chris got the last runner out with this terrific throw to the catcher just seconds before the kid hit home plate?" Sara asked.

"Only twice," Margaret said with a tolerant smile. "But what else are mothers for but to brag about their children?"

"I'm not bragging," Sara said in her own defense. "I'm merely telling it like it is." She handed her son his cold drink.

"TV's on in the family room if you want to watch it, Chris," Margaret suggested. "You can change the station, if you like." She watched the boy walk away, then turned to her niece. "Now then, why was your father's ranch manager looking for you, Sara? I've been on edge ever since that call."

Sara dished out pizza for both of them, thinking she could concentrate better if she kept her hands busy. "He called to tell me that Dad died yesterday." It took her only a few minutes to repeat her conversation with Phil, along with his adamant request that she return to the place of her birth. "I wish I could feel something other than a sad regret."

"Don't blame yourself," Margaret commented. "Noah's the one who should have felt regret. He drank himself to death, I imagine." She'd never liked the man her sister had married, had blamed Noah's alcoholic indifference for Rose's premature death. She'd liked him even less after discovering what he'd done to her niece.

"Phil said his heart just stopped, but it had been damaged by years of drinking, I'm sure."

"He finally got what he deserved, I say." Margaret didn't bother to hide her bitterness.

Leaning back, Sara looked at Margaret, unable to fault her aunt for feeling as she did. Her father had alienated the two sisters and had kept Margaret from knowing Sara those early years. Married to a kind man who'd died ten years ago, Margaret had been unable to have children of her own and was unwilling to forgive Noah for keeping her from knowing her family.

But her contempt for Sara's father hadn't kept her from agreeing to take in his daughter the night he'd called to say he was sending her to San Diego. Sara had learned later that Margaret had waited for her call from the bus station that next day, the call Sara's misguided pride hadn't allowed her to make. Worried when she hadn't heard by evening, Margaret had phoned Noah who'd said they'd put Sara on the bus and that had been the last they'd seen of her. He had no idea where she might have gone.

Perhaps it was fate that finally had gotten her together with her aunt, Sara often thought. When Christopher had been about a month old, he'd developed a serious respiratory infection that had turned into pneumonia. Sara had had no choice but to take him to a hospital. But hospitals demanded money up front and, although Lacie had been willing to help, she didn't have that kind of money. Where she couldn't humble herself enough to beg for assistance for her own needs, Sara willingly did so for Chris.

From the hospital, she'd called the number her father had given her for Margaret Anderson.

Thus had begun a wonderful relationship, one Sara cherished deeply. Margaret had rushed right down, put up the money and embraced both Sara and her son as if they'd been her own. Her aunt had turned out to look so much like the few pictures which she'd hoarded of her mother that Sara had recognized her the moment she'd walked in. Tall, slender and blond, Margaret looked enough like Sara to be her mother. And since that fateful day, her aunt had been like the mother Sara had never known.

Margaret had insisted that Sara move in with her and her husband, John, immediately. As soon as Chris had recovered, Sara had brought him to the lovely nursery Margaret had prepared for him right next to his mother's room. She and Margaret had become even closer after John had died the following year. Margaret had watched Chris while Sara completed several business college courses and found a job in a local company.

Sara felt she owed a great deal to Margaret. She'd done well in that small company and, three years later, she'd managed to buy a small house and work from home so she could spend more time with her son. It was only when Chris had started attending school all day and the volume of her work had increased to the extent that she needed to hire assistants that she'd opened an office outside her home. She knew that Margaret missed having the two of them around, so she visited every chance she had.

And, like tonight, Sara often talked over her worries and problems with Margaret, sharing her concerns with another woman, something she'd never been able to do while growing up. Eventually, she'd told Margaret about her love affair with and feelings for Jesse Morgan. To this day, only Lacie and Margaret, both loyal and trustworthy, knew who Christopher's father was.

"Are you going to be able to handle going back?" Margaret asked, her voice filled with concern.

Sara brought herself back to the present and shrugged. "I honestly don't know." She toyed with her glass of soda, tracing the rivulets of beaded moisture with her finger. "There are so many memories in that house, most of them not pleasant. The thought of going through Dad's things... it fills me with dread."

"Then don't go," Margaret said. She hated the thought of Sara's being upset. "You can give power of attorney to Phil or your father's lawyer."

Sara thought about that, then shook her head. "I've always disliked running from my obligations. Besides, while I was watching Chris play ball earlier, something occurred to me. The ranch should be worth something, even if it needs fixing up before being put on the market. Dad never gave me much except food and the clothes on my back. And he never gave anything to his grandson. Chris deserves his legacy."

Margaret placed another slice of pizza on her plate. Upsetting news took away Sara's appetite, but it only increased hers. "Have you thought about the fact that if Noah really did leave things in a mess, it might take you several weeks to clear things up and find a buyer?"

"Yes, I have." Sara met her aunt's eyes. "Would you watch Chris for me if I have to go?"

Margaret waved her hand impatiently. "You know you don't even have to ask. It would be my pleasure." But she wasn't finished playing devil's advocate. "Have you thought about how leaving will affect your work?"

"It's summer, our slowest time. I could instruct Ginger and Lila tomorrow, then update them by phone periodically. They've been with me two years now. I think they could handle things for a couple of weeks." That was the least of her concerns. Far larger was that she'd never been away from Chris and she knew she'd miss him terribly. But there was no way she could take him with her.

Finishing her food, Margaret sipped her soft drink and decided to bring up another possible problem. "Have you thought of what you're going to tell Clay about this sudden trip?"

Clay Forbes was a nice enough man, a teacher at Chris's school and someone Sara had met when she'd gotten her son involved in Little League, since he also coached baseball. Clay was attractive enough, had a good sense of humor and loved kids. He also claimed to love Sara, a feeling she wished she could reciprocate.

They'd been dating sporadically for over a year, and Clay had asked her to marry him repeatedly. She hadn't led him on, had been honest with him from the beginning, telling him she truly had no interest in a serious involvement. Still, Clay persisted. Sara was aware that Margaret thought she ought to accept Clay's proposal, that he'd be a good father to Chris. But she simply couldn't. And she couldn't easily explain to Margaret that while she liked Clay, his romantic overtures left her cold.

She'd known passion once—wild, unbridled passion. While those sweet, hot feelings had led her onto a difficult path, she had no regrets that at least, for one brief summer, she'd sampled what magic was possible between a man and a woman. She'd long ago decided that she'd rather live without a man than to settle for less.

"Clay will have to understand," Sara told Margaret. "My father's died, and I have things to attend to."

"He'll want to go with you. He's off for the summer."

"That's out of the question." Things would be difficult enough without dealing with Clay hovering over her. But she had thought of something else. "I'll miss that fund-raiser for Christopher House." She'd really been looking forward to the annual event, this year an ethnic dinner Sara and several other "graduates" had organized. It was their way of saying thanks for all the help they'd once so gratefully received. "I'll have to call Lacie. Do you think you and Chris could still go?"

"Of course." Margaret wiped her mouth and folded her arms on the table. "All right, the biggest obstacle. Have you thought about what it would be like to spend several weeks living next door to Jesse Morgan again?"

Sara rose, walked to the window and stood looking out. It was so peaceful here on the outskirts of San Diego. Her own small house was only blocks from her aunt's, her office about two miles away, not far from Chris's school and the baseball field. She had a life here, a happy, serene life she'd painstakingly put together over the past twelve years. Returning would mean walking back into the eye of the storm.

Seeing Jesse again would undoubtedly mean agitation, discomfort, perhaps pain. But what choice did she have? When it came down to it, there was usually no one to do the really dirty jobs in life for us.

Sara turned back to face Margaret. "I've thought about that, and I know it won't be easy. I left years ago to protect Jesse. I'm returning now to help Chris, to get what rightfully belongs to him, and that's more important than a couple of uncomfortable weeks for me. From the sale of the Lazy-S, we can send him to the best schools, get him the best education possible, a head start in life."

"If there's enough, you won't have to work so hard."

She shook her head. "No. I don't want a cent of my father's money. If he didn't give it to me willingly when he was alive, I won't take it now. But Christopher's another matter." She tipped up her chin and found a smile. "And besides, I like my work."

Margaret nodded, pleased at her answer. "Then you've made up your mind. You're going?"

Sara drew in a ragged breath. "It would seem so."

Bouncing along in the white pickup truck, seated alongside Phil, Sara scanned the flat land on either side of the road leading from St. Johns Industrial Airpark to the Lazy-S Ranch. She'd flown into Phoenix, then chartered a small plane along with three other passengers, and landed minutes ago. The Arizona sun was every bit as hot as she remembered.

"Nothing much has changed," she commented as she gazed at the piñon pines, the scruffy bushes among the rocks, the occasional stately saguaro cactus. Off to the right, she saw a very large fenced pasture where seemingly hundreds of brown cows grazed contently. "I see more ranches have added cattle. Did my father ever make the change?"

"Nope," Phil replied in his lazy drawl. "Your daddy wasn't one for changes."

That surely was the truth. "Are you still doing the training?" Phil had been one of the best horse trainers around, plus he'd been giving riding lessons for years, teaching youngsters, teens and on up how to show horses for competition.

"Not as much as when you were home."

Home. A word she no longer connected with the Lazy-S. "So there are no cows, and you no longer train much. How does the ranch make enough money to stay afloat?"

Phil patted down his thinning hair and shifted on the seat. "It's been rough. We have several brood mares, quite a few colts and fillies born this past January. We still raise thoroughbreds for racing, and the blemished ones we sell for workhorses. The market's changed a lot since you left. And your daddy made a few decisions against my advice that cost us this past year."

"What kind of decisions?"

"Well, for one, he sold all but two of our stallions."

Sara had been away from the ranch a long while, but even she knew that that could lead to trouble. Stallions were the backbone of a thriving horse business. Stud fees alone could support a ranch. "Why?"

Phil shrugged as he turned onto the south road. "I suppose 'cause he could get more for them than the mares."

"Is the ranch in trouble financially?"

"I can't say. Noah never let anyone see the books and after he died, I didn't think it was my place."

"Have you and the men been paid regularly and on time?"

"Yup, every week. A couple of the men have left, but mostly 'cause there wasn't enough work to do."

Terrific, Sara thought. Short of stallions, men and money. What had she walked into?

As they cleared the rise in the road, a movement to the far right caught her eye. Straining her eyes against the sun, she made out a man on a horse atop the hill. As she watched, the black horse reared up on his hind legs and whinnied, but the rider controlled him easily. Watching his deft, sure handling, Sara suddenly knew who he was, and her heart lurched against her rib cage.

She watched Jesse pull back on the reins and calm his stallion with the ease of someone born in the saddle. She saw him turn his head and follow the progress of the white Lazy-S truck carrying two passengers traveling down the road along his fence line.

And she wondered what he was thinking.

Chapter Six

It was worse than she'd imagined. Sara stepped across the threshold into the dim interior of her father's house, and felt her spirits sag.

The beautiful hardwood floor that used to be polished and shiny when Gretchen cared for it was grimy with caked-on dirt that had accumulated over a long while. Cobwebs hung from the huge wagon wheel chandelier overhead, trailing downward in ghostly threads.

She let Phil carry her bags upstairs while she wandered around the lower level. The drapes on the living-room windows were sun-faded and thick with dust, the furniture soiled and drooping, the carpeting stained and threadbare. The kitchen was a mess, the tile floor sticky, dirty dishes piled on the messy counters. Noah's den was a nightmare with his huge desk nearly buried beneath stacks of papers, ledgers, folders. Books were missing from the walled book-cases and scattered everywhere—on chairs and the old brown plaid couch, stacked on tabletops. The fireplace was filled to overflowing with ashes that spilled out onto the brick hearth.

"Dear God," Sara whispered.

Behind her, Phil shuffled his booted feet. "I didn't touch hardly anything for fear I'd throw away something you needed," he said, sounding apologetic. "I probably should have had Pete's wife come and clean some."

Pete had been the bunkhouse cook when she'd lived here. Sara remembered the wonderful chili rellenos he'd introduced her to. Sara turned away from the sight of the disorderly den. "Is he still with us?"

"Sure is. And Ruby, his wife, too. You need help, she's a hard worker."

Sara let out a shuddering breath and strolled back into the vestibule with Phil following. "I certainly will need help, won't I?" She swung toward him. "I can't imagine my father living like this. We all know he drank and didn't take good care of himself, but he'd always insisted that the house be clean and neat. What *happened* to him?"

Phil stuck his hands into his back pockets. "He gave up."

"But why?" She honestly wished someone could explain it to her.

"I figure it's 'cause he lost everything and everyone that mattered to him. When that happens to a man, whether it's his fault or someone else's, ain't much left to get up in the morning for."

"I guess you're right." Sara walked over to the oak player piano with its intricately carved legs and ran her fingers over the keys. Puffs of dust sprayed every which way. Turning aside, she brushed off her hands. "Well, I might as well learn all the bad news at once. Why don't you show me the rest of the ranch?"

The rest wasn't as bad as she'd feared, undoubtedly because Phil had been left in charge of more and more of the day-to-day operation of the ranch during her father's steady decline. The barns and outbuildings were well kept, the grounds neatly trimmed, the horses that remained well groomed. She shook hands with the few men who remembered her and hugged Pete who smiled at her warmly, revealing two shiny gold front teeth. And she made arrangements with Ruby to come to the big house in an hour, ready to go to work.

Afterward, she strolled back with Phil, her mood pensive.

Phil pointed off to a grassy knoll shaded by a tall piñon pine. "We buried your daddy over there, just like he wanted. You want to walk over and take a look?"

Sara gazed in the direction he pointed and saw the freshly turned earth mounded in the shape of a coffin, the small wooden cross barely visible at the head. Someone had stuck a clump of flowers at the foot. Again, she felt an overwhelming sadness at all the things that might have been. But she needed to come to terms with her father's death before she could visit his grave. "I'll go a little later."

They walked on, and Sara forced her mind back to the problems at hand. "I kept pretty good track of the horses when I lived here," she began. "I remember we had about eighty of our own, boarded at least another twenty, and you were training eight-to-ten hours a day in the arena. We're down to twenty mares with only three foaling this year, four yearlings and two stallions, one not so young anymore. And we have only six people on payroll besides Pete and Ruby, where we used to employ upwards of thirty."

Rearranging his hat on his head, Phil nodded. "Like I said before, we cut down on staff when your daddy started selling off the horses. Like oil in Texas, the bottom fell out of the horse market in Arizona. We used to have eighteen auctions a year. Down to three these days."

Sara shoved her hands into the pockets of her slacks as her mind tried to analyze the situation. "Grounds aren't bad. Barns could use a coat of paint, but otherwise they show well. Tomorrow I'll take a ride out and check the pastures. I'm sure my father didn't sell off any acreage, did he?" The Lazy-S consisted of ninety acres, and Noah had guarded every inch jealously.

"No, he sure didn't."

They stopped in front of the house and Sara scanned the exterior with a critical eye. "This really needs attention. Outside, we'll have to get new shutters and paint the whole thing. How's the roof?"

"Near as I can tell, it's fine. I can go up and check it."

"Please do. The inside, obviously, needs to be thoroughly cleaned first. From what I've seen, some of the furniture isn't salvageable." She cocked her head and squinted at the upstairs, hoping the bedrooms weren't worse than the downstairs rooms. "Windows seem okay. Drapes have to go, but I can order new ones."

Phil turned to look at her. "That mean you're staying, that you're going to run the ranch, make it like it used to be?"

Slowly, Sara shook her head. Once, that had been her dream. But then, she'd had to give up on more than one dream. "No, it doesn't. But I am going to fix this place up to where it can command a good price on the market. I'm going to go through my father's papers, see if there's any money available in a bank account or somewhere. I can do most of the work in the house myself, with Ruby's help. Once that's done, I'll contact a realtor who deals in selling ranches."

Phil removed his hat and slowly twirled it in his big hands. "Begging your pardon, Sara, but all that sprucing up of the house and all ain't going to be enough. No horseman's going to want the place 'less you can manage to get us two, maybe three, thoroughbred stallions and more mares. A horse ranch needs stock and right now, ours is mighty low. 'Course, you maybe could find a cattleman who wants to all but steal the place as a bare-bones ranch, then convert to cows. Otherwise, you got trouble. You can put a spit-and-polish finish on things, but without stock, ain't no horse rancher going to shell out good money for the Lazy-S.''

Sara had a deep-down feeling that he was right, as much as she struggled against the thought. She had no idea how liquid her father's estate was at this point. How could she afford to fix up the ranch *and* purchase more horses? Frowning, she ran a hand along the back of her neck, already damp in the unrelenting heat. ''Just supposing you're right, where would I be able to get good stock right now when so many ranchers have switched over to cattle or farming?''

''Only place I know of is the Morgan Ranch,'' he answered immediately.

Sara straightened, shaking her head. ''No. Anywhere but there.''

''No other rancher 'round these parts has quality horses to sell. Morgan's got the reputation and the training. Only ones left still doing fine with both cows and horses. That Jesse, he's sure a smart one. He saw this market slump coming long time ago and convinced his daddy. They're making a pile of money when most others are hurting bad. Yes, ma'am, they're the ones you got to see for stallions. Then you'll see some breeding around here.''

Phil had been so busy trying to convince her that he hadn't noticed her expression close down. A cold day in hell, that's when she'd go begging at the Morgans' door again. She'd done that once, when she'd been about to deliver Jesse's son and Lacie Stone hadn't known if either she or the baby would make it. And they'd turned away from her. No, she'd find another way.

Hands on her hips, she frowned at the house, wondering where to begin. "I'll think about it, Phil. Meanwhile, I've got to get to work."

"If you want anything, just holler."

"I would like to know one thing, Phil." For a moment, she studied him—a man somewhere in his mid-fifties who was good with horses and kids, yet who had no real home of his own. He had changed very little since she'd left, still lean and straight, only his beard was a little grayer, his hair a bit thinner. Sara remembered hearing that Phil had been married years ago, but that it hadn't worked out. She'd never heard him mention a woman. "Why'd you stay so long, even when you saw the Lazy-S going downhill?"

Again Phil shrugged. "I liked Noah, especially back in the old days. I understood him. Some men escape in a bottle, others in work. That don't make 'em all bad. Life ain't always fair."

With that she could agree. She touched his arm lightly, then headed for the house. Marching up the stairs, she decided to look upon the whole thing as a challenge. She would accomplish this somehow, fix up the ranch, get more horses and sell it all for a good price.

And she would do it *without* help from a single Morgan.

She found it mighty slow-going. First of all, she wasn't used to hard physical labor on a daily basis anymore, having mostly sat at a desk for the past several years. But, having no other choice, she rolled up her sleeves and went to work.

She located a paid-up insurance policy on her father plus some old savings bonds, freeing up some working capital. While Ruby scrubbed and cleaned, Sara persuaded the men to help her gather all the broken and outdated furniture and stack it in the garage. Then, she called the closest crisis center which gladly accepted her donation. Next, she hired a painting team and put them quickly to work outside.

Inside, after they removed the dirt, the floors, woodwork and cupboards were being refinished and new window treatments were ordered. Though the den had been cleaned thoroughly, she left most of the papers to go over later.

By the late afternoon of the fifth day, Sara felt as if she'd been dragged through a knothole backward, as Gretchen used to say. And she was aching with loneliness for her son.

"How did the game go today?" she asked into the phone minutes later, trying to sound upbeat.

"I only let them have three runs," Chris said exuberantly. "We won five to three."

"That's terrific, honey. I miss you a lot."

"I miss you, too, Mom. When do you think you'll be finished fixing up Grandpa's house?"

She'd told him the truth, the reason she was there, just not all of it. "I wish it were today, but it'll be a while yet. What do you and Aunt Margaret have planned for tonight?"

"The movies, and it's my turn to pick."

Poor Margaret. Chris was currently fascinated with adventure films featuring Indiana Jones types, crusading men conquering monsters and creepy-crawlies for two solid hours. "Have a good time, honey, and don't let Margaret eat too much popcorn."

He laughed that wonderful way he had, telling her he knew the directive was aimed at him and not his aunt. Sara closed her eyes on the sharp need to hold him close. "I love you, Chris."

"I love you, too, Mom. 'Bye."

Feeling emotional but a little better, she hung up, then walked into the kitchen and looked around. It was finally shaping up. Ruby was leaning into the oven, her rubbergloved hands scrubbing hard.

"I think I'll saddle up and go for a run, Ruby. I need to get out of this house for a little while."

Ruby pulled her dark head from the cramped interior. "Sure, sure. You go ahead. I'll finish up here, then make you something to eat."

"Don't bother, Ruby, really. It's too hot to eat." She'd called someone to fix the air conditioner that her father hadn't bothered to have repaired, but the service man had to order a part which would take several days to receive. Meanwhile, with the temperature outside still a blistering ninety degrees at four o'clock, inside it felt ten degrees hotter.

Sara found a rubber band in one of the kitchen drawers she'd cleaned out yesterday, gathered her thick hair in a cluster at her nape and caught it into a neat ponytail. Not exactly chic but a lot cooler, she decided.

"You got to eat, honey," the round little woman said over her shoulder. "You too skinny. Men, they like a little meat on a woman's bones."

"That's handy to know if you're looking for a man, Ruby. I definitely am not in the market." Sara opened the fridge to get a carrot for Golda, the big-eyed two-year-old chestnut mare she'd taken a liking to. Yesterday, she'd gone grocery shopping after cleaning out the fridge, filling it with lots of fruits and vegetables. Maybe later, she'd feel like eating a salad.

Sighing noisily, Ruby straightened, pinning Sara with her intense dark eyes. "You a pretty woman, Sara. No need for you to sleep alone."

"I *like* it that way, Ruby. Women have a lot fewer problems if they sleep alone."

Ruby grinned knowingly. "But you have a lot less fun."

Sara smiled back, uncertain how to answer that. "See you later."

It felt good again, really good, to feel a powerful animal beneath her, the hot wind roaring past her face, the sun pouring down on her bare head. Because it had been a while, Sara had used a saddle, accepting the offer of assistance from Wally, one of the older hands who'd been around since she was a child. She knew she'd be scolded if she'd chosen to ride bareback, though it was what she'd have preferred. Given her lead, Golda raced along, true to the blood of her ancestors.

She'd missed this, Sara acknowledged. In California, she hadn't allowed herself to dwell on all the things she'd loved when she'd lived on the ranch. Despite the indifference of her father, growing up here had had its advantages. She wished she could keep the ranch, turn it into a going concern once more, show Chris how to care for and enjoy horses. Her son would love it here—the open spaces, the animals, the men who could teach him so much. A ranch was an ideal place for a child to learn responsibility and discipline, traits that would stay with him for life.

Slowing Golda, Sara knew that was a pipe dream. She could never bring her son here, never let Jesse know he existed. Apparently, from what she'd heard, the Morgans had become the most financially successful family for miles around. With money came prestige and power. She couldn't risk having Chris taken from her. The Morgans had been kind to her, each and every one, while she'd been growing up. But they'd turned from her when she'd needed them most, not even asking Lacie how she was or where. The irony was that she'd left to protect one of them, and wound up the one being censured.

Easing Golda from a gallop to a canter, she gazed off to the west and saw the orange sun drifting slowly toward the horizon. Sunsets here, Sara remembered, were more beautiful than anywhere she'd been. Her eyes scanning the land as far as she could see, she gazed toward the east.

And she saw a man slowly walking his horse on the Morgan side of the fence dividing the two properties. No one strolled in this heat leading his horse unless there was a problem. She urged Golda closer, then almost yanked the mare to a stop.

The man's problem was that the horse was lame. Her problem was that the man was Jesse Morgan.

He'd spotted her, she could tell by the way he kept his eyes straight ahead. He kept walking on toward her, still some distance away from where she sat atop Golda. Once over the shock of running into him out here, she had time to inspect him.

He hadn't changed all that much. He was just as tall, as straight-backed, with that determined stride. He'd filled out some, his shoulders seemed wider, his chest broader. His hat was shoved back on his dark head, his gaze hooded, his square chin jutting out at a stubborn angle.

He looked every inch a hard man to tangle with.

Heart thudding, Sara wondered how she should play this unexpected scene. Before she'd left California, she'd accepted the fact that she'd probably run into Jesse while in Arizona. As much as she'd tried to prepare herself for that inevitability, she now found she hadn't. Perhaps she never could have.

She could have ridden on, of course, or pretended not to notice him. But her good manners wouldn't allow that. He had at least an hour's walk ahead in the desert heat. She'd never been cruel. Hands trembling, she watched his approach, noticing that his eyes had finally raised to meet hers.

Anger. Frustration. Resentment. Jesse felt them all and more at the sight of her. The incredible sight of her. Then, shocking him, he felt such a jolt of pure longing that his knees weakened.

Damn her for making him feel like this. Damn her for being so beautiful. Damn her for coming back, for making him remember, for reviving the pain.

Jesse stopped a mere ten feet from her and waited.

Sara saw that his stallion had thrown a shoe. "Would you like a ride?" she asked, needing to break the unbearable tension.

"No, thanks," Jesse said in a level voice.

"Fine." Sara said and tugged on Golda's reins, pulling her away from the fence, starting back.

"Wait! Sara, wait."

She slowed, turned the mare in a circle and maneuvered back to sit facing him expectantly.

He didn't want her here, didn't want her anywhere near him. He wanted her more than his next breath. "I wish I could tell you that I'll miss your father," he finally said.

She nodded. "He was a difficult man to understand." She'd certainly never managed to understand him.

She didn't look grief-stricken, but rather sad, Jesse thought. There was an air of quiet confidence about her that hadn't been there before. He wished he could ask what had happened to her over the last twelve years to bring about the obvious maturing. He wished he could ask her a lot of things. "My folks were at the house, helping Phil with the funeral. Mom says Noah left you with quite a mess."

"Yes. How are your parents?" She'd never really blamed Emily for the response she'd had on the phone that long-ago day when Lacie had called. Sara knew that the woman's love and loyalty belonged first and always with her son and the rest of her family. Emily had been trying to keep Sara from hurting Jesse even more.

The stallion shuffled his feet restively and Jesse put a soothing hand on the animal's nose. "They're good. Dad's semiretired now, and they've begun to do some traveling. Mom's the same as always."

Sara brushed back strands of hair that had come loose from her ponytail, thinking she must look a wreck. Yet curiosity kept her rooted to the spot. "And Kay?"

"She's married, about five years now. A lawyer named Will Upton. They live in Phoenix, and Kay teaches fourth grade."

"I remember she always wanted to teach." Through the years, she'd missed her friendship with Kay. She'd never developed another as strong with a woman her own age. "Lisa's undoubtedly married, too." Though Sara hadn't been fond of Lisa, she had to admit she was a beautiful woman, one men had trailed after since her early teens.

Jesse's face, relaxed when he'd been speaking of his folks and sister, tightened a fraction and his eyes cooled. Sara wondered at the change.

"She's still around. Quit college a couple of times. Never did finish. She's in charge of the show horses and lessons."

"As I recall, she loved to perform in the arena."

Jesse nodded, toying with the stallion's reins, wondering why he didn't plunge past these polite inquiries and ask what he really wanted to know. "Yeah, she's still a show-off."

Sara decided she wanted to know it all. Jesse wasn't wearing a wedding ring, but few ranchers did, thinking jewelry would interfere with their work. "And your wife, does she work with you on the ranch?" Or had he married some sweet-smelling society type who didn't like to get her hands dirty, but loved the money ranching brought in? she thought nastily.

Jesse's head came up, and he frowned. "What wife? I've never married. Who told you I had?"

So the other woman that Emily had mentioned to Lacie, the one Jesse was supposedly making a better life with after Sara had hurt him, hadn't hung around, either. Interesting. "I can't recall. Must have been just a rumor."

Despite days of telling himself he wasn't in the least curious about Sara, his eyes slid to her left hand. "You, either?"

"No." They'd run out of small talk, out of family members to discuss. The knot in her stomach had grown huge. She needed to end this. "Do you want a lift back, or not?"

He had more questions to ask, more he needed to know. "I'd appreciate a ride. Can your mare jump the fence?"

By way of an answer, Sara reined Golda about and took off in the opposite direction. When she felt she was far enough away for Golda to work up to a good speed, she turned and nudged her swiftly into a fast run. The two-year-old cleared the fence easily, then slowed as Sara circled back to where Jesse stood watching them.

She'd always been the best horsewoman he'd ever seen. Lisa thought she was good, but Sara was much better, a natural, someone who rode so attuned to the horse that she could predict and control the slightest change in an animal's stride. But he wasn't in the mood to bestow compliments.

Sara drew up close and stopped the mare several feet away. "Your stallion won't nip Golda, will he?" she asked as he tied the lead rope to the back of the saddle.

"All males raised on the Morgan Ranch are unfailingly polite and mannerly," Jesse answered, not looking at her.

She'd walked right into that one, Sara thought as he came around to the side.

"It'd be easier if you got off and I got on, then helped you up in front of me."

He was probably right. The stock western saddle was fairly roomy with a small horn, but Jesse was a big man. At best, it would be a snug fit. Sara's blood began to heat at the very thought of being that close to him as she slipped off Golda's back.

Jesse quickly mounted, then leaned a hand down to pull Sara up. As she settled in front of him, her small bottom tucked tightly between his legs, he felt his body's instant reaction, and wondered if she did, too. There was little he could do about it, he thought with a silent curse as his arms encircled her, his hands taking the reins. The last thing he'd wanted her to know was that he still wanted her, but his recent long abstinence betrayed him.

Or was it *this* woman's nearness and not his self-enforced celibacy that had him painfully aroused at the first contact?

"I hear you live in San Diego," Jesse commented as they started out. He would begin with innocuous inquiries, then ask what he really wanted to know when her guard was down.

Sara held herself stiffly, trying desperately not to lean back into him as her treacherous body longed to do. How could he do this to her, have her aroused in mere moments, when other men couldn't seem to get half this far in hours? With no small effort, she tried to concentrate on more small talk. "Yes."

"You like it there?"

"The climate's wonderful, and I love the ocean."

Jesse had been to California several times and enjoyed the sea. But he loved the ranch more. "What do you do there?" His mother had told him, but he wanted to hear it from Sara.

"I opened a graphic arts studio. Computer design. I do logos, stationery, ads for newspapers and magazines. Recently, we moved into typesetting as well. It's a challenging business, yet there's room for creativity." She was telling more than he probably wanted to know, but she felt safe discussing her work. Odd how long it took to ride a mile when she was so agonizingly aware of the man whose arms were wrapped around her, whose warm breath on her neck was causing her hands to tremble.

The offer of this ride had probably been a mistake, Sara thought belatedly. She should have just ridden back to the house and let him think her rude.

The mare snuffled, shaking her big head as she made her slow way, unused to the heavier burden and undoubtedly aware of the stallion close on her backside. No less aware than Jesse was of the woman whose scent was playing havoc with his weakening control. "Sounds like interesting work," he said, though he believed no such thing. How could she have made such a switch when she'd loved horses and ranching so much? And the bigger question, why?

"I remember you told me how you'd like to run the Lazy-S one day, that ranching was in your blood, the same as in mine."

This was what she'd been afraid of, this delving into the whys and wherefores. "Yes, well, people change. Priorities shift and goals get modified along the way."

"You seemed so certain, so adamant," he persisted, wanting her to feel her back to the wall so she'd blurt out the truth.

Sara released a nervous sigh. "That was twelve years ago, Jesse. I was seventeen. Few of us know exactly what we want out of life at that uncertain age."

He'd known. Perhaps he hadn't yet acknowledged it even to himself, but he'd known deep down inside even at seventeen that he wanted to be a rancher. And he'd wanted Sara Shephard.

She was fencing with him. He could sense it. "But now that your father's gone, you've changed your mind and come back?"

"Not to stay. Just long enough to fix up the ranch and put it on the market."

"You're going to sell the Lazy-S?" He hadn't considered that possibility.

"Yes." She felt oddly defensive, as if she had to justify her reasons to him. "I've built a life in San Diego, one that fulfills me." At least in most ways. "I don't belong here anymore." Which wasn't exactly the truth.

It came to him, the real reason, the one she'd been evading. "There's a man there, waiting for you, one who wouldn't fit in here."

Fleetingly, Sara thought of Clay. He'd fit in here just fine, a man who loved the outdoors. He'd undoubtedly consider ranching a challenge, learn it and love it. If she'd ask him to come with her, to share the ranch with her, she felt certain Clay would jump at the chance. But she wouldn't ask. Inherently she knew her future didn't include Clay, whether in San Diego or elsewhere.

"No, there's no man," she said, then immediately regretted the words. Perhaps she should have let him think there was so while she was here, he'd stay away from her.

Golda swerved to avoid a low bush in her path, causing Sara to place her hands on Jesse's arms for support as she felt herself tilting. Jesse automatically compensated, situating her more firmly between his hard thighs. Swallowing a moan, Sara closed her eyes as she struggled against reacting to the hard evidence of his desire throbbing against her. Memories of a long-ago summer filled with rides such as this when she'd willingly welcomed his nearness, eagerly sought his touch, been desperate for his loving, flooded her mind and senses.

She had to put some distance between them.

Sara opened her eyes and saw that the gate between the two ranches was just ahead. Just a few more moments...

Jesse was well aware of the effect he was having on her. His own discomfort was bearable if he knew he could still arouse her. Maybe then, in a vulnerable state, he could get the truth from her.

As he reined Golda in, Sara swung her leg over and jumped down almost before the mare had come to a full stop. She hoped the sudden drop had cleared her mind and calmed her racing heart.

Unhurriedly, Jesse climbed down and patted the mare's neck. "She's a fine piece of horse flesh," he commented. "How's the rest of your stock?"

Damn him for asking, she thought. Of course, the whole valley probably knew. News between ranches traveled quickly. Her father's selling off of his best horses had undoubtedly caused a fair amount of speculation before his death. Turning, she faced him squarely on. "They're in great shape."

He recognized that tilted-chin approach, that challenging look, and chose to ignore it. "I hear you're a little short. I don't imagine you'll find too many buyers without a larger inventory."

She wouldn't let him see that he was getting to her. "I intend to acquire more before offering the ranch for sale."

And sooner die than ask him if the Morgans had any for sale, he imagined. Time and circumstance were on his side on this one. He knew of no ranches nearby that had horses that would enhance the sale of the Lazy-S other than the Morgan spread. She would discover that in time and have to come to them.

Jesse swallowed around a sudden bitter taste in his mouth. He'd thought himself over her, yet was he? She'd apparently hurt him badly enough that he was eager to have her come crawling to him, if only to beg to buy his horses. His desire for even that minor revenge had him feeling disgusted with himself. Maybe she did have an explanation worth hearing. He took a step closer.

The tight rubber band around her ponytail was pinching, and Sara pulled it off, then shook her head, letting her long hair fall free. Needing to go, she untied the stallion's lead rope and held out her hand for Golda's reins.

Seeing the golden cloud of her hair drift down around her shoulders with the setting sun as backdrop was nearly his undoing. Jesse took her hand, his eyes meeting hers. "Why did you leave like that, Sara? Why did you go without so much as a word?"

Hadn't she known the day she'd received Phil's phone call that if she returned, they'd be having this conversation? Known and feared it. She studied Jesse's face and saw what her son would look like as a grown man, right down to the stubborn, dimpled chin. She drew in a shaky breath, the reminder of Chris sobering her even more. "I called your house, but your mother said you'd already left for Texas with your father."

"You could have left a note, something."

She'd thought of that later, on the long bus ride to San Diego. But if she had and if Jesse had have come after her, her father still could have had him arrested. She'd been afraid to take the chance. "I didn't think of it," she answered lamely, withdrawing her hand from his. "I have to get back."

He wouldn't let her off the hook that easily. "Why did you feel you had to leave so suddenly? What happened?" For years, this had gnawed at him. Had he unwittingly said something, unknowingly done something, that had forced her away?

Sara turned sideways, her gaze swinging to a bird hopping from limb to limb in a nearby tree, then suddenly flying off. She wished she could fly away from his question, from the lingering hurt she could hear in his voice. "My father and I quarreled. Badly. I couldn't handle it anymore. I had to leave."

"What over? Noah said you stole money from him."

Temper flared in her eyes, fast and furious. "What? That's a lie. I never, ever took from him."

"I didn't believe him. Was it me, then? Did he find out you'd been meeting me secretly?"

She turned toward Golda, wanting to end this. "It happened a long time ago, Jesse. Let it go. I have."

"Have you?" Jesse grabbed her by her upper arms and pulled her to face him. "Let's test that." His head dipped, his mouth captured hers while his arms shifted to mold her to his body. He wasn't gentle, wasn't kind, as years of anger and frustration bubbled up within him and boiled over.

He'd had her pinned before she'd realized what he was going to do. With the shock came the need to free herself before he sucked her under. Sara strained to pull back, stiffening her body, raising her hands to pound at his back. She might as well have been a gnat grappling with an elephant.

Clamping her lips closely together, she tried to keep herself from reacting to the onslaught of his kiss. But his mouth devoured, his tongue sought entry and his hands began to wander. She fought back, but her struggles only brought her in closer contact with his hard, exciting male body.

And her own began to respond.

With a small desperate sound of surrender, Sara felt her mouth open under his, felt her hands unclench at his back and bunch in the soft cotton of his shirt. Oh, God, how she'd wanted this, needed this, craved this. When another man had kissed her, she'd wondered if she'd only imagined how *this* man could make her feel, wondered if she'd been remembering what had never been.

But no, this was real. She felt the ripple of need spread through her, drugging her senses, muddling her mind. His hands on her felt so good, so right. His mouth on hers was the first that had ever touched her, the only one she'd ever hungered for. His scent, his taste was achingly familiar. Could that be, after all these years?

She'd lost her ability to reason, lost her reasons for resisting. Lost in a sensual dream she never wanted to waken from, Sara clung to him.

Twelve years erased in a moment, Jesse thought, with that small portion of his brain still functioning. The feelings between them were as they'd always been, from their first kiss when she'd been just sixteen. Explosive, intense, fiery. No other woman had ever been able to make him feel the way Sara so effortlessly had always been able to do.

Breathless, he broke the kiss, but when he heard a small involuntary whimper of protest from her, he took her mouth again—and was rewarded when she met his tongue with hers the same unabashedly passionate way she always had. She'd never held anything back in their physical unions, and that hadn't changed.

But even as he admitted that he wanted her more now than he ever had, he eased away again. For he sensed she was holding back something serious.

All but panting, Jesse gazed down into green eyes still hazy with desire, and loosened his hold on her. "Have you let go, Sara? Let go of all your feelings for me?"

She was annoyed but not surprised when she saw that her hands were trembling as she moved back from him. She had to lie to him. It was the only way she'd be able to walk away. "Yes, I have." She brushed back her hair, avoiding his eyes. "I thought all the males on the Morgan Ranch were unfailingly polite and mannerly?"

"It's only good manners to welcome you home with a friendly kiss."

Sara raised a questioning eyebrow. That kiss had been many things, but friendly wasn't one of them.

"You kissed me back, Sara," Jesse pointed out. "Don't bother to deny it."

She cleared her throat, buying another few seconds to calm her racing heart as she stepped over and opened the gate. "I admit I've always been susceptible to your kisses. But I'm over you, Jesse."

Quickly, before he could read the lie on her face, she scrambled up into the saddle.

He stood looking at her, his feet spread, his stance challenging. "In that case, I hope you'll be happy in California."

She straightened her back and squared her chin. "I will be. Deliriously."

He moved so fast she wasn't aware he had until his strong fingers closed around her leg. "You know, Sara, you never used to be a liar." With that, he gently slapped the mare's flank and stood watching her take off through the open gate.

He hadn't discovered everything he wanted to know, Jesse thought, as he closed the gate. She'd evaded some of his questions, answered others vaguely and lied to him about her feelings. He'd had a hard time convincing himself years ago that Sara would deliberately hurt him, but he'd finally accepted it as the only possibility. But after this encounter, he felt there was more, something she wasn't telling him. He would find out, carefully and methodically.

He would pursue, persuade and get it out of her. He would do it because today he'd learned one important thing, and that was that despite separation, time and distance, and though she would deny it, Sara still wanted him.

Just as he'd never stopped wanting her.

Chapter Seven

Sara set aside the thick stack of papers bound in a blue cover and thoughtfully leaned back in her father's worn leather desk chair. She'd been reading an interesting document, the abstract on the property known as the Lazy-S.

Amos Sidwell, her father's attorney, had told her recently that most properties sold these days required the seller to provide the purchaser with a title insurance policy warranting that the title on the land and dwellings was free and clear. Years ago, however, it was more common to use abstracts which constituted a history of that parcel, adding a page detailing the boundaries and legalities each time the property changed hands.

Because the Lazy-S had been in her family for three generations, handed down from father to son and now to granddaughter, the abstract had remained in Noah's study all these years. The accumulated pages outlining the history of the Lazy-S made for fascinating reading. It dated all the way back to the early 1800s when a Mormon settler from Utah had staked a claim on the land, built his home and proceeded to farm the parcel.

Years later, she'd just read, her grandfather had bought it and built a brand-new ranch house for his bride, and turned to horse ranching rather than farming. The attached survey was very detailed and went back to the origin of the first owner. What she did *not* find was the section that her father had always claimed had once been a part of the Lazy-S and was rumored to have been won unfairly by Jesse's grandfather in a card game.

Twice, she'd looked through the wordy legal papers with their official seals proving they'd been recorded in the county courthouse, and found no trace of her own grandfather's deathbed claim. On the contrary, she learned that the section in question had *never* been owned by the Shephards. So how could her grandfather have lost it in a poker game, fair or otherwise, as Noah had claimed for years?

Sara took a sip of her second cup of morning coffee and considered the situation. Had her father lied? If so, why? Was there some other reason he disliked the Morgans so intensely?

She glanced over at the piles of papers and bulging folders and ledgers that she'd stacked neatly and that now awaited her attention. Maybe there was something in those that would shed some light on this puzzling new discovery. Methodically, she would go through each, though she didn't relish the thought.

She felt melancholy and nostalgic this morning. Perhaps it was partly because of that unnerving encounter with Jesse, or maybe it was just being back here where memories were tucked into every dark corner.

Swiveling in the chair, Sara reached down to the first pile and picked up an old photo album, one she remembered she'd wanted to take with her when she'd left. But she'd been too frightened of her father to ask for it.

Opening the album she hadn't looked through in years, she realized that her mother apparently had loved taking snapshots as there were many from the time she'd been alive. There was one rather faded picture that really went far back, showing four young adults, possibly in their twenties, looking into the camera, their arms laced together. Sara recognized Hal and Emily Morgan, her mother and her father. Noah, on the far right, was the only one scowling.

Had the four of them once been good friends? Sara remembered that Emily had mentioned knowing Rose Shephard, but not well. Had something happened after the two marriages had taken place that had driven such a wedge between the Morgans and the Shephards? Or did it all date back to their ancestors and that questionable land dispute?

She turned the page and found herself looking at a larger five-by-seven black-and-white photo of Emily Morgan, one Sara couldn't recall having seen before. Odd. She wished she could go over and talk with Emily, show her the album, hear what she knew about those days. Had Emily and Rose been close once, and because of their husbands' feud, been forced to choose sides?

Sara wondered if she'd ever know. There was a rather grim picture of her mother and father on their wedding day, both unsmiling. Several baby pictures of her, mostly alone. A couple of Noah, always glancing up as if caught by surprise by the photographer, and obviously annoyed. There were a handful of her mother, looking pale and sickly, her blond hair so like Sara's was now.

She leaned close to examine a photo of a grave site with a headstone and a blanket of flowers, but couldn't make out the engraving. And next to it was the picture of a long white casket draped with roses. Her mother's, most likely. Why had her father wanted such a sorrowful reminder?

Then for years there'd been no pictures added, not until
Sara had asked for and finally been given a camera around
the age of twelve. She remembered how thrilled she'd been,
snapping everything in sight.

There were several sheets of snapshots of her favorite
horses including their names and the dates that she'd written underneath in her childish handwriting. She'd captured
a younger Phil grooming a horse, giving a lesson, riding
fence. Then, continuing, Sara turned the pages and discovered that someone had removed a great many pictures,
leaving only scrawled notations. Reading those, she soon
realized that the missing snapshots had been ones she'd
taken at school and included either Kay or Jesse Morgan.
Sara had thought she'd been safe, taking them on the playground or walking home from the bus. But they'd been
ripped out, leaving the black sheets looking ragged and vi-
olated.

Oh, Dad, what drove you to destroy like this?

Closing the album, she set it aside, feeling lonely and lost,
just as she had so often when she'd lived under this roof. She
hadn't known her mother because of Rose's early death, and
hadn't known her father because of his inflexible self-
isolation. She'd gotten to know and love the Morgans, only
to be forced to leave them.

And she'd loved Jesse.

Swiveling around in her chair, Sara gazed unseeingly out
the window. In her mind's eye, she saw instead the way Jesse
had looked yesterday, that arrogant stance that suited him
so, yet on anyone else irritated her. That black curly hair so
like Christopher's. That hard mouth that had once touched
her where no man before or since had, and still could make
her instantly yearn for more.

Sara forced herself to harden her heart. Jesse's mother
had told Lacie that he was happily involved with another
woman the day she'd called. Poetic justice had somehow

seen to it that that woman had left him, too. Now, her first week back, and he'd grabbed her, kissed her, as if he still had a claim on her.

She couldn't allow that to happen. She had a son to protect, a son he could take away from her. She didn't have the money to fight the rich and powerful man Jesse had become. She had no idea if he'd even want his son, but she couldn't risk finding out. She couldn't risk losing the only good and solid thing in her life.

Jesse had always been able to make her want him. With a look, a mere touch. She would have to fight that, to stay clear of him, to be cool and indifferent.

She became aware of voices in another part of the house and swung back to the desk—a reprieve from all this tedious soul-searching. For answers, for some clue to her father's personality, for something that would help her understand how he'd become such an unhappy, troubled man. And to sort out her own jumbled feelings.

In the kitchen, she heard Ruby talking with Phil, then his footsteps coming her way. Polite as always, he knocked on the open study door, and she waved him in. "Good morning, Phil."

"'Morning, Sara. I got the personnel records on everyone working the ranch like you asked me to." He sat down in the chair she indicated alongside her father's desk and handed her the small stack of folders.

Taking them, she glanced at the top one. "Anyone in this pile not carrying his weight around here?" She was determined to have only good men on the staff, then to hire several more as soon as she figured out where she was going to purchase the horses she'd decided she'd have to acquire.

"Only one I know of is Wally Stump. He's nearing seventy now. Still a good man, and he knows horse flesh. But he can't move as fast as he used to and he's sort of forgetful."

As she so often did in running her small business, although she made her own decisions, Sara thought it wise to get a second opinion before making a final determination. "What would you do with Wally?"

Phil crossed his legs, looking uneasy. "If you're asking does Wally do his fair share around here, I got to say no. If you're asking would I let him go, again I got to say no. Everyone likes him, to a man, and they ask his advice often. He's just plain good people."

"And he has no family, no place else to go and probably very little money saved, right?"

Phil nodded. "That about says it."

Sara found room for the folders on the cluttered desk. "There ought to be a retirement fund set up for cowboys, don't you agree, Phil?"

"Yes, ma'am."

"Wally stays. This has been his home for thirty years. Anyone else?"

The glint of admiration in Phil's eyes was unmistakable. "None as far as I can see."

"Fine. I'll look through them later, but I trust your word." She decided to probe a little. "Phil, exactly when did you start working here?"

"You were just two years old," Phil answered, smiling as he rubbed a hand over his bearded chin. "Cute little thing with all that blond hair."

She smiled at the compliment. "Then you knew my mother?"

"A little. She didn't leave the house much. And she died the following year."

Sara indicated the piles of papers. "I haven't had a chance to go through those yet. Maybe I'll find her death certificate. My father always said she was sickly. Do you know what she died of?"

"Way I heard, it was complications from childbirth."

She frowned, puzzled. "Three years after I was born, she died of complications from the delivery?"

Phil shook his head. "Not that one. The other baby, the one that died."

Stunned, Sara sat back. "I didn't know there was another baby."

"Yes, ma'am. A little boy. Only lived a few days. It was after that that Noah started drinking. He took it real hard."

That certainly put a different slant on things. "I wonder why he never told me."

"Your daddy wasn't a talkative man."

The understatement of the year. "Tell me, back then, did Emily Morgan ever come over, either alone or with her husband, to visit my mother? Did my parents and the Morgans ever visit back and forth?"

"Nope, not once that I saw. Noah had no use for the Morgans far back as I remember."

"Because of the land dispute?"

"That's what your daddy said. Over and over he told me that story."

"I guess he told anyone who'd listen." Sara sighed, then decided she'd had enough of a stroll down memory lane for one day. "I've called Chuck Morris, and he's coming out tomorrow to appraise the ranch and let me know what he thinks I can get for it." The Morris Real Estate Agency had an excellent reputation in the area. "I'd like you to be available to answer his questions, if he has any."

Phil stood. "Sure thing."

"The place is shaping up, don't you think? The outside painting will be finished by the weekend, and next week, they'll start in here. The barns are ready for inspection, horses in fine shape, the pasture land looking good. You and the men have done a terrific job and quickly. I appreciate it."

"All well and good, Sara, but Chuck's going to tell you exactly what I did. No one's going to put in an offer till you get some prime horse stock."

Sara opened the middle desk drawer and removed a piece of paper. "I've got a list right here of area ranches. I'm going to start calling around later this afternoon."

He sent her a doubtful look. "Good luck."

The roar of a powerful engine just outside prevented her from answering. Sara glanced around and saw a red Corvette pull to a stop in front of the house.

Phil peered out, then straightened. "Here comes trouble."

"Who does that belong to?" she asked, then saw a tall woman with long auburn hair climb out.

"Lisa Nagles," Phil said, his tone critical.

Sara glanced over at him. "You don't think much of her?"

Phil shrugged noncommittally. "If she was my daughter, I'd have turned her over my knee a long while ago. The hands tell me she's a wild one, all right."

Sara watched Lisa prop her hands on her slim hips and squint up at the painters on the scaffolding. She was wearing a tight yellow jumpsuit and white sandals, not the sort of outfit one usually saw around a ranch. "Does she date one of our men?"

"She dates 'em all."

Shaking back her hair, Lisa started up the porch steps. Sara stepped back from the window. "I wonder why she's come." She glanced down at her jeans and the San Diego Padres baseball shirt she was wearing, the sort of outfit she usually chose to wear when she cleaned her own house. She hadn't bothered with makeup and her hair hung down her back in a long thick braid, a concession to the heat. Next to a peacock like Lisa, she would look like a pale wren, Sara thought as she left the den.

The doorbell was chiming as she walked into the foyer. "I'll get it, Ruby," Sara called toward the kitchen.

"See you later," Phil said, seemingly anxious to get going as he headed for the back door.

Sara smiled at his hurried departure, then opened the door.

"Well, well. Long time no see, Sara." Not waiting for an invitation, Lisa entered in a cloud of heavy perfume, her eyes inspecting every nook and cranny curiously. "Haven't you just worked a miracle here?" She swung back, on her red lips a smile that didn't quite make it to her eyes.

Sara shoved closed the door, resigned to the intrusion since Lisa had never been the type to go away until she was good and ready. "We do the best we can," she answered, folding her arms across her chest, feeling a shade defensive.

"I'd heard that the best thing anyone could do would be to light a match to this place, but you're fixing it all up again, aren't you?" She toyed with her car keys, her long red nails clicking against the metal. "Planning to live among us again, Sara?"

Funny how often that question came up. Sara was getting a little tired of answering it. She was also feeling perverse today. "Maybe. Should I?"

Lisa's large blue eyes narrowed fractionally, but the smile never left her lips. "Well, why not? Though I don't see how this little hick town can hold much interest for someone who's used to a big city. You're one of those California artists now, aren't you?"

Sara frowned. "Where do you get your information? I do graphic art design. On computers."

Lisa's arched eyebrows rose. "Really? How fascinating. Ever so much more so than working in a smelly old horse barn."

Sara was growing annoyed. She'd never liked Lisa as a child nor as a teenager. Age hadn't improved her. "What is it you want, Lisa?"

"I'm just being neighborly." Strolling past the player piano, she peered into the kitchen where Ruby was hanging new curtains. "What makes you think I want anything other than to welcome you home?"

There was a hidden agenda here somewhere, Sara thought, if only she could figure it out. "That's very thoughtful of you." As far as she could remember, Lisa hadn't done a very thoughtful thing in her entire life.

"I don't suppose you'd care to offer me a cold drink?"

Trying not to grit her teeth, Sara led the way into the kitchen. "You probably know Ruby," she said by way of introduction as she got down two glasses and filled them with ice. Lisa's eyes passed over the small woman as if she weren't there. Sara hid a smile as Ruby glanced over her shoulder at Lisa, then turned back to the window without a word, rolling her eyes as she resumed her curtain-hanging.

Sara poured iced tea, then walked to the butcher-block table where Lisa had already seated herself. Handing her uninvited guest the cold drink, she waited for Lisa to get to the real reason she'd come.

"It's nice in here, it really is." She sipped her tea. "'Course I don't know why you bothered. Jesse will probably tear down this house once the Lazy-S is his."

Sara folded her arms on the table and regarded Lisa. "What *are* you talking about?"

Lisa smiled in her cat-ate-the-canary way. "Have you run across Jesse yet?"

That was none of this nosy woman's business. "I came back here to settle my father's estate, Lisa, not to socialize."

"You and Jesse were once real close, as I recall. That summer before you left in such an all-fired hurry." Her shrewd eyes never left Sara's face.

She might have known their comings and goings over three months had been observed by at least one or two. And she remembered that Lisa had come upon Jesse kissing her once. She kept her face expressionless. "That was a long time ago. Jesse and I have had no contact in twelve years." There, if that was what Lisa was trying to learn, now she had her answer.

"Oh, he'll be around, honey. Don't you worry, because you've got something Jesse wants real bad." Sitting back, Lisa crossed her long legs and waited.

Sara decided to bite. "And what might that be?"

Instead of answering, Lisa jumped in with another question. "Why didn't you tell me that morning you stopped by that you were leaving for good? Did you know Jesse was real upset when he came home and found you gone?"

Sara stirred her tea absently, wondering if she could believe Lisa, wondering why she was bothering to tell her after all this time. She chose to ignore the first question. "Was he?"

"Uh-huh. Made us all wonder if there wasn't something serious between you two." She paused, but when Sara was silent, she went on. "But it didn't last long. You know how men are. Out of sight, out of mind." She laughed, as if sharing a woman-to-woman secret. "Pretty soon he was concentrating real hard on Holly Lucas. You know her?"

Everyone knew the Lucas family, the ones who owned the ranch across the river and bordering the Morgan spread on the far side. She vaguely remembered Holly from high school, a quiet studious girl a couple of years older than she. "I knew her slightly," she answered, wishing Lisa would make her point.

"Well, Jesse really gave Holly the rush. Trouble is, Holly's father figured out real fast what Jesse was up to and hustled his daughter off to some college in the East. That was twice Jesse'd struck out, and he sure was fighting mad." Tossing back her hair, Lisa swallowed more tea.

Sara was losing patience. "You've lost me. What do you mean that he struck out twice?"

Lisa let out a knowing laugh. "Haven't you caught on yet, honey? The ranches. Jesse and Hal want more land. You left, so he couldn't sweet-talk you out of the Lazy-S. In no time, he was nuzzling up to Holly, thinking she'd fall for him and he'd get her family's spread through marriage. Holly's an only child, like you." She hesitated a moment, pleased to see she finally had Sara's full attention. "But now, he's got another chance at the Lazy-S and he doesn't even have to marry you this time. All he has to do is put in an offer. Nobody else around here has the money to buy you out except the Morgans."

Sara swallowed hard. She didn't want to believe Lisa, not a word of it. The woman was obviously trying to stir up trouble. She hadn't come to warn, but rather to upset, which was what Lisa did best. Yet . . . could she be right?

Had Holly Lucas been the woman Emily had referred to in that phone conversation? Had Jesse been angry, not hurt at her leaving, because his plans had been ruined? Could she have misjudged him so?

Jesse had had every opportunity yesterday to mention that he wanted the Lazy-S, and he hadn't. Of course, he hadn't offered to sell her horses, either, which he knew she needed in order to interest an outside buyer. Had he thought that that wouldn't be necessary, that he'd wait until she discovered for herself that the Shephard ranch wasn't worth much without stock? Then he'd move in and pick it up for a song, because by then she'd just want out?

No, she wouldn't believe that. She'd loved him once. He was the father of her son. Jesse wasn't perfect, but he wasn't cold and calculating, so anxious to expand the Morgan holdings that he'd once planned to marry for gain.

"I can see I've got you thinking," Lisa purred.

Sara quickly rearranged her expression. "I'm sorry to say you wasted a trip, Lisa. Because I don't believe you."

Lisa stood, putting on her plastic smile. "You will, honey. Jesse will be around to make his offer real soon. Just you wait and see." She sauntered toward the foyer. "Don't say I didn't warn you. I'll see myself out."

Sara heard the front door close and still she didn't rise. Damn the woman for muddling her mind even more.

"Sara," Ruby said, climbing down from the step stool, "you shouldn't let that Lisa upset you. That woman, she bad news."

Sara got up wearily, taking both glasses to the sink. "You're probably right."

Still, as she turned on the water, she remembered the words her father had screamed at her the evening before she'd left. *It's this ranch Jesse Morgan wants, girl. Not you and not that bastard you're carrying.*

Oh, God, could Noah have been right all along?

In San Diego, Sara did a lot of walking. From her house to her office, to the ballfield, to a nearby park. She missed her walks and decided to go for one after a dinner she hadn't really had much appetite for. She didn't know if it was the unaccustomed heat or her depressing mission, but she hadn't felt much like eating since returning.

Hands in the pockets of her jeans, she strolled down the greenbelt toward the barns, automatically checking the progress of the painting as she walked. Not bad, she thought. A coat of white paint did wonders for an older building. It was dusk, and the automatic sprinklers came on, sputtering and hissing for a moment at start-up, then spraying the grass gently. Maybe tomorrow she'd go into town to the nursery and buy some flowers to plant along the porch. A little color couldn't hurt.

She waved to Pete, who was walking from the mess hall located at one end of the bunkhouse to the small cabin he shared with Ruby. Sara walked on, smelling the heat still hovering over the dusty patches, listening to the crickets already beginning their nightly serenade. The sun was hanging suspended in a pale blue sky, slowly inching downward.

At the horse barn, she rounded the bend and saw Phil calming a horse that had apparently just trotted up to him. Wondering what the saddled mare was doing running loose, Sara hurried over. "Anything wrong?" she asked.

Phil glanced in the direction the horse had come from, frowning. "I don't know. Wally's been out all afternoon checking the west pasture fence. His mare just returned without him."

"We need to go look for him," Sara said immediately.

"I'll get one of the boys to saddle up. Hank and I are working with a sick colt."

"Did you call the vet?"

"We haven't used Doc Myers in quite a spell. Your daddy said he charged too much."

More questionable budget cuts. "You call the vet. I'll go find Wally." Sara grabbed the reins of the mare, stroking her neck, letting her get used to her scent.

"Wally may be hurt. I'm not sure you can manage to..."

She stopped him with an impatient look. "Phil, I grew up on this ranch. I know what to do with an injured man." Gracefully, she swung up into the saddle. "Trust me, all right?"

He smiled at her, his head cocked in admiration. "Yes, ma'am."

"And stop calling me *ma'am*, will you? Makes me feel ancient. 'Sara' will do nicely." Nudging the mare's sides, Sara started off.

It took her quite some time to find him. Lying in the sparse shade of a scrub pine, Wally looked at her with pain in his eyes as she pulled the mare to a halt in front of him. Jumping down, she tethered the mare, then knelt beside Wally. "What happened?"

"Don't rightly know. I was riding fence, looking for breaks in the wire. I got to thinking too hard, I guess, and got too close to that big tree limb up there. Next thing you know, I was flying off, landing on the ground. I must've passed out for a minute 'cause when I woke up, the filly was heading back to the barn." His voice was labored and hoarse from years of chewing tobacco.

"Do you think you can sit up?" Sara asked, slipping her arm under his shoulders.

"Reckon I can try." He did, with her help, but closed his eyes on a wave of dizziness. "I don't feel so good, Miz Sara."

She helped him lie back down, suspecting a concussion. She'd been around the ballfield three years now and had seen several boys receive mild ones. "Does it feel as if any of your bones are broken?" Gingerly, she ran her hand along his arms, then glanced down at his legs. The left one lay at an odd angle.

"Don't know if that ankle's twisted or just broken, but it hurts like hell. Beggin' your pardon, ma'am."

Sara knew that at his age bones were often broke more easily. She stood, wondering just how she should go about getting him up onto the horse. As she considered various options, she heard the sound of an engine approaching from the area of the ranch, but on the Morgan side of the fence. Frowning, she turned to see who was coming.

"Need some help?" Jesse called out as he pulled his Jeep to a stop.

"I can manage," Sara answered. And she would, if she had to carry Wally on her back. She bent to the older man, who lay looking up at her helplessly.

"I feel so dang stupid letting this happen, Miz Sara."

"Don't blame yourself, Wally. Accidents happen." Again, she slipped her arm under his slight shoulders. "I am going to have to ask you to sit up, though."

Jesse jumped out of the Jeep and, wearing his heavy gloves, spread two sections of the wire fencing and stepped through. Going down on one knee, he knelt beside the injured man. "Had a fall, did you, Wally?" With the ease of an experienced rancher, he checked the man's eyes.

"Yes, sir," Wally answered, his voice growing weaker.

Sara remembered that Jesse had never listened well, and apparently that hadn't changed. Still, there was no point in being obstinate when a man lay hurt and needing help. "If you'll help me get him onto the horse, I'll take it from there."

"I don't think that's a good idea. He appears to have a concussion. A horseback ride isn't going to help that. He needs to get to the clinic. I'll take him in the Jeep."

She also recalled how his take-charge manner had occasionally infuriated her. "You can't get through that fence with him in your arms. And he's too weak to make it himself."

Rising, Jesse reached into his back pocket, took out a pair of clippers and cut through the three wires. "We'll stop at the barn and get someone to ride out, repair the fence and take your horse back. Get in the Jeep, and I'll hand him in."

She'd lost control. It was as simple as that. She'd have put up an argument, but it would have been foolish in the face of Wally's obvious pain. Later, she would remind Jesse that he was not in charge of her men. Or of her.

Scrambling through the fence opening, she sat down in the back seat. Watching Jesse, she couldn't help but be amazed at how easily, how gently, he picked up the old man and carried him to her as if Wally were a child.

"He's got some blood on his head," Jesse said. "You want me to get a cloth from under the seat to protect your clothes?"

"Just hand him in. I'm washable." Carefully, Jesse settled the old cowboy on the back seat with his head resting on her lap. "Just close your eyes, Wally, but don't go to sleep. We'll have you to the clinic in no time."

Jesse got behind the wheel and drove off, watching the bumpy terrain so as not to jar his injured passenger too much. At the barn, he pulled over and yelled through the open double doors. "Aaron? Aaron, you still here?"

Wiping his hands on a rag, Aaron came walking over to the Jeep. His eyes swept to the back where Sara sat holding Wally, whose color wasn't good. "Got a problem?"

"Need you to ride out about a mile or so over along the Shephard boundary line. I had to cut the fence, so it needs rewiring. And you need to lead Sara's mare back to their barn."

"Got it. Is he hurt bad?"

"I don't think so. We're heading for the clinic."

His sharp blue eyes danced to Sara, then back to his friend, a smirk on his lips. "Good luck."

Jesse stepped on the gas pedal.

Chapter Eight

The largest of the two clinics inside the city limits was a rectangular building set back off the highway. It shared a paved parking lot with Elroy's Shoe and Saddle Repair. Three registered nurses rotated shifts and the resident doctor was on call, but there only during regular office hours and emergencies. However, because Henry Lapin had nearly severed his little finger in a tractor accident an hour before Jesse's Jeep pulled up, Dr. Roscoe Fields was present when Sara ran in to ask for a wheelchair for Wally.

The nurse quickly wheeled Wally, looking strained and hurting, into an examining room and waved Sara and Jesse to the small waiting room.

Seated on a turquoise, molded plastic chair, Sara frowned toward the double doors closing behind them. "Poor Wally. He looks so frightened."

Jesse crossed his long legs and stretched his arm along the couchback of the orange two-seater opposite her. "I don't imagine he's been in too many clinics. Some of these older ranchhands rely on over-the-counter medication when they feel out of sorts and if none of that works, they discuss their symptoms with the vet the next time he stops in.''

Which wouldn't have helped Wally at the Lazy-S, since she had no idea how long since the vet had been out to the ranch. She hoped Phil had called Dr. Myers as she'd instructed. She'd phone tomorrow and ask him to come back and check the horses before they lost more stock due to her father's penny-wise and pound-foolish approach. "I suppose they figure any doctor who's studied medicine can prescribe for both people and animals. It must work because I don't recall our men getting sick very often while I was growing up.''

"Ours are pretty healthy, too, except for the occasional accident.'' Jesse had noticed that she'd been good with Wally. Cool, levelheaded, not prone to panic. Her blue jeans and cotton blouse were both stained and smudged from Wally's injury. She didn't seem to notice. "Do you remember a fellow who used to work for us called Guitar George?''

Sara smiled. "Sure. He'd come from some sheep ranch in Montana and he used to sit on the bunkhouse steps evenings and play that guitar till all hours. Sometimes, on a very still night, I could hear the music through my open bedroom window. Or at least I thought I did.''

"Probably so. He'd sing these sad, sad songs about love lost and cowboys who left their women behind.''

Remembering, she nodded. "And that tall man with the bushy mustache who never talked much used to get tears in his eyes everytime George played a particular song. What was it, do you remember?''

"*My Old Kentucky Home*.'' Jesse laughed. "I'd forgotten about Buck Thomas. I asked him once if he was from Kentucky, and he told me to mind my own business.'' They both laughed at that.

"What made you think of George tonight?"

"The last time I was in this clinic was with him. He had a freak accident about a year ago. His shirtsleeve got caught in one of the automatic steel doors we had installed in the milking barn. Severed his arm off at the shoulder."

"Oh, God. Did he lose it?"

"Damned if they didn't sew it back on—not here but after an ambulance rushed him over to the hospital at White Mountain—and he's got almost full use of it."

"You're kidding! He can still play the guitar?" When he nodded, she shook her head in amazement. "Medicine's sure come a long way." Again, she glanced at the double doors. "I hope Wally's all right."

"I'm surprised you're so anxious. I thought all you wanted to do was fix up the place, sell it and be on your way." As he'd guessed, temper flashed in her eyes.

"I haven't sold the place yet. Besides, what kind of a person would I be if I didn't care about one of our men who's hurt?"

The kind of person who'd walk away without a word to a man she had to have known loved her. Or had she changed in twelve years, developed heart? Why was it, Jesse asked himself, that he couldn't just let it go, that when he was with her, he couldn't keep from probing to see if he could get her to explain?

The way he was studying her, as if he was silently judging her and she'd been found wanting, infuriated Sara. "Was I heartless or cruel when you knew me years ago?" she demanded.

Jesse was saved from answering when the double doors swung open, and Dr. Fields walked through, glanced toward the waiting room and headed for Sara.

His thin face looked tired, and his white coat hung limply. "Your man's got a concussion and a hairline crack in his left ankle, Miss Shephard. We'll need to keep him awhile."

Sara rose. "Certainly, Doctor. How long before he can be released?"

"Couple of days, I'd say. We need to watch that concussion. I've put his ankle in a soft brace. Tomorrow, I'll call in the X-ray technician, and we'll decide if we need to put him into a walking cast." Shoving his hands into the pockets of his jacket, he frowned. "We have one other problem. Hate to bother you with it, but the desk clerk's not on duty evenings."

"What's that?" Sara asked.

"Mr. Stump says he has no insurance."

Sara wasn't in the least surprised. "I'll take the responsibility. You need me to fill out some papers?"

The doctor looked relieved. "Yes, please. I'll have the nurse get them for you."

"Could I see Wally before I leave?"

"Sure. He's a little groggy, but you can go on back. The last room on the left through those doors."

It took Sara the better part of half an hour to reassure Wally and fill out the necessary paperwork. Walking outside afterward, she blinked into the darkness after the bright lights inside the clinic. Climbing into the Jeep alongside Jesse, she glanced over at Elroy's Shoe and Saddle Repair, closed for the night.

The last time she'd seen it, she'd been pulling away in a huge silver bus while Phil had stood in the rain watching her leave. Twelve years come September. She saw a sign indicating that the cross-country bus still stopped there twice daily. Resolutely, Sara turned her head and focused on the road as Jesse pulled out of the parking lot.

"Noah didn't offer insurance to his men?" Jesse asked, wondering if Sara knew just how costly Wally's bills might be in a day or so.

"I haven't found any record of insurance. But then, I haven't gone through all of his papers yet. Do you offer it to your men?"

"We make them aware that there's insurance available through the cattlemen's association. If they join and they stay with us a minimum of two years, then we pay half the premiums." Stopping at an intersection, he glanced at her in the light from the streetlamp and saw her distracted expression. Was it money problems or memories? he wondered.

"It's difficult for these men who work as ranch hands, especially if they travel around from place to place. No job security, no insurance, no retirement. One day, they realize they're old, hardly able to work and nowhere to go, no money to speak of." She sighed helplessly. "It doesn't seem fair."

"We're trying to remedy that through various organizations. My dad's on the commission, working with other ranchers. Can't do much for the transients, but it's a start for the regulars." About to turn onto the main highway, he paused. "Brenner's Café is still open. I could use a cup of coffee. How about you?"

Sara brushed back her hair, feeling inexplicably tired. Between going through her father's things, dealing with Lisa and then Wally's injury, she felt drained. "I don't think so, but thanks anyway."

Jesse wasn't a man who took no for an answer without a fight. "Do you realize we've known each other for twenty years and we've never shared a restaurant meal together?"

Sara pointed to her bloodstained clothes. "I really would rather not, looking like this. Some other time?"

"All right then, I'll drive you home, and *you* can make us a cup of coffee. What do you say?"

He wasn't going to give up, she knew. As she nodded her acceptance, she thought she saw him try to hide a victory grin. Jesse, she remembered, liked winning.

Leading the way into her father's house, Sara couldn't help wondering what Noah would say if he could see Jesse Morgan walking in behind her. "I'll put on a pot of coffee before I run up and change," she told him.

"Mind if I look around?" Jesse asked, already impressed at what he'd seen in the foyer.

Somehow, she knew he would want to. Had he maneuvered her into this invitation so he could check out the house? "No, go right ahead." In the kitchen, Sara wondered when she'd become so paranoid. Probably this afternoon when Lisa had planted some ugly thoughts in her brain that wouldn't go away.

Later, feeling a little better after splashing cold water on her face and changing, Sara carried a tray into the den where she found Jesse seated on the couch facing the fireplace. Except for the stacks of papers waiting to be gone through behind her father's desk, the room was cozy and inviting, smelling faintly of the pine logs she'd had stacked at the far end of the hearth.

"You've done wonders with this place in a short time. From what my folks said, the whole house needed work."

Sara poured their coffee. "There's still more to be done, but it's coming along."

Jesse accepted the dark brew, took a taste and gave her a look of approval. She made a good cup of coffee. It occurred to him that he knew very little about the grown-up Sara Shephard. He leaned back, wondering just how much she'd tell him. "Do you live alone in San Diego? Are you a gourmet cook or a junk-food junkie?"

Seated alongside him, Sara's heart thumped in her chest as she struggled to remain composed. This was one of the reasons she hadn't wanted to be alone with Jesse. She'd have to answer his questions carefully enough not to reveal anything, yet be honest enough not to arouse his suspicions. "I like all kinds of food," she said evasively. Actually, she gave in to Chris's choices often as not, which ran mostly toward chicken, hamburgers and pizza.

"I understand your mother's sister lives there. Is that why you went to San Diego, to look her up?" *And fell in love with the city and decided to remain, leaving me behind without a thought? Talk to me. Make me understand.*

Sara didn't think she could risk picking up her cup with shaking hands, so she let it sit on the low table before them. "I lived with my Aunt Margaret for a while, then decided to get a place of my own." The thing to do was to counter a question with a question. "Where were you going tonight in the Jeep when you came across Wally and me?"

"Just out riding. Sometimes, things happen in the ranch business, things that are necessary, but upsetting, you know."

This was safer, Sara thought. Keep him talking. "For instance?"

"I've got this one mare, she's kind of a favorite. The lightest chestnut you've ever seen with these soft eyes. I was there when she was born three years ago and I named her Fiona, after my Irish grandmother on my mother's side. The name means fair. I always did go for the fair ones."

Perhaps there were no safe subjects with Jesse. This was when she was most vulnerable to him, Sara reminded herself. When he was gentle and boyish. He looked lean and hard, shirtsleeves rolled up on muscular arms, worn jeans hugging solid thighs. Yet inside, he wasn't as tough as he liked to pretend. Silently, she waited for him to go on.

"Anyhow, we bred her for the first time nine days ago and did the ultrasound today. She's carrying twins so, naturally, we had to prick one of the embryos so the delivery wouldn't kill her. Now, I know that it's in Fiona's best interest. But she lay there looking at me with those soft eyes, making me feel like I'd just killed one of her babies. Which I had."

She was surprised and moved that he would feel that way. It was standard procedure to protect the mare's life in the event of twins, yet it bothered Jesse. "Of course, you had to do it. You've done it many times before, I'm sure."

"Yeah, but it doesn't get any easier. I hate killing living things. Spontaneous abortions I'm used to. Mares have them frequently, as you know. But this..." He shook his head. "It always bothers me. So afterward, I went for a ride in the Jeep."

Sara didn't quite know what to say, so she picked up her cup for a sip of coffee.

"It probably shouldn't trouble me, but it does. I don't know how women do it." Turning to her suddenly, he asked, "Could you do it, Sara? Have an abortion, I mean."

She nearly dropped the cup, saucer and all. Swallowing carefully, she dared not look at him. Had she revealed something inadvertently to Jesse that had him asking such a personal question? How could he know she'd wrestled with that option years ago, but had turned from it? "No, it's not a decision I could live with. But I believe every woman has to make up her own mind on such a sensitive issue."

"It's a tough one, all right. It seems unfair that Kay and her husband want a child so badly and haven't had one in five years while others are able to have them and don't want them."

Sara was more than willing to shift the thrust of the conversation to his sister. "Do you like Kay's husband?"

"Yeah, Will's a nice guy. Too bad he doesn't want to leave Phoenix. Mom would like to have Kay closer. And she's dying for a grandchild." Jesse finished his coffee, wondering why Sara seemed so nervous since they'd come

to the house. Was it his presence in this place where her father would never want him? Or was she just uneasy being
alone with him?

Emily was dying for a grandchild, unaware that she already had one who was eleven years old. Sara tried to keep
her emotions from showing. She wanted to change the subject. Had to. "I'll bet you can't guess who came to see me
this afternoon?"

Jesse didn't think they had too many friends in common
anymore. "Probably not. Who?"

"Lisa." She saw that that caught him off guard. "Surprised? So was I. We weren't exactly close, not like Kay and
I were."

"What did she want?"

"You mean on the surface, or what did she really want?"

He'd rather thought Sara had seen through Lisa too, even
when they'd been teenagers. "Both."

There seemed no point in beating around the bush. She'd
always believed in the direct approach. "Officially, she came
to welcome me back, or so she said. Unofficially, she came
to update me on what you've been doing since I left, and to
let me in on what you plan to do now that I'm back."

Jesse felt a quick rush of anger he couldn't hide, and
knew Sara, who was watching him closely, noticed it. Angling his body, he turned toward her. "This ought to be
good. What did she say?"

Good. Now, she would put him on the defensive for a
change. "According to Lisa, you and your father have been
conspiring to acquire more land for years. You went after
me, thinking I'd marry you and you'd have the Lazy-S."
She saw his face turn stormy and held up a hand. "Wait.
There's more. When I left, you gave up plan A and moved
to plan B, which was to win over Holly Lucas, also an only
child, so you could acquire the Lucas Ranch by marrying
Holly."

He was almost too angry to speak. "Do you believe Lisa?"

That was the big question, and Sara wished she knew the answer unequivocally. Her father would have believed a Morgan capable of that and more. But only this morning, she'd read the abstract on the Lazy-S and discovered that Noah had been wrong about the disputed section of land. Perhaps he'd been wrong about Jesse, too. "I've never wanted to believe anything bad about you, Jesse."

Studying her, he could see she meant that. However, she hadn't said she believed in him, just that she wanted to. He let out a disappointed breath of air as he decided to explain what had happened. "Some time after you left, Holly and her mother started coming over to the house. The visits surprised my mother since she and Mrs. Lucas scarcely knew each other. On one of those visits, Holly walked out to the barn and started up a conversation with me. I'd known her only slightly. She's kind of shy, but a nice enough person. Anyhow, she asked me to take her on some picnic or some event that was coming up, I can't remember just what. I wasn't in the mood and told her so."

She hadn't asked for an explanation, but she was nonetheless interested in hearing him out. "And that's all there was to it?"

"Not quite. A while later, my father came to me, madder than a wet hen. It seems that old man Lucas had approached him, wanting to see if the two of them could cook something up between Holly and me so the two ranches could combine. Dad told him what he could do with that idea, then found out that Lucas was overextended and apparently had thought he'd found a way out. Poor Holly probably wasn't any more interested in me than I was in her, but her parents were using her as a bargaining chip. After that, the Lucases never came around again."

Sara ran a hand through her hair. "I don't understand why Lisa would make a point of coming over here and lying to me, stirring up things and..."

He reached over and touched her arm. "You have a choice, Lisa or me. Who do you believe?"

This time she could answer honestly. "I believe you, Jesse. I've never known you to lie to me." She saw his face soften, his eyes warm. "Does Lisa want me to hate you? Is that her motive?"

Jesse thought he knew. Shortly after Sara had left, Lisa had come to his cabin twice, once drunk, once sober. Each time, she'd had seduction in mind, and he'd made it perfectly clear that he wasn't interested. Never could be interested. The last time, he'd all but thrown her out bodily. Since then, he'd caught her looking at him several times, her eyes calculating.

Yet, he felt stupid telling that to Sara. "Let's just say that she has reasons that are valid in her mind for disliking me. But let's hear it all. What else did she say about what I plan to do now that you're back?"

As she spoke, Sara toyed with the afghan she'd draped over the back of the couch. "She said you had another chance to get the Lazy-S and this time you wouldn't even have to marry me. You'd just sit back and wait until I discover that no one else but the Morgans have enough money to buy me out, then make an offer and finally have the land you want."

"Damn." This was too much. Jesse rose, unable to sit still. "That little bitch." Marching to the fireplace, he braced an arm on the mantel, wishing Lisa were here right now so he could tell her exactly what he thought. For years, he'd covered up for her to his parents. When his friend Aaron had started dating her and asked what she was like, he'd answered noncommittally. And this was his reward.

"What did you do to her that she goes out of her way to discredit you?"

His shoulders slumped wearily. Slowly, he turned. "I'm not sure you'll believe this, but I refused to take her to bed."

"Yes, I do." With his reluctant admission, things shifted for Sara. She went to him, needing to hear just one thing more. "I knew back when I was only thirteen, the afternoon of your graduation party, that Lisa wanted you. She's even more beautiful now. Why did you refuse her?"

He placed his hands on her arms, caressing her skin. She'd changed into cotton slacks and a soft yellow top. Her hair spilled down past her shoulders and she smelled so good, like everything sweet and female. "Because I hadn't gotten over you. Not then and not later when Holly came around. Maybe I never will."

He'd been honest, made himself vulnerable to her. She could do no less. "I haven't gotten over you, either, Jesse. I don't think I know how."

She was exactly what he shouldn't want, a woman who'd left him before and was planning to leave again. Yet, she was everything he'd ever wanted. With a groan, he pulled her to him and bent his head to kiss her.

Unexpectedly, she didn't fight him this time, her mouth opening, inviting him in. His tongue touched hers, setting off miniature explosions inside him. He heard the muted sounds she made deep in her throat, the ones he remembered she used to make when she was fighting her growing excitement. Shifting the angle, he took her deeper.

His hands at her back slipped beneath her shirt, moving along skin that was satin smooth and shivery under his touch. He could feel her breasts grow fuller against his chest, and he ached to renew his acquaintance with them. Experimentally, he pressed her lower body into the cradle of his, and was awestruck when she responded by returning the gentle friction.

Sara felt the long day's accumulation of his beard graze her cheeks and thrilled at the masculine feel of him. His body was rock-hard even as hers softened in remembrance, in unconscious invitation. Hadn't he always reduced her to this in just moments? She inhaled the pine and leather fragrance of the room and the robust scent of man, each sharpening a desire within her already raging out of control.

How many years had she dreamed of this, awakened nights wanting this, Jesse's arms around her, Jesse's mouth on hers? How many times had she told herself to forget the dream, that he would never again be hers to touch freely? How many ways are there to need? She'd felt them all for this man.

Jesse drew back to touch his lips to her eyelids that fluttered closed as she trembled in his arms. He kissed the pulse pounding in her throat while his hands inched between them to fumble with the buttons of her top. His warm breath in her ear caused her to shudder as his fingers moved to unfasten the clasp of her bra.

Then his hands closed around her breasts, and a sigh of welcome that she couldn't prevent escaped from between her lips. She placed her hands on his as he molded and caressed her flesh, and felt her knees buckling. Her last defenses crumbled. She was his all over again.

Jesse felt the change in her as her mouth again sought his, her kiss suddenly desperate. Her eager hands pulled his shirttail free of his jeans and slipped up inside to stroke the skin of his back, her touch setting him on fire. Would she believe that despite what she'd done to him by leaving, despite all their years apart, he still wanted only her?

He moved his hands up to frame her face, his eyes capturing hers. "Do you believe me now, that there's never been anyone for me but you?"

Oh, how she wanted to. She had to. "Yes."

"Tell me it's the same for you."

She would give him that, for it was no less than the truth. "It is. I've wanted no one else."

His eyes darkened. "You're so beautiful. I can't believe that in all those years..."

"Yes, all those years. It was always you."

"Then why, Sara? Why didn't you write me? Why didn't you call me?"

The questions had her feeling suddenly defensive, vulnerable. She drew his hands away from her. "I did, once." How to tell him? she wondered, agonizing over the right words. "I became very ill, some months after arriving in California. They weren't sure I was going to make it. I needed to talk with you. I had a friend call your house."

Gripping her hands, Jesse shook his head. "I never received a call from anyone from California."

"You were away. Your mother answered."

"And she didn't take down a number? Impossible. I would have called back. Hell, I'd have gone charging after you."

"Your mother told my friend that you'd made a new life for yourself with another woman and I wasn't ever to call again."

Jesse was stunned. "No. My mother wouldn't have said that. She knew how I felt about you, what I was going through."

Sara turned, adjusting her clothes, knowing the mood had been broken. "I don't blame her. She was aware I'd hurt you. She was trying to protect you."

Jesse ran an angry hand through his hair. "Something's not right. I'll talk to her."

Buttoning her blouse, Sara shook her head. "Please don't. It all happened a long time ago. Why dredge it all up again?"

"Because I need you to believe I didn't get your message, that I wouldn't have turned from you if I had."

Sara walked to the couch, sat down. "It no longer matters."

But Jesse wasn't one to let things go. "I'll get to the bottom of this." Following her over, he sat beside her. "What was your illness? Pneumonia again?"

She'd had pneumonia when she'd been about ten and had nearly died from it. He'd handed her the perfect answer. She hated to deceive him, but knew she couldn't tell him the truth. "Once you have pneumonia, it's not uncommon to get it again." That wasn't a lie, merely a clever evasion.

"Yeah, so I've heard." He raised a hand to touch her smooth cheek. "So I wasn't there for you, my mother brushed off your friend and you never tried to contact me again. Damn, Sara, I wish you weren't so pigheaded."

Now he was making her angry. "She didn't just brush me off. She said you'd found someone else. If I hurt you, I'm sorry. I was hurting pretty badly, too."

"*If? If* you hurt me? Do you doubt it? Do you still think Lisa was right, that the minute you left town, I ran after Holly? Do you think I would so easily forget how things were between us?"

She shook her head, wondering why they kept going back and forth on this. "Jesse, I didn't say that. I've already said that I believe you. What more do you want from me?"

He was being unreasonable, and he knew it. Maybe it was learning about Lisa and her lying interference. Or that damnable phone call that he'd known nothing about, yet which missing had changed his life. Or having Sara in his arms again, wanting her so badly, yet with problems old and new throwing a damper on both of them.

Why the hell was everything suddenly so complicated? Jesse asked himself.

Rising restlessly, he tucked his shirt into his jeans. "I'd better go." He had a couple of women at the Morgan Ranch he wanted to talk with.

She understood his need for distance. She was feeling a little crowded herself. "Thanks for your help with Wally."

Turning to her, Jesse decided to let her know one more thing. "It's ironic, you know, the things Lisa told you, the way she twisted things around. My father asked me to make you an offer for the Lazy-S a day or so after you arrived. He feels this place needs a lot of work, but that we could use the land. What Lisa didn't tell you was that I wouldn't do it."

Sara felt herself stiffen. "So then you do want this ranch?"

Jesse shrugged, as if it weren't important. "It's a prime piece of land and, with money and work, it could be a good addition to our holdings. But didn't you hear me? I said I wouldn't ask you to sell it to us."

"I heard you. Why wouldn't you?"

"Because, although your father treated you like hell, you know he wouldn't want a Morgan to have his ranch. And because I don't think I could handle another rejection from a Shephard."

Sara felt disappointment dampen her like a cold autumn rain. Despite his seemingly breezy dismissal of his father's request, did Jesse also have a hidden agenda in coming on to her again? "But you and your father still want the Lazy-S?"

He could see he wasn't getting through to her. She hadn't heard a word he'd said beyond the fact that the Morgans wanted to buy the Lazy-S. Stubborn, just like her father before her. He was unwilling to beg her to believe him. "I can't speak for my father. But as far as I'm concerned, you can burn it to the ground."

Turning on his heel, Jesse left the den and slammed out of the house.

Chapter Nine

Sara lay in the large bed of her youth and listened to the crickets serenading outside her open window. The scent of newly mown grass drifted in with the night breezes ruffling the fresh curtains Ruby had hung earlier. Restlessly, her hands stroked the pale yellow sheets she'd purchased in town just days ago. Turning over, she rearranged the pillow under her head for perhaps the fifteenth time, wishing sleep would claim her.

Too much was happening lately, she told herself. In San Diego, her life was relatively calm and free of dissension. Since leaving her father and this house, she was unused to disharmony on a daily basis. Unwillingly thrust back amidst the memories of her childhood, she'd grown restive and tense.

Most of that was because of Jesse. She'd thought she'd prepared herself for seeing him again, but she was light-years away from being strong enough to overcome his effect on her.

On the one hand, as she'd told him tonight, she'd never really gotten over him, never really wanted any other man but him. Lord knows that Clay had tried to seduce her with tender words and kisses that left her sadly unmoved. She hadn't been able to accept Clay as a lover because she knew she didn't love him. Being fond of someone, even enjoying their company, wasn't enough.

Perhaps if she'd never known the passion that Jesse had introduced her to, she might have given in to Clay, believing that that was all there was, that those who said otherwise exaggerated or lied. But after knowing Jesse's touch, no other man would do.

She'd resigned herself to doing without, honestly believing she'd never see Jesse again. But now that she had, now that he'd held her again, kissed her again, touched her again, how could she not long for more? Yet how could she reconcile her need for Jesse with her distrust about his motives?

Tossing aside the sheet and turning over again, Sara thought that perhaps Jesse was right, that burning the place down was the best solution. If there was no ranch for the Morgans to want, then she'd know with certainty whether Jesse was after her or her holdings. But no, the ranch and what the sale of it would bring, belonged to Chris. To Jesse's son, the one he didn't know he had.

Tonight, she'd learned that Emily was anxious for a grandchild, which only added to the guilt she carried over her secret. And she'd learned that it saddened Jesse to have to abort a mare's fetus, a fact that pleased her somehow. It showed his caring nature, his love of living things. It would indicate that if she was to tell him why she'd left—in order to keep their baby and to protect Jesse himself from her father—that he'd feel she'd done the right thing.

Or would he? Would he instead be furious that she'd kept his child from him, and from Emily and Hal, all these years? Would he be angry enough to fight her for custody of Chris? Fathers had rights, too, a fact she knew that courts were beginning to recognize more and more. How could she fight Jesse's anger, Jesse's money?

She couldn't risk it, and it was tearing her apart.

Even if she wholeheartedly believed that Jesse didn't give a damn about the Lazy-S, that he loved her and only her, could they get past the pain of Jesse's missing out on eleven years of his son's life without him holding that against her forever? Would that color his revived feelings for her, perhaps kill them?

You can't have your cake and eat it, too, she often told Chris. Make a decision and stick to it. Well, she'd made her decision years ago, and she was having one hell of a time sticking to it now. The truth was, she wanted Jesse again, perhaps even more now as a mature woman. She wanted to be with him, to be free to love him, to share Chris with him, to make a home with him, to have other children with him.

You can't win 'em all, she'd told Chris on the phone this evening when she'd called him after Jesse had left. He'd agonized over losing today's ball game. No one gets to win 'em all, she'd said so sagely. It was so easy to give advice, yet so difficult to take it oneself.

Sara heard the old grandfather clock downstairs chiming two a.m. and decided to quit fighting lack of sleep. Brushing her hair back, she rose, turned on the bedside lamp and went downstairs. In the kitchen, she remembered that Gretchen had had her drink warm milk on nights she couldn't sleep. The thought had her almost gagging. Opening the fridge, she settled for a soda without caffeine and took the can into the den.

She pulled the chain of the Tiffany lamp on the table alongside the plaid couch and curled up in the corner, arranging her blue satin nightshirt over her legs. She hadn't spent much time in this room during the years she'd lived in this house because her father had chosen it as his personal hideaway. What, she wondered, had he done in here, besides drink? What thoughts had run through his head during those whiskey-laced evenings after he'd banished her from his home?

Sara drank from her can, then set it on the end table. Angling her head, she noticed the family bible on the lower shelf of the table and reached for it. She opened the large leather-bound book and spread it across her bent knees. Turning the fragile sheets, she found several record pages and leaned forward with interest.

There was an entry recording the marriage of her grandparents, then the birth of her father. The final insertion on that page noted the deaths of her grandparents. She turned to the next page and squinted, trying to read the heavily scrolled writing. Her mother's penmanship, perhaps?

The first notation was the date of her parents' wedding, their names and the signature of the minister. Following that was her own birth six years later, recorded by date, hour and minute, plus her birth weight. Two years and nine months later, another child was entered, Noah Andrew Shephard, Jr. His birth and death statistics were on the same line, written in a shaky hand. The brother she hadn't known of had lived only two days. The final entry was her mother's death, scrawled in the firm strokes she remembered seeing on her father's papers. Rose Shephard had died only three months after her baby son.

Sara ran her fingertips over the faded writing, feeling depressed. Entries made in a family bible ought to balance joy with the inevitable sadness. Staring at these, she could feel only an overwhelming sense of sorrow.

Had her parents loved each other once? Was it the loss of his son and, a short time afterward, the death of his wife that had turned Noah into the bitter man she'd known? Had his pain come less from the Morgans and more from his own regrets over the way his life had turned out? Had he used the Morgans as a scapegoat because he felt impotent railing against the fates?

So many questions, Sara thought, as she shifted the bible, thumbing through the pages. The book didn't look as if it had been read often. Certainly she couldn't remember ever having opened it before, though it had rested on that end table for years.

As she was about to close the covers, she noticed the edge of something that had been placed between the leaves of the book. Opening to it, she found a square pale pink envelope addressed to Noah Shephard at the Lazy-S in what appeared to be delicate feminine handwriting that she didn't recognize. Sara could barely make out the nearly illegible postmark. The letter had been mailed thirty-five years ago.

Inside, she discovered a folded sheet of pink stationery and another folded white envelope. The addressee on that one was Miss Emily Ryan in care of the University of New Mexico, and it was postmarked just a week before the pink envelope. The handwriting was unmistakably her father's.

Sara knew that Jesse's mother's maiden name was Ryan. Why had her father been writing to Emily before her marriage to Hal Morgan? Perhaps to ask her to intercede on his behalf to Sara's own mother about a problem? Curious now, she unfolded the sheet of pink stationery.

Her gaze searched out the signature first. It was signed simply *Emily*. Quickly Sara read the few lines in stunned silence. Emily had written Noah that she was returning his letter, that she was very sorry if he'd read something into their friendship that wasn't there. She went on to say that she loved Hal Morgan and intended to marry him, that she didn't want to hurt Noah and hoped they could remain friends.

Staring off into space, Sara struggled to understand. Emily had rejected Noah thirty-five years ago. Had that, rather than the alleged land dispute, been why her father had hated Hal Morgan all these years? Slowly, she removed the letter inside the white envelope.

Written in Noah's bold penmanship, he declared his love for Emily and begged her to leave Hal and marry him. Sara's eyes filled with unexpected tears as she read her father's words promising the woman he loved a wonderful life if only she would be his wife. With trembling hands, she put the letters back in their envelopes and set aside the bible.

All these years the letters had been here, and she'd never known. All those years her father had been drinking himself into an early grave, never having gotten over loving a woman married to another man. That sort of thing might turn anyone bitter.

Yet Sara couldn't bring herself to blame Emily. It appeared from her words that she hadn't led Noah on, but rather that he'd thought there was more between them than there actually had been. She also knew from her own experiences with her father that he wasn't a man who easily forgave someone who'd hurt or disappointed him. Not even if that someone was his own daughter.

Rising, Sara turned off the lamp and carried the letters upstairs with her. It had certainly been an enlightening day. And night. Tomorrow, she would go visit Emily Morgan.

It was time she learned the truth about events that had taken place years ago, events that had shaped her past and now haunted her future.

She looks the same, Sara thought, as Emily held open the door to the Morgan house, her welcoming smile as warm as it always had been. Jesse's mother was still slender, her dark hair cut short now, yet showing only a few white strands, her intelligent gray eyes so like her son's. Wearing a long blue knit shirt over white slacks with tennis shoes, she looked much younger than the fifty-eight Sara knew her to be.

Emily Morgan drew her guest inside and hugged her, then stepped back to look her over. "My, you're even lovelier than you were at seventeen, Sara."

"Thank you for letting me come." When she'd called an hour ago, she hadn't known how Emily would respond to her request to visit. Yet she could see the older woman's innate friendliness, and perhaps a bit of curiosity had won out even if Emily, too, felt a little nervous about their reunion.

"I've been hoping you'd call since hearing you were back," Emily said as she led the way into the sunny kitchen with its bleached white cupboards and red-tiled floor. "I have coffee made if you'd like a cup."

"That would be nice." It felt odd to be so formal with this woman who'd been a mother image during Sara's childhood. As she took a chair at the glass-topped table beneath the fan lazily turning overhead, Sara wished she had a nickel for every time she'd sat in this room—sharing a meal with the Morgans, making cupcakes with Kay or just talking with Emily, who seemed always available to listen to two young girls and their teenage chatter.

At the counter pouring coffee into poppy-red ceramic mugs, Emily noticed Sara looking around, her expression nostalgic. She could only imagine how difficult these past weeks had been for her, returning to the house where she'd been mostly unhappy, facing old memories, seeing Jesse again. After her conversation with her son last night, Emily thought she knew exactly why Sara had come to see her today.

"I've always loved your kitchen, Mrs. Morgan," Sara said sincerely.

"Do you think you could think of me as Emily, Sara? We don't stand on formalities much around here." Taking the mugs over, she sat down alongside the young woman with the vaguely troubled expression. "Jesse tells me you've done wonders with the house. You must have worked awfully hard."

In the sunlight streaming in through the windows, she noticed faint smudges of fatigue under Emily's eyes and thought she looked worried and a bit distracted. "I've had help, so it wasn't too bad." Sara felt a little small talk might smooth the way. "I understand Kay's married and a teacher now."

Emily smiled. "Yes. Will Upton's a fine young man, two years older than Kay. Do you remember him?"

"Not really." Sara listened to Emily tell of their wedding and go on to describe their home in Scottsdale. After a while, she seemed to run out of words and picked up her coffee mug.

Sara decided to forge ahead. "My father was a pack rat, you know," she began. "He saved every piece of paper that came to the house, it seems. He's got file folders filled with receipts and clippings and notes. I'm slowly working my way through the piles in his den."

"Quite a chore, I'm sure. It would have been so much better, for your father and for you now, if he'd have kept Gretchen on after you left."

"Yes. He seemed to get more reclusive after that." Sara reached for her shoulder bag that she'd placed on the table and took out a picture. "I found this in Dad's photo album."

Emily looked at the faded black-and-white. "Goodness, this does go back a ways."

"I don't recognize the background." The snapshot had been taken with the four young people lined up in a grassy area in front of a solid stucco fence with vines trailing along the ledge. "Was it taken around here?"

Dragged back into time, Emily shook her head. "It was taken near the University of New Mexico. We'd all attended classes there. Your mother and I were two years behind Noah and Hal. This was taken right around the time Rose and I graduated."

"Then all four of you were friends?"

Emily gave the picture back. "Your mother and I were never close, if that's what you mean." She took a sip of her coffee. She'd been wrong about the purpose of Sara's visit. Apparently she had more on her mind than Jesse. Sara needed to clear up the past. After all these years, perhaps it was time, before another generation was harmed.

Sara leaned forward. "Emily, will you tell me about what happened back then? I know something had to have, something that changed my father. I need to understand what made him the way he was."

Crossing her hands on the table, Emily regarded Sara. "I'm not sure what you want to know, nor where to begin."

Again, Sara removed something from her bag and placed it in front of her hostess. They were the two envelopes she'd found last night in the family bible. Watching Emily's face, she saw that she recognized them immediately. "How about beginning with these?"

Emily picked up first one, then the other and read them both. Finishing, she set them down, her movements slow. "Thirty-five years. You've thrust me back thirty-five years in time with these."

"I don't mean to upset you."

Emily waved a dismissive hand. "You haven't, not really. I've been doing a lot of thinking about those days since your father's death, since Hal and I stepped into his house after Phil asked us over. The past isn't always a pleasure to recall, Sara."

"I'm very aware of that."

Emily looked into green eyes that appeared to have seen their share of problems, and then some. She'd liked and admired Sara Shephard since she'd started coming around as a young girl. She'd known how difficult it had been for her growing up with Noah for a father, and she'd tried to include her whenever possible in a more normal family environment. Perhaps she'd done more harm than good, too vividly pointing out the contrasts, making Sara rebellious enough to leave home at seventeen.

It was time she found out.

"My family's from Albuquerque, so it was quite natural for me to attend the University of New Mexico. I met your father and Hal the same year, when they were seniors and I was a sophomore. They were both tall and good-looking and I knew they'd grown up on adjacent ranches here in St. Johns. But there the similarity ended. Noah was quiet, studious and very serious. Almost brooding at times. Hal was almost his direct opposite—lighthearted, friendly, outgoing. He had his solemn moments, but he made me laugh a lot." Emily looked at Sara to see how her words were registering. "I feel it's really important to be able to laugh with the person you love, to find joy in life."

"I do, too," Sara replied.

"My father was a stubborn Irishman who'd had to quit school at an early age to help out at home and he'd made it very clear that I wasn't to get serious about anyone until I'd finished college. So, although I dated quite a bit, I had no intention of forming a lasting relationship. But you know, Sara, you can't dictate when you fall in love or even with whom. It just happens and most of the time, we have little to say about the whys and wherefores."

Since Emily was baring her soul here, she could do no less. "I agree. It happened like that for me, too."

"You're speaking of Jesse." It was more a statement than a question.

"Yes." Sara had a feeling that Jesse's mother had known how she'd felt even years ago.

"Your saying that makes it easier for me to tell you my story. At any rate, toward the end of my senior year, I fell head over heels in love with Hal Morgan. He'd graduated by then, of course, and was here helping his father run the ranch. But he'd drive to Albuquerque often to see me. True to my word to my father, I didn't quit school, even when Hal asked me to marry him. But, oh, how I wanted to. That first flush of love can hit you like a ton of bricks."

"I remember," Sara said softly.

"Then there was the problem of Noah. I'd dated him on and off, but I'd told him early on that I wasn't looking to get serious. He took me at my word and was always a gentleman. However, when he got wind of Hal's visits, he started calling and coming around. I tried to dissuade him, but he persisted, claiming he'd loved me all along, that he'd only waited to ask me to marry him until my graduation. I was shocked and I felt terrible, because I'd had no idea that he felt that way. I want you to know I never would have strung your father along."

Listening intently, Sara nodded, knowing Emily to be deeply compassionate. "I'm sure you wouldn't have."

"I had no choice but to tell him that I loved Hal and that I intended to marry him in the fall. Then, just before graduation, I got that letter. I agonized over it, then sent him that answer."

"So then my father just dropped the matter?"

"No. He called repeatedly until I finally had to ask him not to anymore, that I wouldn't change my mind. Just before my graduation, Hal and Noah showed up one weekend. Hal told me that Noah was seeing one of my classmates and wanted us to double-date. That woman was Rose, your mother. We went on a picnic and Noah had someone nearby take that picture you have there."

"My father doesn't look happy. It must have been a strained afternoon."

"It was. Your father was playing the charming suitor and poor Rose was a little overwhelmed, I think. One moment he'd be smiling, then he'd turn all gloomy. Yet later, he'd brighten and pull your mother close, embarrassing her terribly."

"Why did he do that, do you think?"

Emily shrugged. "I've always thought he wanted to rub it in that he'd found someone else after I'd turned him down, to show me that he was happy without me. Which was foolish because I wanted him to be happy. But I don't think he ever was."

Sara fingered the two letters thoughtfully. "Apparently not. I don't think he ever got over you."

Emily leaned forward, needing to tell Noah's daughter. "All these years, I've felt guilty, Sara, that somehow I was responsible for your father's unhappiness. Intellectually, I know I wasn't. We're all responsible for our own happiness or unhappiness. Yet Noah's behavior seemed to indicate I was to blame. Hal and I were married in September. Noah married your mother the following month."

"Were you invited to the wedding?"

"Oh, yes. But after that, we were never invited to the Lazy-S again. And right about then, Noah started telling anyone who would listen that the Morgans had cheated the Shephards out of a section of land and that he wanted nothing to do with any of the thieving Morgans. I called your mother a couple of times, thinking she might need a friend, but she was cool and distant. She either believed Noah or she was afraid to go against his wishes."

Sara let out a long sigh. "How sad. I found the old abstract on the Lazy-S and read it. There's nothing there to indicate that the section of land in question ever belonged to my grandfather. I also just learned that my parents had had a baby who'd died, a little boy who'd lived only a couple of days."

Emily nodded as she got up to refill their coffee mugs. "As you probably know, it's hard to keep secrets within the ranching community of a small town. Though we didn't see them personally, I heard that your mother had a miscarriage every year for five years until she finally carried you to term. I'd hoped Noah would be happy at last with a child of his own. Hal and I already had both Jesse and Kay. But rumor had it that Noah wanted a son, so they kept trying. How it must have crushed him when Rose had a boy only to have the baby die."

"Phil tells me that's when my father started drinking."

"I'm not surprised." Emily sat back down. "I remember once when Jesse was about eight or nine, he wandered over to the Lazy-S even though he'd been told not to. Jesse told me about the incident later. Noah caught him, grabbed him and studied his face. He told Jesse that he had his mother's eyes. Then he shoved him away and yelled at him to never ever step foot on his land again."

"Jesse does have your eyes. I remember another incident, shortly before I left. Dad and I were quarreling one day. He'd been drinking and was accusing me as usual of sneaking over here. We were in the hallway, in dim lighting, and for a moment he seemed confused. He looked at me as if he were seeing someone else. Then he said something like, 'no, you're not her. You're blond and she isn't. And the eyes are all wrong. Hers are gray.' Funny, I never put it all together, even though I knew you had dark hair and gray eyes."

"Why would you have? When we're young, we seldom think of our parents in that way."

"As people who were once young and in love? I suppose not."

"I probably should have talked to you about all this years ago, Sara. And I probably would have, had you remained."

"A lot would have been different had I remained."

Emily thought Sara sounded heartbreakingly sad. "Are you happy in California?"

She was ready for Emily's inquiries, having been awake half the night planning cautious answers. "I'm reasonably contented. I have a nice home near the ocean, work I like to do, good friends. And my Aunt Margaret lives nearby. Did you know her?"

"No. I can't remember your mother ever mentioning a sister. But then, as I said, we didn't talk much." Emily raised her eyes and waited until Sara met her steady gaze. "Reasonably contented isn't quite the same as happy. Even as a child, you always were careful with your words."

She was surprised that Emily saw through her. "I had to be, both here and at home. I was always afraid I'd reveal too much, and you'd all feel sorry for me. And I was worried that my father would find a way to prevent me from coming here." She gazed around the kitchen again slowly. "How I used to love coming here."

"Do you still feel it's necessary to be so careful with your words?"

Sara smiled. "Old habits die hard. I wasn't sure how you felt about me, if I'd be welcome in your home again."

"You mean because of the sudden way you left?" Emily shook her head and lay a hand over Sara's. "You'll always be welcome here. I felt strongly that you had a very good reason for what you did." And when the time was right, Sara would reveal that reason.

"Thank you. I did." Perhaps because she hadn't asked, Sara felt a compelling need to offer a partial explanation, to not have this loving woman think she'd deliberately hurt her son. "My father and I quarreled very badly. He made certain threats, demands. I had to leave."

"I knew it had to be serious, or you wouldn't have left Jesse. You were in love with him."

"Yes."

Emily's smile was hesitant. "You've chosen to love a complex man. Proud, stubborn, independent."

"I didn't choose to love Jesse anymore than I chose the color of my eyes. As you said earlier, sometimes it just happens."

Jesse's mother nodded. "Yes, it does, to those who are truly lucky."

"Lucky? I'm not sure how lucky I am, then or now. Loving someone doesn't always mean smooth sailing. But I was helpless to prevent it." Sara traced the rim of her red mug with a finger, a smile on her lips. "I think I fell in love with Jesse when I was about nine years old and he defended me to Lisa."

Emily sighed. "Lisa. She's such a troubled young woman. I can't seem to get through to her."

"She wants Jesse."

"Yes, and perhaps that's why Lisa's so troubled. She knows that Jesse has eyes only for you." Emily drained the last of her lukewarm coffee. "Jesse came to me last night after he'd been with you, and we talked. Sara, I never spoke on the phone with a friend of yours from California, never said that Jesse was happy with someone else and you were to stay out of his life. When you left, Jesse was devastated. He was by turn angry and hurt, fighting mad, then going for long, solitary rides. Hal and I feared he'd never get over you. He'd been planning to ask you to marry him when he returned from that buying trip."

For the first time, Sara's composure slipped, and she blinked away a rush of tears. Why had their timing been so off? How different their lives might have been. And Christopher's. She closed her eyes, struggling with her emotions.

Emily's strong hands took hold of Sara's. "Is it too late to work things out between you?"

Sara swallowed, brushed aside a lone tear. "I don't know. I left because I saw no way out at the time. I was young and I felt so alone. Then when I . . . when I got sick, I needed Jesse so badly. I asked my friend to call and . . ."

"I wish I'd have been here to take that call."

"I didn't blame you. I knew your loyalty to your son would be your first priority. Although I have to admit, it didn't sound like something you'd say. But I know that my friend didn't lie. She had no reason to. If it wasn't you on the phone, then who would have said that?"

Since talking with Jesse, Emily had wrestled with that question throughout a long, restless night. "Do you remember the approximate date?"

Sara remembered the exact date, the day her son was born. She hesitated, not wanting Emily to wonder at the cause of her certainty. "St. Patrick's Day, shortly after my eighteenth birthday."

Emily shook her head. "Both Kay and Lisa were away at school. Mabel worked for us part-time, but she wouldn't have taken it upon herself to say such a thing. She didn't even know the situation. I can't imagine who could have done it. I hope you believe it wasn't I. I would have gone to get you myself, had I known you were ill and unhappy."

"I believe you. Maybe we'll never know."

"Perhaps not." Emily rose and went to the sink. She thought of the years Jesse and Sara had lost and wanted to weep. So much unhappiness in the world. Unconsciously, her hand went to her breast and she sighed, her worry weighing heavily on her mind.

Watching, Sara frowned. "Are you all right?"

Taking a deep breath, Emily turned. "I hope so. I found a lump yesterday. It concerns me."

Sara empathized instantly. "You need to see a doctor about it right away."

"I've made an appointment to see Dr. Owens next week."

"Please let me know, won't you?"

Emily found a smile. "Thank you, dear. I will."

The slamming of the back door announced Hal Morgan's arrival as he walked into the kitchen. Removing his hat, he smiled at Sara. "Well, look what we have here. You left here a young girl and came back a beautiful woman, Sara." Moving to his wife, his arm slipped around Emily's narrow waist in silent greeting.

Hal's waist had thickened somewhat and his hair had turned completely white. But his smile was just as warm. She'd always liked Jesse's father. "And you're just as handsome as ever, Mr. Morgan."

"I think so," Emily said, smiling up into his deep blue eyes. As always, her heart warmed at the sight of her husband.

Hal kissed her lips, noticing the lines of concern about her eyes, concern that matched his own. "Are you okay?" he asked, keeping his tone light. He wouldn't let her know how worried he was. She had to be all right. She was his life.

"Fine." Emily indicated the pot still plugged in. "There's coffee, or would you like an iced tea? Sara and I have spent the morning reminiscing."

"Tea with lots of ice, please." Hal pulled out a chair and draped his long frame into it. "Reminiscing, eh?" He'd been out with Jesse on the range, knew how tense his son was. And he knew the reason was sitting across the table from him. "Hope those old memories didn't get you both down in the dumps."

Sara had slipped the two letters and picture back into her purse when she'd heard Hal's voice. Now she shook her head at him. "No, not at all. I remember a lot of good times spent in this house."

"That's for sure." Hal took the cold drink his wife handed him and drank thirstily. "So, how's the clean-up project going?"

"Slowly but surely." Sara decided to zero in. "I understand you're interested in buying the Lazy-S."

So Jesse had gotten around to mentioning it to her after all. "You bet. Are you interested in selling?"

"I haven't made up my mind."

"Dad, I thought we'd agreed that we wouldn't bring up the sale of the Lazy-S to Sara," Jesse said from the doorway as the screen closed behind him.

Hal looked up. "I didn't bring it up, son. She did."

Walking to the fridge, Jesse narrowed his eyes at Sara. "Decide to throw in the towel?"

Why did he have to look so damn good? Sara asked herself. He'd apparently cleaned up elsewhere, for his hair was still damp and he'd slipped on a white knit shirt that made his perpetual tan seem even darker by contrast. Always at the sight of him, her hands itched to reach out and touch him. She wondered how much of her thoughts he could read in her eyes. "Not yet."

Slowly, Jesse downed half a can of soda, then sauntered over to where his parents sat around the table with Sara. He'd pictured her here so often through the years, yet now that she was back, he could see she looked a shade uneasy. "Did you talk about the phone call, Mom?" he asked his mother, though his eyes never left Sara's face.

"Yes," Emily answered. "Neither of us can figure out who Sara's friend talked with."

"You sure your friend dialed the right number?" Hal asked, having been told about the situation last night by Emily.

"Yes, very sure."

"Too bad we don't have proof," Jesse went on. "Sara's not real big about taking the word of a Morgan." He was still smarting from their go-round last evening.

"I believe your mother." Sara glanced at the wall clock. "I've got to be going. Emily, it was so good talking with you. Like old times."

"For me, too, dear." Emily rose. "I'll walk with you to the door."

"Nice seeing you again, Hal," Sara added. But she only looked into Jesse's brooding eyes before turning and leaving.

"A little hard on her, weren't you?" Hal asked his son.

Jesse didn't answer, but instead turned to gaze out the window to watch Sara on the porch hugging his mother, then climbing into Phil's old white truck. She carried herself straight and tall, just as she had years ago when she'd climb on her mare and ride home. Proud, self-reliant, magnificent.

Returning, Emily spoke to her son. "Why do you add to her problems, Jesse? She's got a pretty full plate right now."

Slowly, he swung about. "An hour in your company, and she's won you over."

Annoyed, she frowned. "This isn't about winning someone over. It's about being compassionate when someone's troubled."

"No, it's all right, Mom. I'm glad you're in Sara's corner." He set down his empty glass. "She sure as hell doesn't want me there." With that, he walked out the back door.

Hal got up, rubbing his sore shoulder muscle as he went over to his wife. "I wonder if Jesse knows how obvious he is."

Emily turned as he came up close. "You mean about the fact that he's still crazy about Sara? Right now, his impatience is warring with his good sense. Jesse'll come around." Opening her arms, she embraced her husband.

Thunder rumbled overhead, then crashed heartily, the sound reverberating throughout the still house. Through her bedroom window, Sara saw repeated lightning flashes momentarily light up a midnight sky. Rain hit the glass, then slid in thick rivulets downward. Standing at her mirror brushing her hair, she braced herself for the next thunderous clap.

When it came, she shuddered. Electrical storms were common in late June and early July in this part of Arizona. She hadn't witnessed one in years, had forgotten their frightening power. This one had been going on for half an hour. It would be useless trying to sleep. Fascinated, she walked over to stand gazing out the window at nature's show.

From this side of the house at second-floor level, she could look out toward Phil's small cabin, the bunkhouse and mess hall beyond and past those toward the horse barn and arena. She knew how skittish horses were during storms and wondered if she should go down and see how they were faring.

Two quick successive flashes of lightning lit up the sky again, followed in moments by the answering thunder. Through the downpour, Sara thought she saw a figure dashing toward the barn. Probably Phil going to check on the animals.

Since she'd already changed into her nightshirt after her shower, she debated about dressing again. As she leaned closer to the pane, she noticed a sudden bright orange flash at the near side of the barn. Frustrated that she couldn't make it out clearly, she raised the window.

Sara gasped aloud. The orange flash had been real, all right. The horse barn was on fire. She could see several men scurrying from the bunkhouse toward the big structure, could hear horses whinnying above the sound of the rain.

Closing the window, she peeled off her nightshirt and ran to the closet for her clothes.

Good God, fire! The worst thing that can happen to a barn filled with nervous horses. Yanking on her boots quickly, she got up and ran down the stairs, pulling her shirt on over her head as she went.

This couldn't be happening. They had to save the horses.

Chapter Ten

Ducking her head against the rain, Sara made her way around the puddles to the barn. She saw several of the ranch hands gathered at the water tank thirty yards right of the barn, preparing to hook up the fire hoses. Black smoke was billowing up from the corner of the wooden structure near the back. Already Phil and two or three others were leading the horses through the open double doors toward the fenced corrals.

In moments, she was drenched to the skin, but Sara paid little attention as she pushed her way into the barn. The acrid smell of burning hay and wood had her eyes watering. Blinking, she hurried toward the stalls where more horses were waiting to be freed. Their high-pitched whinnies split the air, striking fear in her. She knew how swiftly fires could spread in a high wind and how quickly horses could panic and stampede.

Cautiously, she entered the first stall and slipped a lead rope onto the wild-eyed mare, then led her out and rushed with her to safety. She was intercepted by Phil returning.

"Be careful by the corral gate," he warned. "It'd be real easy to fall and get trampled by these frightened horses."

"Thanks, I'll watch it." She hurried on, almost being dragged by the mare. At the gate, she had to shoo several horses aside before she was able to open it enough to let the mare in. Closing the gate carefully, she turned to go back.

At the barn door, Sara shoved back her wet hair and saw that four of her men were busy freeing the remaining horses. Even Pete was helping out, and she noticed that Ruby was carrying a new foal to a safer place. Perhaps it was a good thing they didn't have but twenty-six horses to worry about. She turned toward the water tank and ran over.

Phil and two other men were wrestling with the hose, having trouble attaching it. Sara leaned down to look. "What's the problem?"

Swearing under his breath, Phil spoke over his shoulder. "We should have replaced this hose a while back. The clamp's old and the threads have worn smooth. We can't get it to hold."

More neglected maintenance. Sara felt like screaming. Turning to gaze at the back corner of the barn where the lightning bolt had struck, she saw that flames were shooting out, licking at the old barn wood while smoke poured through the jagged opening. Despite the rain, the blaze seemed to be building rather than diminishing. "Did you call the fire department?"

"Yeah," Phil answered, still wrestling with the coupling. "They've got their truck out already. Murphy's paddocks just north of us have been hit."

Although Sara remembered it was a volunteer staff, there had to be more firemen available. "Is that all they have, one truck?"

"Yes, ma'am. Said they'd shoot on over when they're finished."

The barn could be a pile of ashes by then, especially if they couldn't get water pumping from the tank. "Phil," she yelled over the thundering noise of the storm, "is there anywhere we could borrow a hose that might fit, some neighboring ranch?"

Phil straightened, swiping water from his face. "Morgans have one. Don't know if it'll fit."

She would swallow her pride to save her stock. "It's worth a try. I'll go call them."

"May not have to," Phil said as he pointed toward the roadway entrance to the Lazy-S. "Here comes help, probably Jesse."

Sara squinted through the downpour and saw Jesse's red truck followed by another pickup from the Morgan spread. As she walked toward them, she saw Aaron and half a dozen others jump from the truck beds as Jesse pulled to a stop and got out.

"How'd you know?" she asked, surprised at how quickly he'd heard of their problem and hurried on over.

"Aaron and I were out checking our barns when we saw the flames." Unwilling to waste precious time, Jesse turned to Phil, listened carefully to what the ranch manager had to say, then instructed two of his men to go back for their hose. Moving with quiet efficiency, he went with Phil to check out the water tank while Aaron inspected the section of the barn on fire. With that authoritative way he had, Jesse dispersed his men, sending some to help with the horses, others to get buckets of water to soak the inside area so the fire wouldn't spread.

Relieved that help had arrived, Sara had to admit she shouldn't have been surprised that Jesse had come to offer aid. He might be angry with her, but that wouldn't prevent him from doing what was necessary. Ranchers all knew they had to be there for one another in emergencies. Often their survival depended on a neighbor's assistance. Growing up on the Lazy-S, that fact had been drummed into her at an early age.

Of course, she'd never really been involved in a true emergency before. She'd heard of barn fires at neighboring ranches but had never witnessed one. Never seen the stark terror in a horse's eyes nor heard their frightened shrieks. Never smelled the black, cloying smoke nor seen the hideous tongues of flame raging out of control. And never wanted to again.

With a twinge of guilt, Sara admitted to herself that she was grateful to let Jesse take over.

Thinking she could be of most use with the animals, she joined Ruby who was already over by the mares' corral, her deep voice soothing the terrified beasts. Sara saw that the two stallions were in the fenced section by the arena, some distance from the others. Moving inside the corral, she checked on the two pregnant mares, making sure they were calm and unharmed. Then she wandered to the corner where the newborn colt hovered near its mother.

"It's all right, baby," she said reassuringly, smoothing down the wet hide. "You're going to be fine." Restlessly, the mother pawed the ground nearby. "You, too, lady."

Ruby walked over. "Never, never, have I seen such a thing," she said, her black eyes anxious. "But the horses, they all okay."

"Yes, thanks to everyone's quick thinking."

"Phil, he tell your daddy over and over about that hose."

"I wish he'd have told me."

Hands on her hips, Ruby watched Morgan men mingling with the Lazy-S crew. "You know, Sara, this is good. Neighbor helping neighbor. Your daddy, he never would believe his eyes. The Morgans, they're good people."

She had to agree as she noticed the Morgan truck returning. "I hope their hose fits our tank." She turned back to Ruby. "I'm going to go check. Why don't you get in out of this rain?"

"I'm okay. The horses, they need me."

Impulsively, Sara hugged the small woman, then slipped out through the gate and hurried to the tank.

"It works," Phil said as he finished attaching the end onto the opening. He handed the nozzle to Jesse. "Yell when you're set up over there, and I'll turn her on."

Sara watched Jesse hurry toward the blaze while several men helped unwind the hose. Finally in position, he shouted to Phil who cranked the large spigot. She could see the water travel through the gray hose, unwrinkling it, rounding its shape. At last, a gush of thick spray spurted out of the nozzle, splashing directly onto the heaviest corner of flame.

Despite her unease, Sara wandered closer, fascinated, and stood watching.

It seemed to take hours. Someone brought a ladder and Jesse climbed up, spraying water wherever the fire still lingered or had been, soaking the boards. At one point, a high support beam broke from the strain and crashed to the ground, sending showers of sparks in all directions. Jesse's ladder wobbled, threatening to tip. As Sara held her breath, two of the men grabbed the lower section and held it steady while he scampered down.

Quickly, they repositioned the ladder and Jesse went back up. Sara thought his arms must surely be hurting badly from the strain of holding steady the thick hose, but he never wavered. His eyes darted everywhere, yelling orders as he saw fit. She saw that to a man, from Lazy-S or Morgan Ranch, they all rushed to obey. The kind of authority Jesse carried men responded to instinctively, for they knew he risked as much as they.

By the time the fire truck arrived, the blaze was nearly out, with just a small section still smoldering. The weary men began leading the soaking wet and still-skittish horses into the arena for the rest of the night until morning, when the full extent of the damage to the barn could be assessed. Besides, the thick lingering smoke had to be aired out in the fresh light of day so as not to damage the lungs of the animals.

Working alongside the men, Sara and Ruby led the reluctant mares into the smaller stalls along the sides of the arena. Sara was grateful the newer arena was built of steel and aluminum and not as susceptible to fire. At the far end, Phil secured the two stallions. As the last horse was shut away, Sara let out a weary breath.

"Might be a good idea to leave the walkway lamps on low for the rest of the night," Jesse said, wiping his smudged face as he came up to her. "The animals will stay calmer if they can see clearly that they're not in danger."

"That's a good idea." Sara moved to the bank of switches, turned off the overheads and left the low lamps burning. Then she pressed another button and the music came on, soft and soothing. "I wasn't sure if the intercom in here was working, but it seems to be." She hoped that the music would soothe the horses.

Wringing rain from the ends of her hair, she glanced out the doors toward the burnt corner of the barn. "How bad is it?"

Jesse ran a tired hand across his face, wiping drips from his chin. "That corner will have to be rebuilt and a section of the roof. Naturally, wiring's affected. Phil will check it out in the morning and be able to tell you more then." Brushing back his hair, he looked at her closely. She seemed to be holding up remarkably well. But then, he'd always thought Sara was stronger than she looked. "Do you know if your father kept up his insurance?"

"Thank goodness, he did. I ran across the policy the other day, and it's in effect." Walking out of the arena, she decided to let her ranch hands finish up. She felt bedraggled. "I wish I'd have known that hose was shot. I'd have bought a new one."

Strolling toward the trucks with her, Jesse knew how she felt. They'd had a minor fire on the Morgan Ranch about five years ago and even that had been a costly ordeal. "I guess Noah was cutting corners toward the end."

"Yes, he was." They passed the barn and she saw that Phil was directing the placement of a tarpaulin over the opening since the rain didn't seem to be letting up. At least the thunder had died down, and only a few errant bolts of lightning could be seen now and then. "They sure were a big help," she commented sarcastically as the fire truck pulled away.

"They can't be two places at once, Sara."

Stopping under one of the lamps shining onto the drenched greenbelt, Sara rubbed her arm, aching from when one of the horses had yanked her along. "I guess you're right. I'm just tired and wanting to take it out on someone."

He stepped in front of her. "Take it out on me."

She shook her head at that. "No, not on you." She was bushed, but she knew she couldn't go in until she'd done one more thing.

Sloshing through the rain, her boots heavy with mud, she walked around and thanked the men from both ranches, one by one, shaking their hands and telling them how grateful she was for their hard work. After she'd spoken to the last man, she strolled back and found Jesse still standing near the lamp where she'd left him. She stopped in front of him.

His eyes slid down her slim frame where her sodden clothes clung to her like a second skin. Under her wet shirt, her curves were outlined clearly. Her face was smudged with soot and her golden hair was tangled and disheveled. He'd never wanted a woman more in his life.

There was something about fighting a natural disaster together that put an edge on your nerves, your emotions. Jesse could feel the tension inside himself, the heightened awareness. There was also something about Sara, the only woman he knew who could look appealing after fighting a fire for two hours in a downpour. Her eyes were misty with unspoken needs. Despite the chilling rain, her cheeks were flushed with excitement. "Are you going to chew me out for taking over?"

Sara looked up into gray eyes dark and assessing. "Chew you out?" She shook her head slowly. "You're the reason we made it through this. Without your help, especially with that fire truck nowhere in sight, the barn would be just a pile of ashes. I don't know how to thank you."

Lazily, Jesse shrugged. "You'll think of a way." He stepped closer until their bodies brushed lightly against each other.

She felt an instant response, felt the echoing thud of his heart against her own. "Are you so sure?"

His hands settled on her shoulders as he dipped his head and let his tongue skim along her lower lip. Her breath shuddered out as he nipped at the sweet fullness. "Maybe you need a little direction." And he crushed her mouth with his.

Mindlessly, he pressed her to him, letting all the accumulated emotion of the past hours pour out of him and into her. A pleasure so sharp in its intensity that he was left swaying as her mouth answered needs he hadn't acknowledged for a long while.

Across the way, the mess hall lights were on and weary men were filing inside to dry off, to warm up.

"Hey," Pete yelled from the doorway. "Come and get it. Hot coffee, eggs and bacon for everyone."

Drawing back, Jesse struggled to breathe normally. The wind had died down, but the rain fell steadily. He no longer noticed nor cared. "You hungry?"

Sara shook her head. "Are you?"

Her eyes were a dark green in the dim yellow lighting. Dark and hotly aware. "Not for food."

Her lips throbbed from his kiss and her heated blood raced through her veins. "Why did you do it, Jesse? Why did you come over and save me?"

"Don't you know?"

Her heart was pounding, full of need, empty of shame. "Maybe. I want to hear you say it."

"I'd rather show you." Bending, he picked her up and headed for the house.

"I look like a drowned rat, like something the cat dragged in," she protested mildly.

"You look beautiful." He kept walking.

"Hey, Jesse," one of the Morgan men called after him. "You want to get something to eat?"

Alongside the ranch hand, Aaron grinned. "I don't think that man's got food on his mind right now, do you?"

The other man laughed as he watched Jesse march off. "Guess not."

Jesse shoved a hip against the back door and carried Sara inside, bumping it closed after them. "I'm going to muddy up your house if I go any farther."

Sara could hardly breathe over the pounding of her pulse. "I don't care." His eyes never leaving hers, he moved to the stairs. He seemed to know exactly where he was going, though she knew he'd never been upstairs in her father's house. Taking her through her bedroom, he pushed into the adjoining bath and there, let her slide down the wet length of his body.

Grasping her hair in one hand, he cupped the back of her neck with the other, dragging her as close as humanly possible while his lips settled on hers. He felt the hot give of her mouth, the steely grip of her hands at his back. He had to have her, to make her his again. He hadn't been sane since touching her flesh the night before.

Almost panting, he pulled back. "Two minutes," he gasped. "I'll give you two minutes to get out of those clothes." Reaching inside the shower curtain that ringed the old-fashioned claw-footed tub, he turned on the water.

She smiled at his impatience. "I can do it in a minute and a half."

He laughed. "Okay, race you."

Hopping on one foot, she tugged off one boot then the other as he did the same. Wet jeans slid reluctantly down damp legs. Sodden shirts hit the tile floor with a moist plop. Then they stepped into the shower.

Jesse wound his arms about her and pulled her directly under the spray with him, letting the hot water wash away the grime of the storm and the stench of the fire. Sara grabbed the soap and ran it over his hard flesh while he rubbed shampoo into her hair, then they switched roles.

But Jesse found himself getting distracted. By the sweet fullness of her breasts, by the satin curve of her shoulder, the soft line of her throat. His hands skimmed and soothed and caressed while her fingers dug into his scalp with a vengeance. Finishing, he clasped her bottom in his two big hands and lifted her until her legs circled his waist. Then he stood under the spray until soap and shampoo were washed from both of them.

Sara stepped out, handed him a towel and grabbed one for herself. Only Jesse had a better idea.

"No, we dry each other." And he raised his hands to rub at her hair.

Within the circle of his arms, she toweled his chest first before shifting to dry his back. Meanwhile, Jesse's attention wandered, and he dabbed moisture from her breasts with slow, sensual strokes. Sara paused, exhaling a soft moan, her body catching fire.

His mouth drawing on her flesh, Jesse felt himself drowning. In her beauty, in the pleasure she offered him. No dreams, no memories could come close to the reality of Sara. Sara with her clean, fresh scent, her green eyes hazy with passion, her slender hands trailing along his rib cage. He'd forgotten how quickly, how effortlessly she could draw him into the cyclone of sensation. He'd forgotten how alive she could make him feel.

"You've been driving me crazy, Sara," he told her. "Awake or asleep, I would think of you. And I would ache with wanting you."

She had a few confessions of her own. "I used to lie awake nights thinking of you, too, wishing you were there with me."

"Thank God for that." Sliding a hand under her knees, he picked her up and carried her to her bed.

"We're still wet," she protested.

"Sheets can be changed." He laid her down and followed her, his movements slow and deliberate. Twelve years of needs too long denied vibrated within him as he buried his face in the softness of her hair. She smelled of soap and still tasted of rain. He pressed his lips to her throat then lower, feeling her heart beat against his tongue. Hot and greedy, his mouth closed over the taut peak of one breast, and he heard her cry out with savage pleasure.

Thrusting her hands into his hair, Sara clung to him. She became aware of the feel of him throbbing against her, waiting and ready, and the knowledge made her edgy and impatient. "Jesse, I . . ."

But instead, his mouth came back to hers and his seeking fingers wandered down to answer that first fierce need. The stunning climax had her pulsing all over, had her reaching for him. Yet he evaded her again.

Floating on a sea of momentary satisfaction, Sara could only let him take her where he would, for she felt limp and boneless. The stubble of his beard grazed across her sensitive flesh, and she gloried in the sensation. With teeth and tongue and eager hands, he drove her up and up again.

Sara felt the anxiety over the barn fire and the tension of the days since she'd returned ease from her. Jesse's mouth making love to every inch of her had her relaxing, had her nearly purring. Gone were her misgivings, her doubts as his kisses continued to arouse. Gone was all coherent thought, all objection, as he took her to the edge. Her body hot and trembling and needy, she reached for him again.

Jesse shifted so that she was beneath him. He knew he had her full attention, had her on the precipice as he looked into eyes smoky with passion. "Tell me again that you're over me, Sara. Let me hear you say it."

She couldn't and he damn well knew it. "Maybe not." She'd give him that much.

"Not good enough, Sara," Jesse said while his arms quivered with the strain of not allowing his throbbing body to lower and join with hers.

Her hands gripped the bedsheets, her need for him raging through her veins like the wild fire had raged through her barn. "I don't know what you want me to say."

"I want to know how you feel."

"Right now? You *know* how I feel. I want..."

"Words, Sara. I need the words and so do you. Okay, just this once, we'll pretend you're a slow study, and I'll teach you." He bent until his face was inches from hers. "Not only have I never gotten over you, but I never will. And there's a very good reason for that. Because I love you."

Then he plunged into her, his mouth taking hers, swallowing her stunned cry of surprise.

* * *

Sara lay beneath him and watched the rain drizzle down the windowpane as the storm outside wound down. But it was the storm inside that concerned her as the last three words Jesse had said to her echoed through her troubled mind. *I love you.*

He couldn't know how long she'd waited to hear them. Waited, hoped, prayed. He wouldn't know how difficult it was for her to believe he meant them now, after so much time had passed.

There had been so little love in her life that even hands that reached out to her in friendship had been suspect. In Sara's youth, there had been Gretchen, then Kay and Emily. Later, there had been Lacie, who was still a good friend, and Margaret, of course. But there had been no man in her life since Jesse—at least not one who meant anything.

For as far back as she could remember, she'd loved Jesse Morgan, first with the fervor of her young heart and then as a mature woman who couldn't seem to forget him. She'd admitted to his mother that she loved Jesse, but loving someone wasn't a guarantee that your feelings were returned. She'd left St. Johns so Jesse couldn't be hurt. Yet, because of that aborted phone call, the fates had separated them.

Finally, he'd offered the words she'd been longing to hear. But, if she accepted his love, if she spoke of her love for him, the very words would imply a shared future. A future that would have to include their son.

How could she tell Jesse about Christopher and still keep his love for her intact?

Jesse shifted, rolling from her, knowing his weight must be crushing her. But he took her with him, unwilling to lose the contact, to allow the closeness of their union to fade. As he settled her within his arms and tilted her chin up to kiss her, he caught a glimpse of a worried frown before she erased it.

"You're thinking too much again," Jesse said.

Her body still throbbed from the aftershocks of his love-making. Perhaps she could lead him away from a serious discussion. "Oh, I'm feeling plenty right now."

He squeezed her arm in reprimand. "You know what I mean."

Sara sighed, giving up. "Yes, I suppose I do." With her hand, she brought the sheet up to cover them, feeling suddenly exposed.

Jesse bit back an oath, annoyed that the mellow mood had been shattered so quickly. "You can handle making love with me, you can invite me to kiss you everywhere, to touch you everywhere. Yet you can't handle hearing that I love you." He touched her face so she was forced to look at him. "Why, Sara? Don't you want me to love you?"

"It's just about all I ever have wanted. But a lot of years have passed since we last made love, Jesse." She sat up then, needing the distance, turning her back. "Things aren't as simple as they were back when we were young."

"What isn't simple?" When she didn't answer, rising instead to go to the closet for a robe, he frowned and came to an uneasy conclusion. "There's someone else. You told me there was no one, no special man in California. Did you lie to me?"

Not a man. A young boy. Your son. She belted the robe before turning back to face him. "No, I didn't lie. There's no other man. It's me. I've changed, and so have you. Twelve years is a long time."

Perhaps she was right. They had changed, matured, grown. He knew the mistakes he'd made back then, not telling her how he felt, not facing down her father. And so he'd lost her. But he was stronger now, wiser, and he knew exactly what he wanted. That much hadn't changed. He still wanted Sara.

Only now, he was willing to fight for her, even if it meant fighting whatever nameless demons haunted her so they could be together. Because they belonged together.

"Yes, we are different people. But the feelings we had for each other are still there, still just as strong. At least for me they are. Tell me that's not so for you, and I'll go away."

Sara walked back to the bed slowly and sat down facing him. "Surely you know I couldn't have made love with you like we just did if my feelings weren't just as strong. Maybe stronger."

Jesse put his hand on her arm, trying to read her eyes. "Then what is it? Don't you believe that I love you?"

"I want to." She shook her head, unable to find the right words. "It's complicated."

"I graduated near the top of my class. I'm fairly bright. Try me."

She shoved back her hair, wishing they'd never started this. "I haven't had much experience with loving, Jesse. I'm not good at it. Possibly I expected too much, of my father, of you. No one's ever cared for me the way I wanted them to." Except Christopher. He loved her completely with a childlike innocence. She closed her eyes with a wave of sadness.

Watching her, Jesse sensed there was something she wasn't telling him, something that was eating away at her, and it wasn't a recent pain. Something that had happened long ago and had kept her away all these years. "Tell me what made you leave here, Sara. Tell me what you and your father quarreled over."

She shook her head, afraid he would guess. "I can't. Please don't ask me."

"Can't or won't?"

She rubbed at a spot above her eyes. "It amounts to the same thing. I don't want to talk about the past."

He wanted to shake her. He was an impatient man who would have to learn patience. She would tell him in time. In her *own* time. He had to believe that. Meanwhile, he had to guard what they did have. "All right. I'll wait until you're ready."

Her hand dropped away as she looked at him with surprise. "Just like that? So easily?"

He sat up so swiftly she scarcely had time to react, then shoved her down onto her back and leaned over her, his eyes hot and hungry again. "Easy?" He saw that she wasn't afraid of him, just surprised and a little intrigued. "You think this is easy for me?"

"I didn't say that."

His eyes bore into hers. "Do you think we can work things out between us eventually?"

"I don't know, Jesse. I've been on my own a long time. You're a very strong man. I'm not sure we're a good mix." She was being painfully honest, though it cost her to admit it.

"We've got a hell of a lot of chemistry going for us here."

She had to smile at that, very aware that only her thin robe separated her flesh from his hard, naked body. "You have a point there."

Lowering, Jesse touched his mouth to hers, brushing his lips slowly along hers, and felt a sigh tremble from her. His hands slid up her arms and paused to note her erratic pulse through the thin skin at her wrists. His tongue slid inside, met hers in a slow dance, then he deepened the kiss, drawing it out exquisitely until they were both breathless. "Do you like the way I kiss you, Sara?"

Her skin was already humming, her blood beginning to heat. This she could handle, the physical part. This she craved more than the air she breathed. "Mmm, yes." This was much better than thinking or talking.

His hands began to roam, untying the sash of her robe, opening the folds. The passion between them that had been so carefully banked he brought to life again as his mouth retraced the contours of her face. He could see the mists closing in on her as her eyes darkened, as her restive body began to shift.

"Do you want me, Sara?" he asked as his fingers wandered, exploring.

She stretched like a sensual cat under his clever ministrations, her mind beginning to float. "Yes, I want you."

"More than all the California men you've known?"

"Apparently, or I would have given in to at least one of them." His hand closed over a breast, achingly gentle, infinitely arousing, and she sucked in a deep breath.

"Why didn't you, Sara? Why didn't you give in to at least one man in twelve long years?" His hand slipped down and his fingers touched her intimately. She jerked in response, and her eyes flew open. "Tell me why."

Perhaps he was right. Perhaps words were necessary. Maybe they didn't have a future together. But they could have this.

Sara wound her arms around his neck and met his intense gaze. "Because none of them were you. Because, for me, it's always been only you."

This is how he'd wanted her, all of her his, heart and soul his, aware this minute of no one on earth but him. This time when he slipped into her, it was as if he were coming home. He watched her features soften as he began to move, saw the warm glow in her eyes as they stayed on his. With a studied control he hadn't thought himself capable of, he drew out their pleasure.

She'd known passion with this man before, yet each time, she learned something new, something glorious. Here was the patience that was so seldom a visible part of him. Here was the tenderness, the concern for her enjoyment. As his mouth touched hers, Sara's eyes closed and her hands dived into his hair. Finally, she felt his control shatter as she whispered his name, then let go of the world and joined him in one of their own making.

Chapter Eleven

Sara finished her chicken salad, set her empty plate on the coffee table and leaned back on the couch in the den. It had been an incredibly long day.

The rain had finally stopped by early morning. Phil had gone out early to assess the damage to the barn and had come to her kitchen door to let her know what he'd found. She had just poured Jesse's coffee and joined him at the table when she heard the knock. She'd had no choice but to invite Phil in.

It had been an uncomfortable moment for her, Sara thought, remembering. Fortunately, she'd changed from her robe into her usual jeans and shirt before she'd come downstairs, and nothing looked amiss. Perhaps if she hadn't been filled with the guilty knowledge that just an hour before Phil's visit she'd been awakened by Jesse's wondrous lovemaking, she could have pretended her neighbor had just arrived to check on things. However, the men had taken both Morgan trucks back last night, and so it was plain that Jesse had spent the night.

Phil, too, had looked a little uneasy as his eyes had skipped from one to the other. Jesse had been the only one apparently unshaken. He'd calmly asked Phil what he'd discovered regarding the barn.

Sara had been relieved to learn the news wasn't terrible. The damage had been fairly well contained to that one corner section of the barn. Due to other storm damage last night, the insurance adjuster Phil had phoned had said he couldn't make it out to the Lazy-S for a day or so. Meanwhile, Phil and the men had secured the gaping hole and were in the process of cleaning things up and airing the place out so the horses could be returned to their stalls. She'd thanked him, and he'd seemed relieved to hurry off.

Smiling, Sara remembered how Jesse had teased her about being suddenly self-conscious in front of Phil. As he'd said, she owed no one explanations since they were both free and consenting adults. However, since no man had ever been seen leaving her bed before—for the simple reason that she'd never taken a man to her bed before last night—it was only natural that she'd feel awkward.

Sara sipped her iced tea and stretched out her legs. After more lingering kisses, she'd driven Jesse home and then spent the rest of the day working alongside the men. The horses all needed attention. Grooming, comforting, thorough exams for small cuts and bruises that might fester later if unnoticed. Stalls had to be cleaned out, fresh hay brought in, the animals fed and watered, exercised and pampered a bit more than usual. Lanterns had been strung up until the electricity could be repaired.

By five, Sara decided that things around the Lazy-S looked pretty good. She'd made her weary way back to the house and taken a long shower, then fixed herself a light dinner. That had been an hour ago. Now, wearing a long green shirt that trailed down nearly to the hem of her white shorts, she contemplated the last stack of her father's papers that she had yet to go through.

It was warm in the den since the air-conditioning still hadn't been repaired, and she didn't have a lot of energy, but she decided she'd tackle at least some of the paperwork. She hadn't slept much last night due to Jesse's distractions and thought she might turn in early tonight. Not that she'd minded missing sleep for that reason. It had been the best night of her life.

And sometime during the night, she'd decided to put off thinking about the future, at least for a few days. It wasn't like her; she'd always faced problems head-on. Perhaps because she was deathly afraid that there was no happy solution to their situation and therefore delaying the inevitable a few days couldn't hurt. Didn't she deserve a few days—and nights—of happiness in Jesse's arms before she lost him again?

For lose him she would, either way. If she didn't tell Jesse about Christopher, then she'd have to leave and forever live in fear that no matter where she and her son went, he might find them this time. If she did tell him, which deep inside she knew was the *right* thing to do, she'd lose him still, for she doubted he could forgive a woman who'd deceived him this long, even if she'd started out with the best of intentions.

Sara rose with a frown on her face. If she pondered this much longer, she'd give herself another headache. Instead, she walked to the final stack, shuffled through some of the few remaining folders and picked up a green journal. Returning to the couch, she opened the thick book.

The pages were dated, the handwriting her father's. It took her a few minutes to realize that it was mostly a journal relating to the running of the ranch that went back to

Noah's early years when he'd first taken over from his father. Stock purchases were recorded along with acquisition prices, the birth of foals, sales, etc.

Leisurely thumbing through the pages, Sara skimmed the information until her interest picked up about a third of the way through. The focus of the journal shifted to diary-like entries, random thoughts, even occasional ramblings about the weather and personnel problems. Again, she scanned the notations briefly, going on. About halfway through, there was a marked difference in Noah's handwriting and the tone of his words.

The year was the same as that of his wedding to Rose and detailed his agony over losing Emily Ryan. He spoke of being unable to eat or sleep or concentrate, so filled was his mind and heart with the memories of the woman he'd wanted. He didn't blame Emily, but rather himself for not speaking up sooner, for letting Hal Morgan move in on her while his reticence had kept him away. And he blamed Hal most of all.

Reading her father's words, written while in obvious pain, Sara could understand his disappointment, for she, too, had been parted from the one she loved. Only casually did Noah mention Rose, that he'd married her because she was a good woman and he needed sons to help with the ranch. At that, Sara felt her dead mother's probable misery at finding herself in a loveless marriage, one where her primary function was to provide her cold husband with sons.

Next, Noah began mentioning the land dispute between the Shephards and the Morgans, explaining that he'd come up with the story in order to explain to neighboring ranchers why there was suddenly so much animosity between Hal and himself. Admitting that he knew it was wrong, Noah nonetheless had felt he had to save face, that he couldn't attend functions or pretend to be friends with Hal nor stand off to the side and watch Emily, already big with Hal's firstborn. It hurt too much.

Closing her eyes a moment, Sara felt empathy for her father and his suffering. Surely to love and not have that love returned was one of life's cruelest things to endure. Perhaps if she'd have known this years ago, read this journal much sooner, she'd have been able to communicate with him better.

Moving on, she turned the page and read how things got worse. Emily delivered a healthy baby boy while Rose miscarried year after year. Noah's mood darkened, and apparently he'd spent all his energies on the ranch and very little on his wife who must have been going through a similar hell. Kay's birth was also noted along with Noah's undaunted determination to have a child of his own.

At Sara's birth, Noah's entry read as more a triumph over Hal than a blessing of a healthy baby at last. How that must have hurt her mother, for she doubted if her father had spared his wife's feelings. He'd never spared hers.

But Noah wasn't finished, for the child had been a girl and he wanted, *needed,* a son. So he insisted they keep trying, against the doctor's orders. Three years later, when the baby boy died and Rose nearly followed, Noah finally seemed to come to his senses. He wrote page upon rambling page of his self-hatred for pushing Rose into another pregnancy when physically he'd known her weakened body couldn't handle it.

But the worst was yet to come. When Rose died, his world spun out of control. He wrote that it was his fault that the boy hadn't lived and his fault that his wife had died so young. All his fault. And he confessed that the only way he could stop the pain was to lose himself in drink.

Awash in sympathy, Sara felt her eyes fill. What her father had done—and done deliberately and with a terrible purpose in mind—had been awful. But surely the death of his son and wife had been punishment enough.

Picking up the book, she read on and learned that the punishment he doled out for himself was far worse than others might have given him. He refused to allow anyone to get close to him, for he felt unworthy of even the smallest friendship. He watched his daughter grow from a thin awkward girl into a lovely teenager, he wrote, yet he never allowed himself the pleasure of accepting the love she might have given him.

It was his self-hatred that ate at him, Sara finally determined. He wanted to be punished, to atone for the deaths he'd convinced himself he'd caused. Noah felt he shouldn't be allowed happiness, not even his own daughter's affection. He'd lost his right to happiness.

Noah's handwriting became almost illegible and his entries decreased, appearing only occasionally during her growing-up years. Yet he wrote of pride in his daughter's intelligence, her school record, her blossoming beauty, her natural ability with horses. By now, tears trailed down Sara's cheeks unnoticed as she wept for his loneliness.

The next page had once been torn out, the left margin jagged, as if ripped in a frenzy of anger. Yet later, it had been smoothed out and reinserted. Sara read it slowly.

Noah spoke of becoming aware that Sara was meeting Jesse Morgan secretly, and all the anger he'd felt for Hal shifted to his son, the son who had Emily's eyes. The night he'd learned of Sara's pregnancy, heard her beg him to allow her to go to Jesse, he filled the page with his anger and frustration. He felt the gods were punishing him further and that the only thing he could do would be to cast his daughter from his house.

Sara wiped her damp cheeks as she read how Noah had sobbed after he'd watched Phil drive her away on that rainy morning. Noah was convinced he'd only ruin Sara's life if she remained, for his punishment would go on, touching her life, too. In a shaky hand, he wrote of his love for Sara, but that he couldn't tell her, couldn't show her. He didn't deserve her or the grandchild yet to be born.

But he'd see to it that the Morgans wouldn't have that child, either. He wrote of Jesse coming to see him to demand to know where Sara had gone, but Noah hadn't relented. Jesse had threatened, argued, finally begged. Noah had stood firm.

The final page had been written some time after she'd left the Lazy-S and was filled with incoherent jottings, Noah's disjointed thoughts, his fear of dying alone. He'd promised himself he'd never try to contact Sara or Margaret, for he didn't trust himself not to beg his daughter to return. He wanted a second chance desperately, yet he knew he didn't deserve one.

After that, the ledger pages were empty.

Slowly Sara closed the book, wiped her eyes and blew her nose. She was left with an overwhelming sense of sadness. And she felt profound pity for her father who'd literally ruined his own life. His misplaced sense of guilt and his tortured mind had sentenced him to a friendless, miserable existence that had been bearable only when he was in an alcoholic fog. What a terrible waste.

Thoughtfully, she set the book aside. Even if she'd have known all this back then, she probably couldn't have reached her father. No one could have. By the time she was born, he'd already been well on his way down his own path of destruction.

She couldn't do anymore tonight, Sara decided. Her emotions were too close to the surface. Rising, she picked up her empty plate and glass and walked into the kitchen. Drained yet restless, she wandered outside.

The setting sun streaked the sky with orange and mauve strokes, the clouds ringing the distant mountains appearing almost purple. She could smell the red dust of day settling on the shrubs along the side of the house. She missed the scent of the sea that drifted to her backyard in San Diego, but the desert aromas were the ones she'd grown up with. Crickets were already singing their monotonous tune, and an occasional whinny could be heard coming from the barn. Twilight wrapped around the Lazy-S, its muted shades softening the harsher realities of daylight.

Sara started walking away from the house, up along the grassy area. She was scarcely aware of her destination until she saw the tall piñon pine atop the knoll and the grave still fresh beneath it. Perhaps now she was ready to say good-bye to Noah Shephard.

The small wooden cross seemed appropriate, for her father had been a man of simple tastes. Someone had placed fresh flowers at his feet, possibly Ruby. They were limp from the unrelenting heat, yet added a touch of color to the clay-reddened soil. Slowly, Sara sat down on the grass alongside the mound.

He'd given her life, yet she hadn't known him. He'd loved her, or so he'd written, yet she'd never heard him utter the words. And he'd loved Emily, and that unrequited love had ruined his life. Again, Sara could feel a permeating sadness that seemed to linger in the air above her father's final resting place.

Finally, though, she could let go of the anger, truly this time. People don't always love us the way we'd wish, but that doesn't mean they don't care in their own way. A lesson she'd had to learn, one that perhaps would help her accept Jesse's love more easily. And she could forgive Noah at last, for though he hadn't treated her as she'd wanted, he'd done the best he could. It wasn't up to her to judge him. She would find comfort in that thought.

"Goodbye, Dad," she whispered. "Sleep well."

Dry-eyed, Sara rose and made her way back to the house. As she rounded the bend, she saw Phil standing on the front porch. When he spotted her, he came over.

"Sorry to be bothering you, but I saw your light was on," Phil said.

"That's all right. I've been walking." She opened the door and stepped into the foyer, motioning him to follow. "Is something the matter?"

"Well, I'm not sure I should be doing this, but I got something here that belongs to you." He held out a plain white envelope with her name on it.

Puzzled, Sara took the envelope, not recognizing the writing, though the bold strokes seemed to indicate a masculine hand. "Did someone leave this for me?"

"A long time ago." Phil faltered, searching for the right words, unused to lengthy explanations. "Jesse... came to see me couple of times... after you left that day. He was awful upset, wanted me to tell him where you were. I finally told him... I'd put you on a bus to San Diego... told him that was all I knew. He wouldn't believe me, kept hounding your daddy, the other hired hands." Phil shook his head, remembering. "Finally, one day he came to me with this here letter. Said *if* I happened to find out where you went, to mail this to you. I guess he thought I knew but wasn't saying. Trouble is, I didn't."

Sara turned over the envelope and saw that it was still sealed. "And you've had it all this time?"

"Yes, ma'am. From time to time, I asked your daddy if he knew where you was living, thinking he'd slip up and tell me and I'd mail you the letter. But he never would say. I wasn't going to bother you with it when you came back 'cause I thought the way you was talking then, that you didn't have any use for the Morgans, just like Noah.'' Phil shuffled his feet awkwardly. "But then, this morning when I saw how things are between you and Jesse, I got to thinking maybe you'd want the letter, after all.''

Sara gave Phil a smile tinged with sadness. "Thank you, Phil.''

"I hope I done the right thing.''

"You did.'' She touched his arm briefly, then saw him out. Strolling to the kitchen, she opened the envelope and sat down at the table.

Slowly, she read Jesse's words. Again, her eyes filled with tears. Not of unhappiness this time, but tears of joy. He had loved her years ago, just as he'd been telling her. He had wanted to marry her, asking her to let him know where she was and he'd go get her no matter how far.

Slipping the letter into her pocket, Sara stood, found the truck keys and hurried outside where the white pickup was parked. Climbing behind the wheel, she rushed off.

As she turned into the Morgan compound, she saw that lights were on in the big house and also in Jesse's small cabin. This morning when she'd dropped him off, she'd fortunately not run into anyone. Now, she parked the pickup alongside Jesse's porch, ran up the steps and knocked on the door, not giving a thought to who might see her. Something far more important was on her mind.

Jesse heard the knock as he dried his hair after his shower. Wrapping the towel around his waist, he walked to the front to open the door.

She was wearing green, which was certainly her color. Her long blond hair hung past her shoulders and her face looked as if she'd been crying. Yet her eyes were shining. His face broke into a welcoming smile. "Sara.''

"I love you, Jesse,'' she said simply.

Taking her hand, he drew her inside.

Across the compound, Lisa Nagles stood under a tree and watched Jesse invite Sara inside his cabin. Disappointment settled on her like an invisible cloak. In another moment, she saw the light in Jesse's living room go off. Obviously, they were going to the back of the house. To his bedroom.

"Damn," Lisa said aloud and slumped to the grass. She'd been walking back from the arena to the house after checking on her horses when she'd seen Sara drive up, seemingly in a big hurry. It appeared that she hadn't come to Jesse by prior arrangement, but rather on impulse. But what did her motivation matter? Sara was here and apparently welcome in his cabin, where Lisa was not.

For years, Lisa had tried to get close to Jesse. Twice she'd played the fool by throwing herself at him. Twice he'd turned her down. She'd had other men friends, lots of them, in college and around here. But none measured up to Jesse Morgan.

Yet try as she would, he never really saw her.

Lisa had been watching both Jesse and Sara from afar for these past couple of weeks, and she hadn't thought they were seeing each other again. She'd known that Jesse had helped Sara out once when one of her older ranchers had gotten hurt and last night because of the fire. But his truck had been parked by his cabin this morning, so she was certain he hadn't stayed overly long with her.

Yet the way Jesse had pulled her in just now and him wearing only a towel was proof positive that their relationship was way beyond casual. Lisa felt she'd fought the good fight and lost. Defeat was a bitter taste in her mouth.

"Still at it, Lisa?" a lazy voice nearby asked.

Lisa swung around and saw Aaron watching her. "What do you mean?" she countered.

Shaking his head in disbelief, Aaron folded his long legs under himself as he sat down beside her. "You know what I mean."

Lisa shook back her thick auburn hair and leaned against the tree bark. Aaron had worked for the Morgans off and on for ten or twelve years and, for some reason, he was able to see right through her. "My timing's always been rotten, Aaron," she admitted reluctantly. "I never can seem to do the right thing when it comes to men."

Aaron picked up a blade of grass and stuck one end between his teeth. "Oh, you probably could if you'd just let go of this notion you have that you want Jesse. Don't you know that carrying a torch for somebody who doesn't return that interest only hurts *you.*"

She wasn't quite sure why, but Lisa felt comfortable speaking her mind to Aaron. They'd dated a few times— nothing serious—and had gotten along well. Oddly enough, he hadn't tried to get her into his bed, and she hadn't tried to seduce him, either. It was as if they were friends. And Lisa didn't have a lot of friends, male or female. Aaron was solid, someone you could trust. Maybe that's why around him, she let her guard down. "I can't seem to let go, Aaron. I've wanted Jesse for as long as I can remember."

Aaron shifted, gazing over toward the small cabin. He was undoubtedly Jesse's closest friend and had known Jesse was nuts about Sara probably before the man himself had admitted it. He also knew that Jesse had never looked at Lisa the way a man who wants a woman looks at her. He, on the other hand, had. But Lisa had to change, to do some growing up before he would let her know. "Do you suppose your wanting Jesse has to do with really caring, or do you want him because someone else has him?"

Surprisingly, she took the question seriously. "I'm not sure anymore. I didn't want Sara to have him years ago, and

I still don't. But even when she was gone, he never noticed me really." She looked at Aaron, her blue eyes imploring. "What's wrong with me?"

He smiled. "Nothing far as I can see. You look damn good to me." Then he sobered, deciding to tell her the truth. "The thing is, you can't put your finger on why someone's attracted to one person and not another. Take Peggy, for instance. She wasn't a raving beauty, so it couldn't have been her looks. More chemistry, I'd say."

"Who's Peggy?"

Aaron leaned back on an elbow. "A girl I met my last year of college. Fell like a ton of bricks for her. She knew it, too. I had a little bit of money saved, a flashy car, and I was a jock. I spent every dime I could get my hands on on her, and she let me. My dad was losing his ranch and I was borrowing money from him so I could impress Peggy. Nice guy, huh? All my friends told me she was using me, but would I listen? Hell, no."

Interested now, Lisa turned toward him. "So what happened?"

"After I ran out of money, she dumped me. Trouble is, I couldn't stop thinking of her and wanting her back. I knew what she was like. Hell, I saw her snag some other guy and go to work on him. I still wanted her. I nearly flunked out of school my senior year and would have if Jesse hadn't brought me around, helped me pass my finals."

"But you did get over her then and got on with your life."

"I wish. Even after graduation, I couldn't forget her. I dated, but no one else could measure up."

Lisa sighed. "I sure know what that's like."

"It took me a couple of years, honestly. My mom and dad moved away, and Jesse got me a job working here. And I was still a mess, walking around like a lovesick idiot."

"What finally worked, what got you over Peggy?"

"No blinding flash, no big moment of truth. I had to bring myself back up, to convince myself that the memory of Peggy will always hurt. But I can't have her. I have to go on with my life. I'm a decent person and one day I'll find someone who's probably a damn sight better than she ever was."

Lisa made a hopeless sound. "That's just it, you see. You *are* a decent person. I'm not. I . . . I've done things, things to try to get Jesse to notice me. Things that if he knew about—or if *anyone* knew about—they wouldn't forgive me." She flopped back onto the grass and lay an arm across her eyes.

"You mean about pretending to be Emily and telling Sara's friend on the phone that Jesse was happy with someone else and to leave him alone?"

Lisa shot back up. "How do you know about that?"

Aaron shrugged. "Jesse told me what he knew of the story the other day, and I figured it out. That was that St. Patrick's Day weekend, and you were home from school because you had the flu. I remember because I'd asked you to a dance and you couldn't go."

"You guessed but you didn't tell on me?"

"Why should I? It wouldn't serve a purpose. But I understand Emily's real upset about it, so she just might remember you were home, too. If she does, you could be in hot water."

Slowly, Lisa lay back down, near tears. "I don't know why I did it. The phone rang and no one was around, so I saw my chance and I took it. And the other day, I went over to see Sara and . . . and told some lies about Jesse being involved with Holly Lucas after Sara left. I figured that if I couldn't have him, she shouldn't, either." She brushed at her eyes. "I'm not a very nice person."

Aaron angled toward her, wishing he could convince her. Lisa was a lovely woman with a lot to offer. But if she didn't shift the focus of her life, she'd mess it up even further. "Don't be so hard on yourself. Loving someone makes us do stupid things sometimes. You need to forget Sara and forget Jesse. You need to butt out of their lives and let them work things out. Maybe they will, maybe not. But you can't force Jesse to care about you by shoving Sara out of the picture. You tried that. It didn't work."

"You're right. Oh, damn." Lisa rubbed both her temples in slow circles. "If they find out about that call, they'll all hate me, Aaron. Maybe I should just go away."

"Running won't help."

"You have any better ideas?"

"Yeah. Tell Emily and Jesse *before* they find out. Tell them you're sorry and mean it. Then concentrate on your own life, on finding someone who returns your feelings. Trust me, pining away after someone who doesn't want you just messes you up."

"Oh, God, I don't know if I can do it. Emily will be *so* disappointed in me. And Jesse will be furious."

"Emily's always willing to give people a second chance. When I was going through all that with Peggy, I was pretty rotten to be around. The Morgans had given me this job, and yet I couldn't seem to concentrate. I made mistakes, got another guy hurt one day 'cause I wasn't paying attention, got drunk and couldn't work. Emily used to talk to me by the hour, helping me to work things through."

Lisa knew he was right. "She is a pretty terrific person."

"As for Jesse, now that he has Sara back, he won't be as angry as you may think."

"I don't know what made me act so terrible. Maybe because when I first came here, after my father left and my mother couldn't take care of me, I felt like a loner, like I

didn't belong. Kay liked Sara better than me and that hurt.
I thought if I could get Jesse to notice me, I'd be a part of
the family, an accepted member. If not Kay's sister, then
Jesse's girl.''

"I understand that. And so will Jesse.''

Sitting up, she touched his hand. "Would you go with me
when I talk to them? Please?''

Aaron gripped her fingers with his own. "Sure. When do
you want to go?''

"Give me a little time.'' She gave him a nervous smile.
"You're a good friend, Aaron.''

Sara dumped the last of the outdated papers into the trash
bag and closed it with a twist-tie. Her father's den was all
cleaned out. Hands on her hips, she surveyed the room.

In the weeks she'd been back, she'd discovered a lot of
secrets, most right here in this, her father's sanctuary. She
would always live with the regret that she hadn't learned of
them while he'd been alive. But, as Jesse had told her last
week, time spent regretting was effort wasted. After she'd
told him about what she'd read in her father's journal the
night she'd gone to his cabin, he'd also said something else,
something that gave her a small measure of hope. Knowing
that *The Wizard of Oz* had been her favorite movie as a
child, he'd used that to illustrate his point.

"Maybe Noah was only trying to find his own Emerald
City. He drank to escape his unhappy life, searching for a
better one. Let's hope he found it.''

She would try to remember that, Sara thought.

Sara carried the final bag of trash and set it outside the
back door. Then she took a tour of the downstairs, room by
room, inspecting with a critical eye. Earlier this afternoon,
she'd done the same upstairs, then walked the entire compound, checking barns, buildings, fencing.

The painting was completed, giving a fresh look to the ranch as a first impression to a potential buyer. The air conditioner was finally fixed. Work had begun on the fire damage to the barn and she expected it to be finished by week's end. Everything was in good repair and the horses in top condition. The Lazy-S was ready to be offered up for sale, even though she had yet to purchase those additional horses. She had accomplished what she'd set out to do, the easy part.

The hard decisions awaited her.

Back in the kitchen, Sara put on a pot of coffee since it was an unseasonably cool afternoon. Strolling in to the den, she sat down in her father's desk chair, her mood thoughtful.

Many times before in her life, she'd had to make difficult decisions, and she'd always faced them head-on. It was time now to face this one. What to do about Jesse?

He'd been so moved the night she'd gone over and finally openly declared her love for him. She'd told him that Phil had given her his old letter and she'd apologized for not having believed him before reading it. He'd just been happy that she cared and wanted to put the past behind them.

There was the rub. The past involved an eleven-year-old boy, Jesse's son. Her son. She believed Jesse loved her and knew she loved him. Yet she agonized over how to tell him about Christopher.

Her shoulder bag was on the desk and she opened it, finding Chris's photo. Propping it against the penholder, she studied the grinning reflection, the curly black hair, those wide-set gray eyes, that stubborn, clefted chin. The picture of his father. And how would she tell her son that she'd suddenly run across his father?

So far, she'd answered Chris's occasional inquiries about his father with vague explanations that hopefully left him with the feeling that his parents had loved each other, but circumstances had made it impossible to remain together. That had satisfied him. So far. But Sara knew the day was coming when nebulous answers no longer would.

She'd talked with Chris last night, and he'd sounded lonely for her, as she was for him. She had to go home soon, for she missed him terribly. And she'd talked with both Lila and Ginger who were holding down the fort at her office, but she needed to get back to them, too.

Maybe she should go home for a few days, then return and finish up. Or should she have Margaret bring Chris here for the balance of the summer while she acquired the necessary stock and hired more hands, until the ranch sold? And one day drive over to the Morgans with him and...

And what? Introduce him as Jesse's long-lost son and the Morgans' grandson? Oh, God. Sara leaned back in the chair. No, she couldn't put Chris through that, or the Morgans, either. She'd have to tell Jesse and let the chips fall where they may. He would either understand and embrace them both or... or...

Or he'd never want to see her again. Or he'd take her to court and demand paternal rights. No. He wouldn't be cold and cruel, not now that he knew she loved him. Would he?

If only she could be certain, if only she could find a way to tell him without losing him. If only...

A knock at the door had her swiveling around. She couldn't see the porch from the den windows so she rose. Quickly, she tucked Christopher's picture back into her purse and walked to the foyer.

As soon as she saw Jesse's face, she knew something was wrong. "What is it?" she asked as he stepped inside.

"I just need you to hold me," he said, his voice strained.

She went to him, sliding her arms around his waist, laying her head on his shoulder. But after a moment, she eased back, needing to know. "Tell me, Jesse."

Jesse swallowed. "It's Mom. She came back from the doctor an hour ago. They suspect that the lump in her breast is malignant."

"Oh, no." She held him close again, offering comfort, seeking comfort. Not Emily. Not when she'd just found her again.

"They're going to do a biopsy in the morning. They'll know more then." He buried his face in her hair.

"We have to think positive." She leaned back to look into his eyes, to brush his hair off his forehead. "She's otherwise very healthy. Even if they have to operate, she'll beat this thing."

"God I hope so," Jesse said. "I've never seen my dad so upset. He's trying not to think the worst. We all are."

"Shall I go see her?"

He shook his head. "She's packing to go to the hospital. Dad's with her and so is Lisa, who suddenly is being really good. I called Kay, but she and Will are away. I forgot that they go on vacation every June after school lets out. Camping somewhere in the Northwest, so I can't reach them. If you want, you can go with me to the hospital in the morning."

"Of course. I want to be there."

Jesse let out a ragged breath. "I'm sorry. I didn't mean to lay this all on you so suddenly." He saw that his hands were shaking as he released her. "It's funny how we always expect the people we love to be healthy and whole forever."

"Yes, we do. Why don't you go into the den and I'll bring in some coffee? I just made it." And he looked as if he could use some.

In the kitchen, she arranged cups and napkins, moving automatically. Sara had thought Emily looked worried when she'd mentioned finding the lump last week, as any woman would. And, as most women, she'd prayed they'd find it was benign. That wasn't to be, it seemed. Picking up the tray, she removed her frown, knowing Jesse needed her to keep his spirits up through this.

She walked into the den, set the tray onto the coffee table, then turned to where Jesse stood by the desk. The moment she noticed what he held in his hands, the blood drained from her face.

Puzzled, his eyes raised from the picture to meet hers. "I saw your purse had fallen, so I came over to pick it up. And this fell out." Frowning, he looked again at the smiling boy and felt as if he were staring into a mirror that had erased about twenty years. Or going through an old photo album of his mother's. Slowly, he turned the picture over.

The inscription was in a childish handwriting. "To Mom, with love, Chris."

Mom. The picture in Sara's purse was inscribed to Mom. The boy was her son. The boy who looked just like him. Her son and *his* son. He felt the heat of anger move through him as he met her eyes again. "I guess now we both know why you left town in such a hurry."

Swallowing, Sara moved several steps closer. "Please, Jesse, let me explain."

"Explain? You think it's possible to explain why you kept my son from me for twelve years? Why didn't you tell me back then, back when you found out you were pregnant with my child?"

"I tried to. You weren't home and . . ."

"But I came home. Didn't you think I'd marry you? Didn't you know I loved you?"

Sara's voice was low, trembling. "You never said the words. You never mentioned marriage, either."

Jesse ran a frustrated hand through his hair, not hearing her, his mind filled with objections. "I don't understand. Why didn't you call later? Why didn't you write? You knew where I was, even though you saw to it that I didn't know where you were. You *and* my son."

It was happening exactly as she'd feared. "Jesse, I was going to tell you . . . I—"

"When?" He slammed his fist down hard on the desktop, needing to express his anger. "When were you going to tell me, Sara?"

"I'm not sure. I . . ."

"Were you punishing me, because I wasn't home when you called, because some unknown woman answered the phone that day?"

She brushed back her hair, hating the anguish in his eyes. "Maybe. Maybe I was. I needed you so badly and you . . . you weren't there. I almost died. I almost lost the baby, and I couldn't reach you. I thought you didn't care."

"So for twelve long years, twelve stinking years, you kept my son away to punish me. And what about my parents? They have a right to know they have a grandchild, too."

"I know, and I'm sorry. Truly. If I could change things . . ."

"Sorry? Sorry doesn't cut it, Sara." Taking the picture with him, Jesse turned and marched past her out of the den. Out of the house. Out of her life.

Sara stumbled back to fall onto the couch, stuffing a fist into her mouth to keep from sobbing out loud. Oh, God, *had* she been trying to punish Jesse for not being there for her? Would he ever forgive her, even after cooling down and thinking things over? Would he listen to the rest of her explanation, that she'd been trying to protect him back then?

No, she thought, straightening at last. He probably wouldn't. He was too angry, too hurt. She'd lost him a second time.

Again, she was on her own.

CRITICAL

Table texture with it buys, the checkbook as
selfless of the buy. He

America with other feet

Chapter Twelve

Malignant. The very word made Jesse shudder as he heard Dr. Owens explain his mother's condition. Holding himself in tight control, he forced himself to listen, to let the words penetrate.

They'd taken a small sample of breast tissue at eight this morning and done the biopsy while Emily was still under anesthetic. The results were indisputable. The lump was malignant.

Dr. Owens addressed Hal but was aware that Jesse, Lisa and Aaron were also listening. "If the lump had been benign, we'd have gone in and removed it, and that would have been that. But in the event it wasn't, I'd notified Dr. Horvath to stand by. You'll recall, Hal, that I told you I've known Dirk Horvath for years. One of the best oncologists in the state. He studied at the Mayo Clinic."

Hal's hands in his pockets were knotted into fists as he swallowed past a huge lump of fear. Yes, he damn well wanted the best for Emily. But he also wanted to know more. "So what happens now?"

"Dirk's scrubbing. We'll operate as soon as he's ready. I'll assist."

Beneath his ruddy tan, Hal grew pale. "So quickly?" He'd never trusted things that happened too fast. What if they'd made a mistake? What if something went wrong? What if Emily...no! He couldn't complete the thought.

"The sooner the better." The doctor's compassionate gaze took in the whole family. "Take heart. She's a strong, healthy woman. I'll be back to talk with you as soon as it's over."

Jesse touched the doctor's arm. "Can we see her before...before the surgery?"

Dr. Owens shook his head. "Your mother's asleep. She wouldn't know you anyhow." With a comforting pat on Hal's shoulder, he left the waiting room.

Lisa slipped an arm around Hal. "She's got to be all right. She simply *has* to be."

Hal nodded, then went to sit in the farthest chair propping his elbows on his knees, gripping his hands tightly together as he stared at the polished floor. He wasn't a man who prayed regularly, but he was praying now.

Lisa moved close to Aaron, who held her lightly in the circle of his arms. She'd never in her life been as frightened as she was now. She'd never realized how much she loved Emily Morgan till she was faced with the possibility of losing her. Closing her eyes, holding onto the solid support of Aaron Strong, she promised she'd confess all her transgressions and make it up to those she'd hurt if only God would let Emily be well again.

Alone with his thoughts, Jesse turned to gaze out the window at the White Mountains in the distance. Funny how your life could fall apart in less than a day, in about twenty-four short hours, he thought.

He'd been on top of the world yesterday morning, crazy in love, looking forward to a great future for the first time in years. Then his parents had come home to tell him about Emily's lump, and he'd gone over to Sara's and learned she'd deceived him.

Not a little deception, mind you. But one she'd not even hinted at for twelve long years. Deliberately, without a thought to his feelings, with but one small attempt to reach him in twelve years. How could she explain that away?

There was joy in all this, too, Jesse reminded himself. He had a son, a boy who looked as if he'd spit him out of his mouth, as his grandfather used to say.

Christopher. In his anger at the mother, he'd hardly thought about the boy. Well, Sara had had their son all to herself all this time, and now it was his turn. No judge on earth would deny him his rights, once he'd heard the story. He'd bring Chris here, raise him on the ranch, teach him about horses, send him to the best schools, then have him work right alongside his father and grandfather. On the Morgan Ranch, the one that would one day be his.

Jesse hadn't told his mother or father yet about Chris. They were too distracted right now. But he would, as soon as his mother was over the surgery. And they'd be thrilled. They'd help him get his son and the four of them would be a family.

And to hell with Sara who had lied to him.

"How are you doing, Jesse?" Lisa asked, at his elbow.

He hadn't heard her come up, but he nodded briefly to her. She'd been acting odd the last few days. Kinder, softer. Jesse wasn't sure if he trusted her actions, wondering what had brought about the change. He'd even remarked on it to Aaron, who'd just shrugged and said enigmatically that people do change. Lisa couldn't have picked a better time to warm up since they couldn't reach Kay and he was sure his mother would need a woman's touch during her recovery. Jesse had hoped that woman would have been Sara, but...

"I'm okay. How are you holding up?" he asked Lisa.

"I'm worried, of course. But I'm confident. Emily will make it just fine." She met his eyes, hesitant but determined to ask since no one else had. "Where's Sara? I thought surely she'd be here."

"I don't know." A muscle in his jaw clenched as he turned back to the window.

So there *was* something wrong. "I know it's none of my business, but you two seemed so close again. Did you quarrel?"

"You're right. It's none of your business."

Lisa knew that tone, knew she'd get no further with Jesse. Reluctantly, she went back to sit alongside Aaron. They'd probably fought over that phone call or perhaps what she'd said about Holly Lucas, Lisa decided with a familiar pang of guilt. She should have said something before this. She couldn't tell Emily right now, and certainly Jesse was too angry to listen. She'd go to Sara as soon as Emily was out of danger. She'd make things right. Aaron had convinced her that she couldn't really find happiness until she straightened out the past.

Glancing at the clock, Lisa sat back to wait.

At the Lazy-S, Sara, too, was waiting, and she found the minutes creeping by. She hadn't dared go to the hospital, knowing that Jesse would be there and he wouldn't appreciate her presence. So she'd been phoning regularly, keeping informed that way.

She'd had to lie, claiming she was Kay so they'd give her information. She thought the small deception forgivable under the circumstances. She'd nearly burst into tears when she'd heard Emily's lump was malignant. That had been several hours ago and they'd told her she was undergoing surgery immediately.

How long could a simple lumpectomy take? she wondered as she paced. Had they found more?

She was just about to phone for an update when she saw a pickup from the Morgan Ranch swing into her drive. For a wild moment of hope, she thought that Jesse had decided they could work things out, that he was coming in person to tell her that Emily had come through with flying colors. She swung open the door and was disappointed to see Lisa and Aaron climb out of the truck and come toward her.

"I thought you'd like to know that Emily's doing very well after the surgery," Lisa said as she stepped onto the porch. "The doctor feels they got all of it and that her recovery should go well."

"Thank God." Sara was too relieved to be annoyed at the messenger. "And thank you for letting me know." Her eyes swung to Aaron and back to Lisa, wondering why they didn't appear ready to leave. "Is there something else?" Jesse? Was Jesse all right?

"Could we come in for a minute?" Aaron asked. "Lisa has something she wants to tell you."

Sara couldn't imagine what Lisa would have to say that could possibly interest her, especially not on this upsetting day, but she couldn't be rude. She ushered them into the den and took the chair by the fireplace as they settled onto the couch. As she waited for her to begin, Sara couldn't help noticing that Lisa didn't seem self-confident and superior today, as she so often did.

Lisa found that confessing her past sins wasn't nearly as difficult as she'd feared. With Aaron close beside her offering silent encouragement, she told Sara of her jealousies since childhood, of her infatuation with Jesse, of pretending to be Emily that long-ago day on the telephone. When she saw the way Sara closed her eyes at that piece of news, looking momentarily shattered, she almost didn't finish.

But she made herself go on and add that she'd also lied about Jesse's involvement with Holly Lucas. By then, Sara had recovered and sat quietly watching her.

"I have no excuses to offer for my behavior, Sara. All I can say is that I wanted Jesse, and I didn't want you to have him. I've come to realize that he...he doesn't want me whether you're in the picture or not. I've done some terrible things, and I don't know if you can forgive me."

Silently, Sara got up and went to stand by the window, her emotions in a turmoil. "Have you told Jesse?" she finally asked.

"No, not yet. He's preoccupied and worried about his mother. I tried to talk with him earlier, and he brushed me off. But I will tell him. And Emily, too." Lisa glanced at Aaron hesitantly, then rose and went to Sara. "If there was a way I could make this up to you, I would, gladly."

Sara turned. "I've made a few mistakes myself, Lisa. I'm no one to judge you."

Eyes brimming with tears, Lisa hugged the woman she'd always considered a rival. "I'm truly sorry. Please forgive me."

"For what it's worth, I do."

Lisa pulled back, blinking. "I had the feeling this morning that Jesse's upset over more than Emily's surgery. Then, when you didn't show up at the hospital and he wouldn't talk about you, I felt it had to do with all the troubles I've caused you. Maybe if I make him listen to me tonight, the two of you can start over."

Sara shook her head sadly. "There are more problems between Jesse and me than you can fix. But tell him anyhow. At least one mystery will be cleared up."

Aaron joined them as they left the den and walked to the door. "Lisa's not a bad person, Sara. She just wanted to belong to the family and didn't know how to go about it."

Sara nodded. "We all need to belong."

"Thanks for being so understanding," Lisa told her as she walked out with Aaron. "Jesse will come around. You'll see."

As Sara closed the door, Aaron helped Lisa into his truck. "There, that wasn't so hard now was it?"

"No, mostly because you were with me." She squeezed his hand. "But I get the feeling something's terribly wrong between them, something that has nothing to do with what we just talked about."

"We'll corner Jesse when he gets home tonight from the hospital and make him listen." He started the motor. "Meantime, what do you say we get something to eat? I'm starving."

Lisa smiled, feeling as if at least a partial weight had been lifted from her shoulders. "You're always hungry," she said with a laugh. He was such a pleasure to be with. Maybe, just maybe, life would be good again.

Inside the house, Sara hung up the phone. The hospital said that Emily was resting comfortably in ICU and that the prognosis was good. What a relief.

Then she picked up the phone again and dialed Phil's number. During a long, sleepless night and a worrisome day, she'd come to a decision. There was something very important she had to take care of, and there wasn't a moment to waste.

Hal Morgan walked outside into the bright sunshine of late afternoon and blinked. His eyes stung, his head ached.

Hell, his whole damn body hurt. Probably from the tension he'd been under for some time now. But it was finally over and he forced his shoulder muscles to relax, then his arms and finally his fingers, flexing them slowly.

"I never want to go through anything like that again," Hal told his son as he sat down on the low stucco ledge outside the hospital. It felt good to take a deep breath of fresh air, to gaze at the distant mountains, to allow the sun to warm his cold limbs. "I've been so damn scared." A hard admission for a man to make, but it was nothing but the unvarnished truth.

Jesse squinted at a roadrunner scurrying off through the scrub bushes in the adjacent field. "I know. Me, too."

"I have to tell you, Jess. If I'd have lost your mother, I wouldn't have wanted to go on. She's everything to me." Hal ran a shaky hand across his face, unused to sharing such a heartfelt emotional moment. But when the person you loved most in the world comes close to death, life becomes more precious.

He glanced at his son and saw that the worry hadn't left Jesse's face. Hal had just spent five minutes with Emily in ICU. Maybe he could reassure Jesse. "She opened her eyes and smiled at me. The doctor was there and said things looked good." He grinned. "She's going to be okay now. I *know* it."

Jesse nodded. "Thank God for that."

Hal frowned. He'd been so self-absorbed the last couple of days. He hadn't noticed that something was bothering his son, but he saw the signs now. And it wasn't just his mother's illness. Sara hadn't been with them and Hal had thought, after seeing her truck parked all night at Jesse's cabin last week, that things had changed for the better between them. "What is it, Jesse?" he asked, deciding that life was too short to spend time fencing.

Jesse rose, stuck his hands into his back pockets and walked a short distance away. "I found out something last night. I didn't want to bother you with it until we knew Mom was all right." Turning, he met his father's gaze. "I have a son. I figure he's about eleven and his name is Chris."

Hal's face registered surprise, then a rush of pleasure. "That's wonderful. Sara's, of course. Where is he?"

Jesse's jaw clenched, then unlocked as he made himself relax. From his pocket, he withdrew a picture he'd memorized since taking it from Sara yesterday. He handed it to his father. "In San Diego, I imagine. Sara was pregnant when she left here, but she didn't see fit to tell me. All these years, she's kept him from me." His eyes filled with pain. "She robbed me of eleven years of watching my son grow up."

Hal studied the photo. "He's a Morgan, all right. A fine-looking boy." From long habit, Hal's mind moved to the practical rather than the emotional. Certainly Jesse was entitled to some anger, but Hal had the feeling that all the cards weren't out on the table. "How old was Sara when she left here?"

Jesse wanted to talk about his son, not Sara. Yet he couldn't be short with his father. "She'd just graduated from high school that June, so I imagine she was eighteen. Why?"

"Oh. I thought . . . wait a minute! No, she was seventeen. That's right, a year younger than Kay. I remember that she'd skipped a grade when she was fairly young."

Fresh out of patience, Jesse paced. "What's the difference, seventeen or eighteen? She was old enough to know I cared about her." *You never once said the words. You never mentioned marriage either.* Sara's soft-spoken statement echoed in his mind, but he resolutely ignored it.

"It makes a hell of a difference. Did she tell you why she left?"

"Just that she'd quarreled with her father, and he'd made it impossible for her to stay. Hell, she was always quarreling with him. And if she'd have come to me, I'd have stood up to him." Again, he felt uneasy. All right, so she'd tried to reach him, but she hadn't tried hard enough, dammit.

The picture was clear to Hal, but he could see that Jesse's emotions were blocking his view. "Yes, she quarreled with Noah constantly. And all those years, she'd hung in there. But this time, she couldn't wait even the few days it would take you to return home. She left suddenly and hurriedly. I think I know why."

Jesse turned to face his father. "All right, tell me."

"Noah threatened you with statutory rape. His daughter was only seventeen, a minor, under the age of consent. You were twenty-two. He could have had you jailed."

"But I didn't rape her. We could have fought Noah in court. We could have won."

"Maybe. Maybe not. No, you didn't rape Sara. But the law says she was too young to give her consent. The law would have been on the outraged father's side."

Stunned, Jesse considered that. "If that's the reason, why didn't she tell me?" *Please, Jesse, let me explain.* "No, you're just guessing. She *wanted* to leave here, wanted to keep my son from me." Unwilling to let go of his resentment, Jesse turned and paced to the far wall that faced the parking lot.

Hal rose and walked to him. "Since she's returned, before you learned about the child, would you say that Sara's words and actions indicated that she cares about you?"

"I'd thought so."

Placing his hand on his son's shoulder, Hal squeezed hard. "I know this has been a blow, finding out about your boy this way. But I believe Sara loves you and I don't believe she'd have kept your child from you unless she was facing a worse choice. You told me that Phil drove her to the bus and saw that she got on it in broad daylight on a Sunday morning. That doesn't seem like the actions of an angry girl running away from a father's quarrel. It seems like a frightened girl being forced to leave town by a threatening father."

Jesse narrowed his eyes, weighing the possibilities.

Hal watched Jesse consider the logic of his argument. He knew his son was stubborn but never thought him unreasonably so. "Do you believe that Noah would have been furious enough to send her away if he'd have discovered that Sara was pregnant with your child?"

Jesse let out a huff of air. "Yeah. If he'd have thought the baby was mine, he'd have done whatever he could to hurt Sara."

"And to hurt you. What better way than denying you your child? And denying me my grandchild, too, for that matter."

Jesse's hands curled into fists filled with fury. Alive or dead, Noah Shephard had hurt all of them badly. "Do you honestly think that's what happened?" If it was, if he'd jumped to the wrong conclusions, he would have to beg Sara to forgive him. He'd been blaming her when she'd been trying to protect him.

"Sure sounds logical to me. What explanation did she give you?"

Jesse shuffled his feet. "I was so damn mad I didn't let her explain. She tried, but I cut her off." Remembering, he almost groaned aloud. "That phone call. She'd been in labor when she asked the friend to contact me. She . . . she almost died, almost lost the baby." *Oh, God, and he hadn't listened to her.*

"Pretty tough to handle for a girl of seventeen, far away from everyone she knew." Hal knew that Jesse was beating himself up, but he also knew that his son would do the right thing. "Maybe you ought to go talk with Sara again. You know, Jess, some men love only once. I'm one of them. I think you are, too. Just now, in there with your mother, I got to thinking that life doesn't offer us many second chances. When you see one, you'd better grab on to it."

Jesse swallowed hard. "Thanks, Dad."

Hal gave him a brief, hard hug. "Go to her. I'll keep watch on Mom."

But Jesse was already digging for his keys and racing toward his truck.

"Gone? What do you mean she's gone?" Jesse's anxiety turned to fury once more as he faced Phil outside the Lazy-S barn.

"I put her on a plane 'bout two hours ago," Phil said in his slow drawl. "She's headed back to San Diego."

"Damn." Jesse turned, his mind racing. He hated leaving now with his mother still in ICU and his father planning to spend all his time at the hospital for the next few days. The ranch couldn't run itself. Maybe he could get Aaron to...

"I wouldn't worry none," Phil went on. "Sara said she'd be back in a couple of days."

Jesse whirled around. "She's coming back? Why'd she leave?"

Phil shrugged. "Didn't say."

Puzzled, Jesse looked around at the buildings. Sara had made a hell of a difference. Everything looked great. "Did she put the place on the market?"

"Nope. Said she'd make that decision when she returned."

"Do you have her address in San Diego?"

Phil shook his head. "Her aunt's phone number and Sara's office number's all I got. You want those?"

With those numbers, he could find out her address. He could fly to San Diego, force her to listen. Jesse took a deep breath. Maybe the better way to play this was to see what Sara had in mind, to be patient. His last impulsive move hadn't worked out too well. He'd waited twelve years. Surely a few more days wouldn't change things. If she didn't return when she'd promised, he could go after her then. "No, not now. But I would like to know the minute she comes back. Will you call me?"

"Sure thing."

"Right." Slowly, Jesse walked back to his truck. It was going to be a very long couple of days.

It was the first of July, ninety degrees and sweltering. Jesse wiped his damp face on his sleeve. It was late afternoon and he'd been hard at work since five in the morning. It was time for a break.

He walked to the water fountain in the corner of the barn, took a long drink, then cupped his hands and splashed his face in an effort to cool off. He'd been helping Aaron artificially inseminate cows most of the day, and it was hot, grueling work. Using his kerchief, he dried his hands thoughtfully.

Three days since he'd learned that Sara had left. How did one define *a couple of days?* To him, it meant two, three at the most. By tomorrow, he'd have to take some action, Jesse decided.

He hadn't heard a word from her, nor had Phil called. This morning, they'd taken his mother out of ICU, and she was recovering slowly but surely in a private room, her spirits good. His father still spent most of his days with

Emily, but confident of her progress, the strain was gone from Hal's face. And Jesse had talked with Aaron about the possibility of his friend's handling the ranch for a few days in case Jesse had to leave. So he was all set to take matters into his own hands if Sara didn't return by tomorrow.

Wiping the damp cloth along his neck, he thought for a moment about the conversation he'd had recently with Lisa. It hadn't really surprised him to learn she'd posed as his mother on the phone with Sara's friend that day long ago. What had surprised him was her confession and her apparently sincere apology. Aaron had been with her, lending Lisa support—another surprise. Aaron had always been able to see the good in people that had sometimes escaped Jesse.

He'd given Lisa the forgiveness she'd asked for, and that hadn't been easy. If only his mother had answered the phone that day, how different all their lives might have been. But when he'd discussed Lisa's confession with his father, Hal had warned him not to dwell on the might-have-beens of life. He'd pointed out that that kind of thinking had ruined Noah Shephard's life. Jesse had had to agree.

Glancing toward the far end, Jesse spotted Aaron checking the freezer where the sperm cylinders were kept. "I'm knocking off for a while, buddy," he yelled across. "Got a couple of calls to make."

"Righto," Aaron answered.

Picking up his hat, Jesse turned to walk out the double doors. And stopped short.

Sara was standing in a shaft of light, her long hair turned golden by the sun. She wore a long red shirt over white slacks and a hesitant look on her face. Until this moment, Jesse hadn't realized how much he'd missed her. Acting on instinct, he opened his arms to her and waited.

Her smile broke through and she rushed to him. He grabbed her into a tight embrace, swung her around, burying his face in the sweet fragrance of her hair. She was back. She was home.

He lowered her feet to the ground slowly. "I'm getting you all dirty," he said inanely.

"I don't care." Rising on tiptoe, she offered her mouth. He touched his lips to hers, not in the crushing kiss she'd been expecting, but in a tender coming together that was all the more powerful in its gentleness. If he hadn't welcomed her return, she wasn't sure what she'd have done. Reluctantly, she drew back and looked into his eyes. "Please forgive me for what I've done. I'll make it up to you, Jesse. I swear I will."

"It's okay. Dad helped me see why you left like that, why you didn't tell me you were pregnant. Noah threatened to have me jailed, didn't he?"

Thank you, Hal, she silently whispered. "Yes. He said the law was on his side. Statutory rape. It would have ruined you, embarrassed your family. I couldn't let him . . ."

Jesse pulled her close again in a fierce hug. "I know. And I know about Lisa answering the phone that day." Now he met her eyes, needing to tell her. "I'm so sorry I wasn't there for you when you needed me."

She smiled from the heart for the first time in days. "It seems the fates have been conspiring to keep us apart for a very long time."

"But it won't work anymore. I love you, Sara. Will you marry me?"

"Yes. Oh, yes." The kiss was filled with promise, with love.

"Why did you leave again?" Jesse asked. "I wasn't sure if you wanted me to follow you or . . ."

"I needed to do something." Taking his hand, she led him through the open doors. "I want you to meet somebody."

Jesse blinked as his eyes adjusted from the dimness of the barn to bright sunlight. Then he blinked again at what he saw.

The boy was tall for his age, his dark curly hair worn a little long, like his own. He'd been roughhousing with a gray cockapoo, but straightened when he saw his mother walk out of the barn. Christopher's eyes were a familiar shade of gray and his chin bore the Morgan trademark, a deep cleft.

Jesse's eyes filled as he walked forward to meet his son, his arm around the woman he loved.

Epilogue

Emily Morgan walked into her comfortable living room carrying a tray laden with cups, a pot of hot chocolate and a plate of freshly baked cookies.

"Mom, you shouldn't be handling such a heavy load," Sara said, setting aside the book she'd been reading, rising from the corner of the sofa and taking the tray from her mother-in-law.

"Nonsense. I'm feeling fine, and the doctor says I'm to resume all my usual activities." Her last checkup, thank God, had gone better than expected. Emily sat down at the opposite end of the couch. "And what could be more usual than baking cookies at Christmastime?"

"Mmm, they smell wonderful." Sara poured them each a cup of hot chocolate, then picked up a cookie. It seemed she was always hungry these days. "I've got to fight this, or I'm soon going to be as big as that barn out there."

"And what's wrong with that?" Hal asked coming in the front door and stomping the snow from his boots. "Pregnant women eat for two, don't they?"

Sara smiled. "I feel as if I'm eating for three."

"I don't think we have twins on our side," Emily said. "What about yours, Sara?"

"Not that I know of. I'll settle for one, thank you." Sara filled a cup for Hal as the door opened again. She looked up in time to see Chris, his cheeks red from the cold, come dashing in, oblivious of his snow-crusted boots.

"Mom, you should have been out with us. Dad and I helped deliver a colt. He's beautiful, Mom."

Sara smiled at his enthusiasm. "I bet he is. Chris, your boots are wet."

"It's only a little snow," Emily said, drawing her grandson over to sit beside her. "What're you going to call the colt?"

"Dad said I could name him." Chris spotted the cookies and reached for one as Jesse came in, shrugging out of his coat. "Right, Dad?"

"Yes, indeed." Rubbing his hands together to remove the chill, Jesse moved to sit between his wife and son. "A guy who delivers his first colt ought to get to name him."

"I like Sundance," Chris said. "Like the stallion you told me you used to have, Dad."

"A good choice." Slipping his arm around Sara, he pulled her close and kissed her lightly. "Looks like someone's been busy," he commented, nodding toward the newly wrapped gifts under the Christmas tree in the corner.

"Wow, look at that." Chris scooted over and knelt to inspect the brightly colored packages.

"Mom and I helped Santa out a little. Aunt Margaret will be coming in tomorrow."

Emily sat back. "And Kay and Will are driving up the next day." They'd invited Phil over for Christmas dinner and, of course, Lisa and Aaron would be joining them. Those two had been cozier than ever lately. Emily suspected that they might be attending another wedding soon. It seemed as if Lisa had met her match and was ready to settle down, finally over her obsession with Jesse. "It will be so good having all of us together for the holidays."

"Yes," Hal agreed, "but I don't want you to overdo."

"Hal, I'm just fine. Stop fussing. It's Sara who shouldn't overdo."

Jesse squeezed his wife's shoulder. "Hear that?"

"Oh, come on, you two. I'm pregnant, not ill."

"It's the new house," Jesse added. "Ever since it was completed, she works too hard decorating it. She's got her office all set up on the first floor. Chris's room is finished and now she's fixing up the nursery."

Sara rose, shaking her head. "I repeat, I'm not fragile." She walked over to where her son was still examining the gifts. "Let's take off your boots and hang up your coat, Chris." Following him to the vestibule, she gave him a hand.

Hal reached for another cookie. "You sure didn't waste any time after the wedding, Jess," he commented as he gazed at his pregnant daughter-in-law.

Jesse stood. "We wasted twelve years, Dad. I don't want to squander another minute." Moving to his wife's side in the archway, he turned her toward him. "Mrs. Morgan, you're standing under the mistletoe."

Sara glanced up, then slipped her arms around his waist as she smiled at him. "Wasn't that clever of me?" And she rose to meet his kiss.

* * * * *

A Note from the Author

We run across a lot of special women in our lives. The trouble is, we often don't know just how special they are.

The single mother who works in our office and is raising two children without assistance, as well as going to night school. Our neighbor who uncomplainingly takes care of an invalid mother along with her own family. Perhaps a relative who takes in foster children, making a real difference in many young lives.

What does it take to be That Special Woman? To me, it's courage against all odds, strength of character and that indomitable spirit. Someone like my heroine, Sara Shephard.

Sara lost her mother at a young age and was raised by a father who didn't neglect her physically but rather emotionally. Despite that shaky beginning, she never lost faith. Then she met the warm and caring Morgan family and her lonely heart reached out. Just when she thought she'd found

the love she'd dreamed of with Jesse Morgan, fate stepped
in and separated them.

Because she had to, Sara built a new life, loving Jesse
from afar for twelve long years. Suddenly, she has to go
back to face her past and the secret she's been guarding, a
true act of courage, for, in doing so, she could lose everything. But Jesse Morgan is exceptional, too, and he's never
forgotten the dauntless young woman who lived next door.

In this decade of the nineties, nowhere is the year of the
woman celebrated more beautifully than in Silhouette's That
Special Woman! series. I hope you enjoy Sara's story.

Take 4 bestselling love stories FREE

Plus get a FREE surprise gift!

Special Limited-time Offer

Mail to Silhouette Reader Service™

3010 Walden Avenue
P.O. Box 1867
Buffalo, N.Y. 14269-1867

YES! Please send me 4 free Silhouette Special Edition® novels and my free surprise gift. Then send me 6 brand-new novels every month, which I will receive months before they appear in bookstores. Bill me at the low price of $2.71 each plus 25¢ delivery and applicable sales tax, if any.* That's the complete price and—compared to the cover prices of $3.50 each—quite a bargain! I understand that accepting the books and gift places me under no obligation ever to buy any books. I can always return a shipment and cancel at any time. Even if I never buy another book from Silhouette, the 4 free books and the surprise gift are mine to keep forever.

235 BPA AJH7

Name	(PLEASE PRINT)	
Address	Apt. No.	
City	State	Zip

This offer is limited to one order per household and not valid to present Silhouette Special Edition® subscribers. *Terms and prices are subject to change without notice. Sales tax applicable in N.Y.

USPED-93R

©1990 Harlequin Enterprises Limited

Silhouette Books has done it again!

Opening night in October has never been as exciting! Come watch as the curtain rises and romance flourishes when the stars of tomorrow make their debuts today!

Revel in Jodi O'Donnell's STILL SWEET ON HIM—
Silhouette Romance #969
...as Callie Farrell's renovation of the family homestead leads her straight into the arms of teenage crush Drew Barnett!

Tingle with Carol Devine's BEAUTY AND THE BEASTMASTER—
Silhouette Desire #816
...as legal eagle Amanda Tarkington is carried off by wrestler Bram Masterson!

Thrill to Elyn Day's A BED OF ROSES—
Silhouette Special Edition #846
...as Dana Whitaker's body and soul are healed by sexy physical therapist Michael Gordon!

Believe when Kylie Brant's McLAIN'S LAW —
Silhouette Intimate Moments #528
...takes you into detective Connor McLain's life as he falls for psychic—and suspect—Michele Easton!

Catch the classics of tomorrow—*premiering* today—
only from V. Silhouette

**And now for
something completely different
from Silhouette....**

SPELLBOUND
R O M A N C E

Every once in a while, Silhouette brings you a
book that is truly unique and innovative, taking
you into the world of paranormal happenings.
And now these stories will carry our special
"Spellbound" flash, letting you know that you're
in for a truly exciting reading experience!

In October, look for *McLain's Law* (IM #528)
by Kylie Brant

Lieutenant Detective Connor McLain believes
only in what he can see—until Michele Easton's
haunting visions help him solve a case...and her
love opens his heart!

McLain's Law is also the Intimate Moments
"Premiere" title, introducing you to a debut
author, sure to be the star of tomorrow!

Available in October...only from
Silhouette Intimate Moments

SPELL1

Share in the joy of a holiday romance with

1993
SILHOUETTE

Christmas

STORIES

Silhouette's eighth annual
Christmas collection
matches the joy of the
holiday season with the
magic of romance in four
short stories by popular
Silhouette authors:

**LISA JACKSON
EMILIE RICHARDS
JOAN HOHL
LUCY GORDON**

This November, come home
for the holidays with

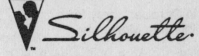

where passion lives.

TAKE A WALK ON THE
DARK SIDE OF LOVE WITH

Silhouette

SHADOWS '93

October is the shivery season, when chill winds blow and shadows walk the night. Come along with us into a haunting world where love and danger go hand in hand, where passions will thrill you and dangers will chill you. Silhouette's second annual collection from the dark side of love brings you three perfectly haunting tales from three of our most bewitching authors:

Kathleen Korbel
Carla Cassidy
Lori Herter

Haunting a store near you this October.

Only from ▼ *Silhouette*® where passion lives.

SILHOUETTE.... Where Passion Lives

Don't miss these Silhouette favorites by some of our most popular authors!
And now, you can receive a discount by ordering two or more titles!